Published By RDF Publishing

ISBN-978-1717574428

Cover design by Jamie Lynn

First Edition

THOUGH POPPIES

GROW

By

Robert Farnsworth

1

Verdun, France, 1918

John Bayer crouched in a shallow crater, waiting for the flare to disappear. Looking around before jumping to his feet, he darted from one mound and mud hole to the next. Heart pounding. Sweat dripping. Hands shaking. Mask fogging. Rifle bouncing. Darting.

He squinted through a hazy mask and searched for a place of cover. All that remained were stumps, dirt piles, and holes filled with putrid water. Mustard gas hung in the low spots like fog. Daylight would come soon. John could hide in the shadows, but he could not hide in the light.

No one survived in the dead expanse of no man's land. Only rats, big as house cats after gorging on the flesh of dead soldiers, lived here. John knew if he remained here long, they'd smell him.

Another flare soared into the sky. The light gave the gas in the atmosphere an eerie yellow glow. Shadows crawled across the landscape like a lion stalking its prey. John needed to find a hole. Not a deep hole. Anything deeper than his chest would trap him.

The flare exposed his position. Gunshots exploded around him. A voice screamed from the trench nearby. John spotted a place of cover surrounded by a low dirt mound and jumped in. Shallow, the hole was up to his knees. He could lie on his stomach and not be seen, his head raised enough to keep the mask out of the water. Not just water though, but dirt and blood and who knows what else. A bullet crashed into the ground nearby, spraying his body with dirt.

The flare hissed out and darkness reigned again. John raised himself into a squat. He craned his head in every direction before

3

he dared move. He darted again. Shots rang out. Blasts of dirt slammed into the ground nearby. The earth trembled. Mortars exploded.

Another flare soared skyward. More explosions. More gunfire. More darting. More ducking. More crawling. Another flare. Another explosion. The ground quaked under his feet. He lost his balance.

John found himself in a crater deep enough that, with the muddy walls, he could not easily escape. He knew he would die here. He closed his eyes and breathed heavily. *I could call out and surrender,* he thought. *No, this is war. Deserters are not captured, they are executed.*

John leaned against the side of the crater, his right foot sinking into the sludge. He shifted his weight to his left foot and sank again. He shifted back to the right. His left foot came out slower this time, heavy with clayish mud. Back and forth he rocked, with each movement the weight bearing foot sank quicker, deeper. John knew he must get out now, or he would not get out alive.

He only had room to take one small step when he jumped for the edge. His right foot, still gripped by the mud, held him down. He jumped again and made it no further. His breathing quickened. His heart pounded in his ears. He kept jumping. Each time he leapt, he slid down the side of the hole.

Another flare flew into the sky. John crouched below the berm of the hole. He drew slow, purposeful breaths. His chest burned with the labor of forcing air through the mud-encrusted mask. He closed his eyes and thought about home. *My brother was right. I should have stayed on the farm. I'm going to die and I accomplished nothing.*

A new sound reached his ears. Hissing and squeaking and growling. The rats. He'd heard stories. He hoped they weren't true.

The flare fell to the ground and darkness retook the landscape. Red eyes peered into the hole. Eight eyes, no ten, maybe twenty. How many?

John stared at the rats and knew what they wanted. He could not stay in the hole. After one jumped on him, the others would follow. He could hold off one or two, not ten or twenty. Not rats this large and savage.

He dared not lunge. The quick movement would spark a frenzy. John drove the barrel of his rifle into the muddy floor of the hole, leaving the stock to act as a sort of stepping stool. He stood with his right foot on the butt and pushed himself over the edge of the berm. The rats backed away as one.

John's legs dangled in the hole. A wall of red eyes peered at him. Yellow teeth glowed in the twilight. John shuddered. He started to slip back into the hole, rocks and splinters and metal shards shredding his exposed chest. He drove his fingers into the mud and pulled himself forward.

The quick movements set the rats into a violent fury. He rolled and kicked and punched and tried to get to his feet. One jumped on his back and tore into his shoulder. Another latched onto his calf. John screamed. Bullets peppered the dirt nearby.

The taste of fresh blood incited the rats to more violence. John swung his arms wildly, knocking the rat off his back. Blood poured out the wound. He pushed himself to his knees before struggling to his feet.

He gave the rat attached to his calf a horse kick with his left foot, driving it into the mob. They tore into it with a viciousness that made John shudder.

He stood motionless for a moment and watched the animals tear into each other. They forgot about him. He forgot about his pursuers. The light of another flare exposed him.

An explosion thirty feet away shook the ground. He ran. He needed to reach his own trench. He ran straight this time. No darting. Just running.

John ran straight for an opening in the twisted barbed wire. The gap wasn't large, but he would try to wiggle through. He clawed at the wire with his bare hands. He ignored the pain and crawled forward. He was close enough to making it through this hell, he believed he might survive. He saw the edge of the trench. His heart rate quickened.

John ignored the gunfire and the spray of bullets landing nearby. He was going to make it. Ten feet from safety, he yelled, "American, I'm an American." He fought with the wire, his hands bleeding and torn. He didn't care. "I'm American. Don't shoot. American."

A blow to his back knocked John forward. He landed in the soft mud, almost through the barbed wire. Warm blood dripped down his back and side. He struggled to inch forward, pulling himself ahead on his elbows. Everything around him became a blur before he collapsed into the mud. A hand grabbed him by the wrist and jerked him forward. He heard a voice with a strange accent. "I've got you, mate. You're gonna…"

The words trailed into darkness.

2

One week earlier.

John leaned against the white handrail on deck of the elegant passenger ship and vomited over the side. One hand gripped the metal rail, the other clutched a linen handkerchief. He wiped his mouth before looking over his shoulder.

The ship glided up the smooth Garonne River toward the French city of Bordeaux on a warm August morning in 1918. John ran his fingers through his hair, now damp from a cold sweat. He closed his eyes and inhaled the salty air lingering on the brackish river.

Growing up on a farm did not prepare him for a seven-day voyage at sea, especially not a journey through the treacherous waters of the North Atlantic. Even on the now calm waters, waves of nausea rolled over him.

Laughter from a group of soldiers nearby drew John's attention across the ship deck. None of the men smoking or playing cards noticed him. A gentle breeze gathered their cigarette smoke into streams funneled toward John. He stumbled against the handrail as the tugboat guiding the huge ship to port struggled against its enormous load. One more nauseating lurch reminded him he was better suited for land.

John returned his gaze to the city of Bordeaux while he patted his uniform. He imagined the murmur as people and horses and a few automobiles passed by. Other than the night he spent in New York before leaving for Europe, John had never seen a city larger than Lincoln.

The vessel slowed to a crawl before the rumble of an enormous metal chain vibrated the ship. John leaned over the rail to watch the anchor sink to the harbor floor. The ship jerked when the anchor hit bottom. Ripples rolled away from the boat.

"Thirty minutes!"

John turned to the top deck of the gleaming white ship where an officer yelled through a brown bullhorn. "You have thirty minutes to retrieve your belongings and assemble on the main deck."

Through throngs of soldiers, John made his way to his room to retrieve an already packed bag. He shared a room in the lower portion of the ship with Thomas Schlicting, a fellow lieutenant with whom he became friends during basic training. After their initial six-week training, they roomed together during the four-week officer preparation school. John shook his head and thought about his friend. Tom also grew up on a farm, but didn't seem to mind the movement of the ocean.

When he arrived to his room, John found Tom furiously stuffing his belongings into a duffel bag. Throughout the voyage, he had unpacked his entire bag and had clothes, toiletries, and pictures lying haphazardly around the room.

"Running late I see." John tossed his bag over his shoulder. "You know it'll take longer than thirty minutes, right?"

"Not late, right on time," Tom answered, with a wink.

That was his thing, a wink. Tom winked almost every time he said something he thought was clever.

"Besides," Tom continued stuffing his bag with unfolded laundry, "we don't have more than thirty minutes. The General and his staff will be on the first boats to shore. That makes us important."

John laughed. "Yeah, the only two German-speaking guys on this entire ship. I guess they might need us when they get to the front."

John exhaled and gave his temporary home one last look. He reached for a pile of envelopes left unpacked, tied together on his bunk.

Tom nodded at the envelopes. "Gonna drop those letters in the mail before you get off the ship?"

John shook his head and thumbed through the envelopes. "Not yet."

"I don't understand you." Tom looked out the corner of his eye. "When we met in camp, you were certain you would marry Rose. Now you won't even send her a letter?"

John thought about the girl from home, Rose Austin. Before he shipped out, he thought he loved her. Now he wasn't sure. A few weeks is not a lifetime, and she did say, "We don't know what will happen when the war is over. Let's just enjoy our time together. The future will take care of itself."

John scratched his cheek. He'd shaved that morning, but already had a shadow in early afternoon. "I want to make sure it wasn't the war that brought us together. I don't want to break it off but I also don't know if I want to make it permanent."

"Well, at least *I'm* still free to chase the French girls when we get there." Tom winked again before he swept a small table full of hair cream and pictures off the desk into his bag. "Maybe you'll find a nice French girl, too. Keep your mind off other things."

"That's the last thing I need," John said, before pointing to a large ball wrapped in white paper. "What is that thing?"

"It's a salted ham." Tom inspected the bundle before nonchalantly stuffing it into his bag.

"Where did you get a salted ham?"

"I won it from one of the cooks at cards last night." Tom chuckled.

John gestured to the rest of the items scattered on Tom's bunk. "Looks like you won more than that."

Tom winked for the third time. "You're gonna be happy we have all this. You'll see."

"I probably will." John stepped into the hallway. "I'll see you up there … maybe."

"I'll make it, don't you worry." Tom's voice echoed off the metal walls while John trudged through the passageway.

Soldiers from three corridors emptied into one hallway, causing a small traffic jam at the final stairwell to the loading deck. John shuffled toward the door, getting squeezed tighter and tighter with every step. He reached the salty warm air in time to see Tom push through the door on the opposite side of the deck. John zigzagged through the crowd until he reached his friend.

"How did you get here already?" John dropped his bag to the deck. "You weren't even finished packing when I left."

"Work smarter." Tom lowered his overstuffed bag to the floor. "I knew to avoid the main corridor. I took the back one instead. Longer walk but quicker trip. Told ya I'd make it."

John nodded. "Yep, you always make it."

In training camp, Tom was the soldier who made it to assembly barely in time. When it was lights out, he slid through the barracks door as it closed. John couldn't remember a time when Tom was late. He couldn't remember when he was early either.

John was the opposite—on time and prepared for everything. Chow at 6:00, John arrived at 5:55. Drills at 7:00, John was there by 6:50. What a pair he and Tom made. John, a vision of the perfect soldier. Polished, pressed, and ready. Tom, a disheveled mess.

Not that John minded. He didn't expect the same standard from others he set for himself. He remembered rushing through his chores on the farm. His father lectured in a thick German accent, "If you aren't willing to do something right, why do it at all?" This became John's manner of life. Even so, he became friends with the most disorganized soldier in his company.

Although they couldn't have been more different, they looked so similar many people assumed they were brothers. Tom, at five nine, was only a few inches shorter than John, but had the same cropped black hair and olive complexion. His beard didn't grow as fast as John's, but since he refused to shave, he sported the same five o'clock shadow as John by three o'clock every day.

John considered the growing mass of soldiers on deck before glancing at his watch. "Any idea when we'll get to shore? It's getting crowded up here."

Tom nodded toward the side of the ship where landing craft had been lowered into the water. "Like I told you, we'll be first, and it doesn't look like it will take very long."

As if on cue, the General came through the doors at B deck. He walked down a set of stairs onto the main level. John stood at attention with the rest of the soldiers on deck while the old man passed their ranks. The General nodded at the troops before climbing a rope ladder into the front landing craft. Grabbing hold of the rope that held the little boat steady, the General swung his left leg into the smaller vessel. No one offered to assist him, and it was clear he required no help.

"I wonder if he practiced after lights out so he wouldn't fall overboard?" Tom spoke loud enough to cause those around him to laugh.

After the General was seated in the boat, the officer with the bullhorn announced, "General staff load in the front two boats."

A silent army of about twenty soldiers surged toward the landing crafts. Tom elbowed John and nodded toward the second boat. A few soldiers jockeyed to get in the same boat with the General. John wasn't interested in getting noticed by the old man. He wanted to make it through the war unnoticed and unscathed.

Bordeaux was the picturesque European city John imagined, although he didn't get to enjoy it. The only sights he witnessed rushed by on the ride to the troop staging area near the train depot. Being on the General's staff had its advantages, as John was transported to the train station in the back of a flatbed truck. The bumpy ride was preferable to walking the seven miles with the enlisted soldiers on the warm summer day.

John watched the beautiful limestone and marble structures that lined both sides of the boulevard pass by en route. Having looked forward to seeing the city, he was not disappointed. He suspected his hosts intentionally took the longer route to display the city to their American guests. Along the way his French counterpart, a young soldier named Alain, said, "Many of these buildings are older than your country, you know?"

John laughed when Tom blurted, "If it wasn't for us, these would all be old German buildings soon."

The Frenchman scowled at Tom and the rest of the ride to the station was quiet.

The wait at the depot lasted much longer than the ride from the harbor. John observed train after train, filled with men, steam out of the train yard. He wondered aloud why it was taking so long.

"The French leadership won't allow the General and his staff to ride in ordinary troop transports," Tom said. "So we wait for a passenger train."

John pointed to a farmer down the road with a horse drawn wagon full of hay. "The General probably wouldn't care if he rode in that cart to the front."

Tom leaned against the warm red brick wall with his hat over his eyes. "You know how the French are about appearances. The

11

General has to appease them *and* fight a war. Not that we'll actually get close to the front."

John's eyebrows furrowed. "I know. I can't help but feel guilty about it though."

3

Tom pushed himself to his feet. Pacing on the wooden platform, he pointed at John. "Do you really think it's heroic to sit in a muddy trench, filled with water and filth, wearing a gas mask, waiting to charge the Germans and hope they don't shoot you before you turn around and jump back into the same putrid hole?

"Really, is that your idea of a hero?" Tom pulled his hat off. "I know we won't be killing Germans, but we'll be reading dispatches and translating prisoner interviews. That'll be a lot more important than running into a wall of machine gun fire."

"I know, I know." John waved his hands. "You're right. But how do I stop feeling guilty knowing other guys are dying in trenches and we'll be safe behind the front?"

Tom lowered himself to the floor again. "Do you even read those newspapers you have your nose stuck in all the time? If you did, you'd know this war will not be won by those guys in the trenches. It'll be won by knowing the Germans' next move. That's what we're here for. And yes, we might do it safer than those other guys. But it will save many of their lives too.

"Ahhh, hell." Tom returned his hat to his head. "Feel guilty if you want. I'd be happy I grew up in a house that spoke German and sent me to law school so I don't have to get shot in the trenches.

"Besides," Tom said, with a French accent. "The French Mademoiselles won't be at the front. They'll be back where it's nice and safe."

John shook his head. "Mademoiselles huh? That's all you need to take your mind off, uh, what is it you do around here anyway?"

Tom laughed with a snort. "I told you, we're here to do all the work to win the war. I just make it look easy."

John and Tom reclined in the sun outside the depot for almost four hours. Wheat in a nearby field swayed in the breeze. John thought about walking with Rose through a similar field in Nebraska a few days before he boarded the train for boot camp.

Rose wore a green cotton dress that matched her eyes. She knew green was his favorite color. They'd lived down the road from each other their entire lives, but only went out together for the past few weeks. Until then, they had avoided talking about the war. John knew how Rose felt about him. He stopped and looked into her eyes. "You know I'm leaving soon. I might not come back."

"I know." Rose tilted her head.

"I can't promise I'll come back to Nebraska when the war is over." John stepped closer. "If I make it back at all."

Rose placed her hand on John's arm. "I'm not asking you to make any promises. We have this moment and we have the next three days of moments. Why torture ourselves when we don't know what will happen after you leave?"

"You're right." John exhaled. "I like being with you. I like talking to you. I wish we had realized this sooner; I wish that I—"

"But you're leaving." Rose took both of his hands. "And we can't change that. What we can do is enjoy this time. The future will take care of itself."

All four sets of tracks at the station hummed with activity every moment of the day. Thousands of soldiers climbed into hot train cars while John and Tom rested in the comfort of the shade of the depot. For every train that left filled with soldiers, another returned loaded with wounded men.

Cars arrived, too, with soldiers who never would go home. They were destined for a final resting place in a cemetery in France. These were the bodies recovered. Many soldiers were shot

14

in "no man's land," the area between opposing trenches. Rats, bombs, or mud devoured them. Their final memory, a cheap telegram to their family from the War Department.

After a long silence, Tom pointed in the direction of a boxcar. "That's what I mean." He spoke quietly. "Do you think their families will be happy that they were so heroic as to fight and die in battle? I don't think so. Every one of them has a mother wishing her son was home, or at least twenty miles behind the front line."

John's stomach churned. He closed his eyes and took a deep breath. The odor lingering from nearby soldiers who hadn't bathed in a week didn't help his unsettled stomach.

"Do you think we can survive this?" John asked. "All afternoon, we've watched trains full of wounded and dead men steam into the rail yard. We probably won't be at the front, but will that make any difference? When a pilot drops a bomb on your head from his airplane, it won't matter if you're at the front or if you work for a General twenty miles behind the line."

Tom rubbed his sweaty forehead. "Sure, we'll make it. If we're smart, keep our heads down, and don't volunteer for anything crazy, we should be fine."

"And," Tom added with a smile. "If you happen to hear a plane flying overhead, run straight toward the General's command tent."

John glanced at the smirk on his friend's face. As usual, Tom took a serious conversation and turned it into a joke. "Okay, I'll play along. Why should I run toward the old man's tent?"

Tom shrugged. "It's simple. We constantly hear about wrong targets getting blown up. So run straight for the center of the bull's eye and they're bound to miss you."

A murmur spreading down the row of troops interrupted their laughter. Time to board the train. John jumped to his feet. Tom was slow and deliberate, stretching as he stood. "Relax," he said with a yawn. "They can't win this thing without us. They'll have to wait."

Walking by a now unloaded train, John knew this was not his transportation to the front. He recognized them as former cattle cars that packed men like sardines for the half-day ride to the front. John stopped at the open doors of one of the cars.

The inside of the car wasn't quite what he expected. He'd imagined pools of blood and amputated limbs, along with blood-

15

covered clothing strewn about the car. He was surprised at how clean it appeared. No blood or limbs, just an empty boxcar with a few buckets in one corner. The only sound, other than the shuffle of feet behind him, was the buzzing of flies in the car.

What he had not expected when he stepped closer to the open door was the odor. John was accustomed to the smell of blood. Having worked around livestock his entire childhood, he often helped his father and brother butcher cows, pigs, and chickens. He remembered watching them work all day cutting meat. He also remembered having to help clean up when they finished. Back then, he inhaled the smell of blood so much, it tasted like metal in his mouth. That was fresh blood.

This was not the smell of fresh blood. It was the odor of old blood, soaked into wooden planks. It was the smell of feces and urine. It was the odor of rotting wounds; the first time John smelled gangrene. It was the smell of men, unwashed men, sitting in hot boxcars while the summer sun pounded on them. These smells culminated into one, horrific stench that saturated the boxcars.

"It's a shame." Startled, John turned to find another officer behind him looking into the boxcar.

"What?"

"The cars." The soldier pointed inside. "They try to clean 'em up and use 'em for cattle when the army is done with them. The cattle can smell the death, though, and won't go in. The only way to get rid of the stench is to burn the cars. What a waste."

John nodded. "What a waste."

He knew Tom was right. If he were a fighting man, this would be his transportation. Could he even survive a twelve-hour ride in this train car, let alone endure the horrors at the front? Yes, better to ride with the General staff in a passenger car. Better to be a nobody in the rear than a hero at the front.

Heroes die, John thought, as he stepped onto the train. *And I don't want to die.*

4

S quealing brakes and the rattling of the train woke John from a sound sleep. Outside, darkness. John rubbed his eyes. City lights shone inside the car when they pulled into the station. Tom slept in the seat opposite him.

Still looking out the window and in the kind of a fog that only waking from a deep sleep could bring, John stretched before kicking Tom's leg. "Any idea where we are?"

"Paris." Tom yawned. "The city of love."

John marveled that his friend knew where they were even though his hat was pulled over his eyes. Confused and a bit alarmed, he said, "Paris? That's ten hours from Bordeaux. I didn't sleep that long, did I?"

Tom laughed as he stretched and twisted himself out of his seat. "Yes, you did. Slept the entire way. I stopped by a few times to see if you were awake for dinner or cards, but you were sound asleep. I came in a few hours ago to catch a nap before the last leg of the trip."

John yawned as the sleep wore off. He stretched his neck to work out the pain from the angle he had slept.

"I guess I was tired." John massaged the area where his lower neck and left shoulder met. "Where do we go from here?"

"There are trucks waiting to take us to Verdun." Tom tried to pull his bag from under his seat. "Well, just outside Verdun. That's where we're stationed. Not too close to the front."

John leaned over and helped Tom pull his overstuffed bag free. "Both of us?"

"Yeah. Disappointed?"

"No." John shook his head. "Surprised. We're the only two officers from our training class who speak German. I expected they'd need us in different locations."

"I don't know all the details. I was able to find out they set up a camp near Verdun for German prisoners. They need more than one of us to do interviews or translate interrogations with them. Something like that anyway." Tom heaved his green duffel bag over his shoulder and wrestled it through the door.

John wondered how Tom ever got the overstuffed bag through the door in the first place. "Well, maybe that's good. My mom will be happy to hear I'm away from the front. She might be even happier that I'm talking to fellow Germans."

Tom hesitated at the door. "I don't think your mom will know anything about it. From what I've heard, this isn't the sort of situation we're allowed to talk about. Your mail might not even get out, at least not unedited, if you catch my meaning."

John squinted and waited for a laugh that didn't come. Tom wasn't joking. "I guess you're right. It could be dangerous if I wrote a letter telling her where I was and what we're doing, if the Germans got their hands on our mail."

"If they found that kind of information, our location would be target number one. All those huge guns that shoot for miles would be targeted right on our heads." Tom made an exploding gesture with his hands "Kaboom! They wouldn't even care about killing their own. Secrets are more valuable than soldiers."

John scratched his head. "I have to admit I'm relieved about the change in plans. I expected to be translating German telegrams day and night. This could be somewhat exciting."

Tom leaned against the wall in the corridor and dropped his bag on the floor. "Don't get too excited. I don't think we'll be allowed out much."

"I'm not the one they have to worry about." John elbowed Tom in the ribcage and laughed. "How do you know all this anyway?"

"The General's chief of staff had too much to drink last night." Tom patted his front pocket and smiled. "He probably doesn't even remember talking to me or who he lost all his money to."

As they laughed, two soldiers from the first car walked through the sliding door between the train cars. The first soldier gestured to the front of the train. "Lieutenant Bayer, Lieutenant Schlicting. The General wants to speak with you."

Tom smirked and gave John a look that meant, "Here we go" before they picked up their bags and followed the two soldiers. Stretching to step across the gap between cars, John looked back at the soldier behind him. "Why are we needed in the General's car?"

The soldier shrugged "I don't have any idea."

John and Tom stepped into a smoke-filled car similar to the one they had just exited. The only difference was that the windows and blinds in this car were closed, holding in the smoke and heat.

They came face to face with a short, dark haired officer. "Are you the interpreters?"

"Yes, Sir." John and Tom snapped to attention.

"Dismissed." The officer waved his hand and the escorts left.

"I suppose you're wondering what's going on?" The soldier stood slightly shorter than John. A tuft of hair protruded from the man's shirt at the neck that matched his black moustache.

John and Tom nodded.

The officer rotated his hat in his hand. "I'll start by introducing myself. I'm Major Bill Jacobson. I'll be commanding our little endeavor."

John lowered his eyebrows. "Little endeavor? What kind of endeavor?"

"I'll answer that." The General, who had been leaning against a table with a cigar resting between his lips, stepped forward. He stood close enough to John that he could smell the cigar on the old man's breath.

Major Jacobson stepped back, acknowledging the superior rank of the General.

"You fellas probably want to know what the hell you're doing here?" The General's thick accent reminded John of a soldier he'd met from Boston.

"Yes, Sir."

"You know, we've watched you two for a while now." The General leaned on the back of a seat, cigar still in his hand. "We've been planning a special unit that will help us get information. You see, we're having a hard time getting the German prisoners to tell us anything useful."

The General took a slow drag off his cigar. "They come in fresh from battle, recently captured. We assume they know something about their side of the war. Our boys interview them, interrogate them, try to get information, but their lips are sealed tighter than a whale's ass. That's where you two come in."

Tom coughed a little laugh when he heard, "whale's ass."

The General eyeballed Tom. He slowly raised the cigar to his lips. This gave John the opportunity to ask, "What can we do that would be any different, Sir?"

Tom added, "We're not exactly experts at this. I've never even seen a prisoner let alone know how to get information from one."

"I'm not asking for your ideas on how to get information." The General pointed at John and Tom. "You two *are* the idea."

"Come again?" Tom said.

"We don't need someone else to interrogate prisoners. We have hundreds of boys that can do that. We need someone on the inside."

The General looked at Jacobson. "Major, explain it to them."

"Yes, Sir." Major Jacobson returned to the center of the train car, clutching his hat in his hand. "I know you're confused. Let me start from the beginning. Do you remember when you first signed up to serve?"

John nodded. He was aware of perspiration rolling down his back in the broiling train car.

Major Jacobson used his free hand to wipe the sweat building on his brow, a luxury John didn't have standing at attention. "You remember you did a few things when we found out you spoke German. You gave a writing sample and took the oral examination, right?"

"Yes." John squinted the sweat out of his eyes.

"Well, we needed something different. If we only wanted interpreters, we could have gone to any university to recruit German language students. Easy. In fact, that's how we got the interpreters we have." Major Jacobson wiped a bead of sweat from his nose. "No, what we need are soldiers who not only speak German, but speak the language like a German."

"Wait a minute." Tom's voice rose with excitement. "It sounds to me like you want us to be spies. Is that what you're saying? Sneaking behind the lines?"

Major Jacobson laughed. "Not exactly. We want you to be spies in the prison camp."

"Prison camp?" Tom's eyebrows furrowed. "Why us?"

"We've tried this before." Jacobson shrugged. "And it didn't work. The guys we sent into the camps didn't sound like real Germans. They sounded like Americans speaking German. It took no time for the real prisoners to figure out what was going on."

The Major reached for a glass of water on the table behind him. Before he could continue, John said, "I understand you need someone to speak German with the right accent. But why not grab someone fresh off the boat from Germany? They'd probably be more convincing than us, because they are actually *from* Germany."

"We thought of that too. The problem is we don't know if we can trust them. Just because they chose to immigrate here before the war doesn't mean they're loyal Americans."

The General stepped forward again. "This brings us to you boys. You're Yankees, born in America, raised in the cornfields of Nebraska and Kansas. Born to immigrants with real German accents. Hell, you probably spoke more German at home than English. Am I right?"

John and Tom nodded.

The General slapped his hands together. "That's exactly what we've been looking for."

"So you picked us." John ignored protocol and wiped the sweat off his brow. "What if we get found out? This whole plan depends on two amateurs who've only been in the army about ten weeks. What happens then?"

The General laughed. "You're not the only two. We didn't think it would be smart to have all the guys meet before they go in. Too much risk of giving each other away."

"So why allow John and me to know about each other?" Tom pointed his thumb at John.

"Do you want to go in there all alone?" The General took another drag from his cigar.

"I guess not," John said.

The General's lips turned up into a smile. "Alright then. You'll want at least one person you can trust. You won't be at risk of accidentally giving up the whole operation. You also have

21

someone who might get you out of a pinch, if needed. The guards won't even know you're not real POWs."

"Just so we're clear." Tom's eyes darted to John before returning to the General. "You want us to pretend we're German POWs, live in one of the camps, and try to gain intelligence of unknown importance? Not only that, but only the people in this car will know who we really are? What happens to us if you get bombed while we're in the prison camp?"

Major Jacobson waved his hand. "We won't be the only ones who know. When we said the guards wouldn't know, we meant most of the guards won't know. Our interrogators will know who you are. That's how we'll get information from you. We'll pull you out for interrogation just like we would any other prisoner. And, of course, the officers training you will know."

"Got it," Tom said. "So how *long* are you asking us to do this?"

Jacobson shook his head. "I know what you're really wondering. Will we stick you in for the rest of the war? The answer is no. The plan is to have you work on your backstories for the next week or two and then place you in a camp with the fresh arrivals. When you get information from them, we pull you out for a while, then back in when another new group has filtered in."

The major took a deep breath. "It's important we get you with new arrivals before they get acquainted with the old timers. Those prisoners who have been there a while know this game and will warn the new guys to keep their mouths shut. That only gives us about three or four days per group. More time would be nice, but space won't allow it."

John took a breath and prepared to ask a question. Before he could speak, Tom slapped him on the shoulder. "I don't know about John, but I'm in. Sounds fun."

The others looked at John. He knew he didn't really have a choice, but was glad they gave it to him straight. Or seemed to. "Yeah, me too. What now?"

Nodding with a smile, the General moved toward the door. "Good, good. Bill here will fill you in on the details. Good luck, fellas." Before they could ask another question, the General was gone, leaving behind a trail of smoke.

John and Tom were also soon on their way. Major Jacobson gave them two sets of directions, one for their living quarters at a former parochial school and the other for the old church they would train at each day. It was expected, they were told, that they would arrive on time each day and their mission was strictly confidential. As far as anyone was concerned, they were translators in language services.

On the walk from the train to a waiting flatbed truck, John spread his arms to allow his soaked shirt to dry. "So what do you think about all this?"

Tom ran his fingers through his sweaty hair before slinging his jacket over his shoulder. "I was serious on the train. I think it sounds like fun."

"Really?" John's eyes lowered. "That's your idea of fun?"

"I'm not kidding. Don't get me wrong, I'm not looking forward to living in a prison camp, but think about it. We get to be spies without ever actually crossing enemy lines."

John copied Tom and slung his sweat soaked army jacket over his shoulder. "It doesn't sound terrible. It'll keep us out of the trenches at least. I don't think it's going to be as easy as the General makes it out to be. It's not like we'll be living in those camps with General Ludendorff. It's going to be regular soldiers. What are those guys going to know?"

Tom shook his head and laughed. "You're looking at this all wrong. Whether we get any good information or not doesn't matter. We get to tell our grandkids we were spies in the war. Stop overthinking this and go with it. It's gonna be fun."

Their conversation stopped when they reached their truck. They were instructed to never talk about their mission around anyone, including fellow soldiers. Climbing into the back of the truck, Tom winked. "It's gonna be an adventure."

5

A jostling three-hour ride in the back of a small green Model T field truck brought John and Tom to the converted school in Verdun. The clerk at the front desk gave them a mini tour and showed them to their room. Along the way, Tom paused to watch two French girls cleaning the old school library. After the tour ended, the clerk told John about a small tavern on the same block as the school.

Tom pointed to the small building. "That must be it. The kid at the desk said it was down the street."

John raised his eyebrows. "I thought you were too busy ogling the French girls to hear anything the clerk said."

"I'm always paying attention, my friend. It's how I've made it this far." Tom slapped John on the back and pulled the door open.

The atmosphere of the inn was a mixture of cigarette and grease smoke combined with French music that played on the gramophone in the corner. Quiet conversation wafted through the air. A large bar took up most of the wall to the left of the entrance. A door behind the bar led to what looked like a small kitchen. A huge rock fireplace, currently dormant in the summer heat, sat against the wall to the right of the door.

John and Tom chose a table near the bar and waited for service.

"Oh, Americans." A short, white-haired man entered the room and spoke with a thick French accent. He pointed to John's uniform. "So clean. You must be new to our country?"

John raised his head. "Yes, just arrived. That obvious?"

"Oh yes." The old man waddled in their direction. "Usually, soldiers come in here on their rest time from the front. Even if they've taken a bath, they can't get the dirt out of the clothes. Not that I mind. Soldiers from the front have a big thirst."

"We got off the boat yesterday and have a big thirst too." Tom laughed. "I'll take a beer, or ale, or whatever you call it here. And one for my friend."

The old man shuffled behind the bar. "I'm Gautier, if you need anything. This is my place."

John quickly drank two beers before he decided it was time to head back to the old school. Tomorrow would be a long day, he explained, and he needed to get some sleep. Tom wanted to stay and see if he could get in on a card game with some of the other soldiers in the restaurant.

"Gonna write a letter to that girl back home?" Tom asked.

"Yeah, I think so." John stood. "I don't know what I'm going to say though. It's only been three months since I saw her, but I'm not sure I'll go back to Nebraska when this is over."

"By the sounds of it, she'd go with you anywhere." Tom reached for his billfold. "If that's what you want."

"That's the thing." John shrugged. "I'm not sure it's what I want. I thought it was, but now with a little time to think about it, I'm not sure."

Tom patted John on the back. "You'll figure it out. Have fun writing."

"And have fun losing your money."

Tom winked. "I never lose."

On the way to the exit, John glanced through the door behind the bar and smiled at a young woman working at a small stove. Her dark hair was tied up in the back. One curly strand dangled near her neck. When she looked at John, her mouth curved into a smile.

"Who's that?" John asked Gautier.

Gautier glowered at John.

"That," he said with a clenched jaw, "is my niece Margrit."

"Oh, Okay." John rubbed his eyes and turned from the kitchen. "Thanks for the drinks."

Gautier glanced over his shoulder into the kitchen before smiling at John. "Have a good night. And welcome to France."

Walking out the door, John looked over his shoulder for one more glimpse and mumbled, "Thank you."

#

The next day, John and Tom returned to Gautier's for lunch following their first morning of training. After the old man delivered their food, John said, "One Week? They think we're going to be ready to fool a bunch of Germans after only one week?"

"That's the idea." Tom took a bite of his sandwich.

John shook his head before taking a long drink of water. "I don't know how this will work. We're supposed to have grown up in these little German towns. What if one of the prisoners happens to come from the same area, or has a cousin from that city. What then?"

"I guess we improvise." Tom leaned back in his chair and took a sip of beer, even though drinking while on duty was a violation of regulations. "They're interviewing all the prisoners, so we won't be in that situation. But if we get into trouble, we'll figure it out."

John made a coughing sound and nodded toward the kitchen. The beautiful woman from the night before walked toward their table. His heart pounded.

"Anything else?" she asked. She spoke in broken English they barely understood. Like the day before, her hair was wrapped up in the back with one little strand dangling down. John assumed she meant to leave the strand free, and it drew his attention to her long, slender neck.

Tom smiled at John with a look that meant, "Why yes, as a matter of fact there will be something else."

John tried not to stare at the attractive girl. He told himself he wasn't interested, but his eyes kept rolling back in her direction. "No, just the check please."

Her forehead creased. "Check, what is check?"

John smiled. "The bill. You know, so we can pay for our food."

"Oh yes." She nodded before walking away.

Even though it was dark in the wood paneled room, John could tell she wore a plain red summer dress that somehow looked much less plain on her. His eyes were glued to her.

"Hello?" Tom waved his hand in front of John's face. "You awake?"

"Oh, sorry, what?" John blinked at Tom.

26

"Wow, so you are interested in girls, or a girl other than the one back home. I couldn't tell until now." Tom laughed and leaned so far back in his chair, John thought he might tip over. "Now that I know, I'll leave her to you."

"What are you talking about?" John felt heat rising in his face. "I'm not interested in anything like that, especially when I haven't figured out what I'm going to do about Rose."

Tom's head cocked to the side. "What did you tell her in the letter?"

John was still a little dazed. "What?"

Tom smirked. "The letter. You know, the one you were going to write last night."

John rubbed his neck. "Oh, that. Nothing. I mean, I don't know what to tell her so I didn't write anything."

"And how do you feel about her." Tom swung one leg onto an empty chair at the table across from him.

"You mean Rose?" John didn't want to admit he couldn't get his mind off the beautiful girl after he saw her last night, and that was the real reason he hadn't written to Rose.

Tom said. "Yes, Rose. Who else?"

"Well, I think I love her. Or thought I did." John stumbled over his words. "But now that I'm here, I don't know. This is why we made no promises to each other."

Tom jerked his head in the direction of the kitchen. "You like what you see with that one though, don't you?"

John shook his head. "Well sure, she's beautiful. But you know my situation. There is something about her that I can't..." John scratched his chin. "Was there something else you wanted to say?"

Tom nodded in the direction of the kitchen. "While you were drooling, I asked if you noticed anything about her accent?"

John stared at his friend for a second. "No, not really."

"Nothing?" Tom asked.

"Well, now that you mention it, there was something a little different." John paused. "She didn't sound French, did she? Not that I'm an expert on French accents."

"You don't have to be." Tom spoke quietly as Margrit re-emerged from the kitchen holding a small slip of paper. "She didn't sound French at all. It's hard to tell, but it sure sounded like a German accent to me. We are experts on that. At least the Army thinks we are."

Margrit arrived to the table as Tom's words trailed off. She set the paper in front of John and reached to collect an empty plate and glass. Her bare arm brushed against John's. He felt goose bumps up that side of his body and wanted to hear her speak again.

"Gautier is your uncle, right?" John asked.

"Yes."

John's curiosity wasn't satisfied. He enjoyed her arm against his. "What brought you to work here with your uncle? I mean, are you from around here?"

Waiting for an answer, John noticed her perfume. He caught himself taking a deep breath, trying to inhale as much of the intoxicating scent as he could. The girls he knew in America didn't smell like this.

John flinched when Gautier yelled from across the room. "Margrit, the vegetable delivery is here." Before she could answer John's question, Margrit was behind the bar without a word. As she entered the kitchen, she turned her head with a half-smile at John.

Gautier ambled from behind the bar in the direction of John and Tom. Arriving at their table, he picked up John's empty bowl and plate. The entire time he stared at John. "So, you came back to my place? I hope you enjoyed your lunch."

"Yes, it was delicious," John stammered. He couldn't stop thinking about Margrit's smile. The scent of her perfume lingered in the air around him. "The girl, your niece, is she your cook?"

Gautier's eyes narrowed. "Yes. Why do you want to know?"

John felt uncomfortable under the Frenchman's gaze. He tapped his foot under the table and tried to respond as casually as possible. "It was delicious. I wondered if she is cooking a family recipe, you know, since she is part of your family?" After a short silence, John added, "I know how important it is to protect those sorts of family secrets. You can't be too careful with whom you share them."

"Yes." Gautier eyed John. "We must protect those things that are most dear to us, no?"

The old man didn't wait for a response before he grabbed John and Tom's cash with his free hand and left the table. "I'm glad you enjoyed your meal."

"What do you suppose that was all about?" Tom asked, after the old man was gone.

John shrugged. "I suppose he's protective of his niece. If she is German, he might want to keep it quiet. I know I would."

Almost thinking aloud to himself, John added, "But why do you suppose she's here?"

"I don't know." Tom took the cloth napkin from his lap and tossed it onto the table. "I'll come back for the food, but I think it's safe to say the girl is off limits."

John nodded. "Yeah, you have plenty of other game to hunt anyway."

"Yes, I do." Tom laughed. "But do you?"

6

After lunch, John and Tom returned to the old monastery that housed the language-training center. The massive wooden pews were pushed to the side, replaced with an assortment of worktables scattered throughout the church.

John sighed and held the tall oak door open for his friend. "Do you think they have anything else planned for training? Other than screaming at us, I mean?"

Tom shrugged. "Doesn't look like it. Why?"

John stood holding the door. "It seems like a poor way to prepare spies, even if we aren't going to be crossing into enemy territory."

"I don't think they know what to do with us," Tom said. "These guys all used to be German professors at university before the war. It doesn't look like the army gave them much direction."

John shook his head. "So they're making it up as they go?"

"It looks that way," Tom answered.

John stepped into the foyer of the church and let the door slam shut. The sound echoed through the hallow building. "How does that help us prepare?"

Tom smiled. "You're over thinking this again. Think about it. We're using the names of our parents and grandparents as our backstories. We know our family history backward and forward. The yelling is just trying to put a little pressure on us to see if we slip up."

John frowned. "How can you be so dismissive about this? What happens if we screw up in camp because they didn't train us properly?"

"Nothing." Tom waved his hand. "If one of us makes a mistake, they pull us out for more practice. Nothing to worry about."

"I hope you're right."

Tom winked. "I'm always right."

#

When the afternoon training session ended, John asked Tom if he wanted to eat dinner at Gautier's.

"No, I'll eat at the school tonight. I think I'll have better luck with the French girls than you will with your mystery cook."

"Oh, come on," John said. "I like the atmosphere. That's all. And the food."

"Well have fun, with the, uh, atmosphere." Tom called over his shoulder. "Your interest in that cook answers your questions about the girl back home though, doesn't it?"

John mumbled, "I think it might."

John's shoulders slumped when he entered the restaurant and didn't see Margrit. Only Gautier worked behind the bar. The room was about a third full of customers, so John was able to find a table with a good view to the kitchen.

"I just want to hear her accent again, that's all." John tried to convince himself he wasn't falling for a woman he didn't even know. He was only curious, he told himself.

John turned to the massive rock fireplace. A fire roared inside the hearth and a chunk of meat hung on a rotating pole. A small electric fan hummed next to the fire and a makeshift pulley system connected the fan to the pole, rotating the meat. Hanging from a hook in the top of the fireplace next to the meat was a large black vat of what John assumed was the soup of the day.

John's stomach rumbled at the smell of roasting meat and soup. The heat of the flames could be felt from John's table halfway across the room. Closing his eyes, the aroma of onions and garlic from the soup almost tricked him into thinking he was in his parents' dining room back home.

When Gautier arrived at his table, John asked, "What's with the fire?"

Gautier kind of snorted before answering with a frown. "Our stove is broken and won't be fixed until tomorrow. We have to cook dinner somehow. The menu is only soup and roast beef tonight."

John leaned in his chair, trying not to show his interest in the kitchen. "That sounds good to me. Can I have the roast beef put on a piece of bread for a sandwich with my soup?"

Gautier laughed. "You Americans love your sandwiches. Don't you even want to know what kind of soup we have?"

"Well," John answered with a smile. "As good as it smells, I don't need to know."

Gautier's chest puffed out. "Yes, we have an excellent cook."

John sensed his opportunity. "So your niece, where did she learn to cook?"

Gautier's eyes twinkled. "Margrit learned from my wife before she died. But she has something my Joceline didn't. She adds to a recipe and creates a masterpiece. Even cooking over an open fire in the summer heat."

"May I ask what happened to your wife?"

"We don't know for sure." Gautier closed his eyes.

John leaned forward in his chair. "What do you mean?"

"It was only about a year ago." The old man opened his eyes and took a deep breath. "It was a summer day much like this one, only not quite as hot. Joceline went to the bakery with Margrit, buying bread for the day. She was teaching her about buying the best foods, so they went from place to place. They were in line at the bakery when my Joceline collapsed. That was it. She was dead."

"You don't know what caused it?" John was surprised at how much the old man shared.

"No." Gautier shook his head. "Most of the doctors are at the war. Those that are left only help the sick. They said they don't have time for the dead. Without checking, the best guess was a stroke or heart attack, you know, because it was so quick."

John stared at his hands, unable to look at the Frenchman. He tried to express his condolences. "I'm, I'm so sorry."

Gautier lowered himself into a seat next to John. "I know Margrit blames herself, but I don't know what she could have done. When it's your time, what can stop it?"

John nodded, still not making eye contact. "I guess it must have been hard for her, and for you, not being able to say goodbye."

Gautier had a faint smile and sort of waved his hands at John. "You know, you Americans are so different from us French. We live life differently. At least my beautiful Joceline and I did. She knew how much I loved her. I didn't need to have extra time to make sure she knew it."

John shrugged. "That's true. Maybe we could learn something from you. I've never experienced that kind of loss, so I don't know what I am talking about."

"And I pray you never do." Gautier patted John's shoulder.

John glanced in the direction of the kitchen. "And your niece, she lives with you, right? How long has she been with you?"

Gautier pulled his hand from John's shoulder. "Why do you want to know?"

John froze for a moment. "Um, I'm curious. That's all."

Gautier stared at him. "My niece has been with us since before the war."

"May I ask why?" John swallowed hard. "Did something happen to her parents?"

Gautier scowled. "Her parents thought it would be safer for her to stay here after the war started. Their home was much closer to the front than ours."

John rubbed goose bumps on his neck. "So she is French?"

Gautier clenched his teeth. "I can tell you have a question you want to ask. So ask."

"It's just that," John took deep breath, "well, she sounded German to me. My parents grew up in Germany, and I know the accent. It wasn't French."

Gautier looked over his shoulder before he replied. "If you found out she's German, what would you say then?"

"Nothing," John said. "I mean, I'm American, but I have family in Germany. I am only curious."

Gautier stared hard at John before speaking in a near whisper. "Yes, she is German, well half-German. Her mother was French. As I said, she came to visit before the war broke out. Her town was mostly destroyed during the first year of the war."

"What about her parents?" John asked.

"They moved from their home before it was destroyed. Margrit's grandparents took them in. They live close to Berlin, away from the fighting. That's all we know. It's been a few years since communication across the front stopped," Gautier said.

"It's not illegal for her to be here," the old man added. "But there are those who wouldn't like it either. I don't want the government paying attention to her."

John nodded. "No, I suppose not. I won't tell anyone. My friend Tom noticed her accent, but he won't say anything. His folks are German too."

Gautier exhaled and got to his feet. "You have discovered our little secret. I hope I can trust you."

John looked Gautier in the eyes. "You have my word."

Gautier smiled. "Then let's get you something to eat."

He turned toward the kitchen and yelled, "Margrit, we need you up front."

John liked how Gautier said, "we need you," as though he still included his wife in the daily operation of the inn.

The beautiful silhouette glided across the dark room toward the huge fireplace. When she arrived at his table with a sandwich and a bowl of soup, John laughed to himself to think he came all the way to France, home of exquisite food, and all he'd eaten were sandwiches, soup, and an unpleasant stew at the school the night before.

"You're a wonderful cook." John wanted to talk to Margrit before she was gone again. He didn't know why. He did have feelings for Rose and he wouldn't be in France forever, so why even bother learning about Margrit?

"Thank you." Margrit avoided eye contact.

John's heartbeat pounded in his ears. "Your uncle told me about your aunt. That she taught you how to cook."

"Yes, my aunt was a good cook." Margrit spoke in broken English. John wanted to talk to her in German, but suspected Gautier wouldn't appreciate it. In truth, he enjoyed the way she spoke his language.

He sat at the table with his hands folded in his lap, feeling awkward and not knowing what to say. "I'm sorry about what happened to her."

"Thank you. It was a hard time for us." Before John could continue the conversation, Margrit stepped away from the table. He could tell she wasn't comfortable talking with him in a room

34

filling with people. He decided to wait and see if he might have a chance to talk more later in the evening.

Later turned into closing time. John sat all evening, trying to blend in. After almost three hours, the restaurant was finally empty enough for John to resume his conversation with Margrit while she cleaned a table near his.

Dizzy, it occurred to him he might have had too much to drink. He watched her move across the room and thought she didn't really walk. She glided, as if her feet never really hit the ground. The red dress she wore at lunch was replaced with a white blouse and long black skirt. He didn't realize he was staring until she stopped and looked at him.

John spoke more seriously than he meant to. "Your uncle told me about where you're from."

Margrit's eyes widened in alarm.

"I didn't mean for it to sound like that." John rubbed his forehead. "I just wanted to talk."

"Why do you want to talk to me?" Margrit sounded relieved, but still apprehensive.

John shook his head. "I really don't know."

Margrit frowned.

John realized how he must have sounded but stumbled as he searched for the right words. "I don't mean I don't know. I do know, but I can't explain it. You know? Okay, let me start over. Why do I want to talk to you?"

He took a deep breath. "Relax, just relax."

"Why do I want to talk to you?" he repeated. "I can't explain what it is about you that I want to get to know. At first it was the mystery of the girl with the German accent cooking in the back of a French restaurant. Now, after talking to your uncle, I want to hear more about you."

Gautier's laugh roared behind John. "It doesn't hurt that she's pretty, eh Yankee?"

John half shrugged. "Yeah, that doesn't hurt either."

"You know Yankee, I like you. I'm not sure if I trust you yet, but I like you." Gautier slapped John on the back. "You've been sitting in here all night, waiting to talk to a girl you haven't even been properly introduced to, not even sure of what you'll say. I like your spirit. What's your name, anyway?"

"John," he said with a slight slur, "John Bayer."

Gautier squeezed John's shoulder. "Well, John Bayer, this is my niece Margrit Kahler."

Heat crept up John's neck. He stood and tried to do a quick bow, placing his hand on the table to steady himself. He knew he'd drank too much. "It's a pleasure to meet you, Margrit."

Margrit stood silent while Gautier spoke. "You can talk to her, but first I need to know you aren't married. If I find out you are, you won't be welcome in my place. After all, what kind of man sits in my tavern all night waiting to talk to a pretty girl, knowing he has someone trusting him at home?"

Gautier spoke with the conviction of a man who loved his wife.

"No, I'm not married. I don't even have a girlfriend, well not an official one anyway."

Gautier's eyes narrowed. "What does that mean?"

"There is a girl, we went out a few times before I left. But it wasn't serious." John started to lean forward, nearly tipping over.

Gautier reached his thick arm up and placed his hand on John's chest to steady him. "Well then, if the girl wants to talk, you can talk."

Gautier removed his hand from John's chest and walked away.

"What was that all about?" John spoke in German.

"Oh, you speak German?" Margrit expression brightened. "You speak it very well. Where did you learn it?"

John ignored that she didn't answer his question. "My parents are from Germany. They went to America when mom was pregnant with me, twenty-three years ago. I grew up speaking German and English."

John flicked his hand at Gautier. "So what was all that about with your uncle?"

Smiling, Margrit looked across the inn. "With the restaurant so close to the front, we see many soldiers in here. Sometimes more, other times less. My uncle has seen plenty of men, with rings on their fingers, sitting with girls who aren't their wives."

"And he wants to protect you?"

"Yes," Margrit said. "It usually helps that I am in the kitchen. Out of sight. Camille, our waitress, has been sick. So I have had to come out from the back the last few days."

John nodded. "You don't mind spending so much time alone in the kitchen?"

"No, I love to cook. It reminds me of my aunt." Margrit smiled with a faraway look. "Sometimes I can almost feel her with me."

"Your uncle told me about her." John leaned on a chair.

"And you know the other reason I stay in the kitchen. My uncle says it's not safe for a German, even a girl, to be known so close to the front. So I stay in back." Margrit nodded in the direction of the kitchen.

"And it probably works, too, unless two Americans who speak German happen to stop in on the same day you have to come out from the kitchen." John shifted his feet.

Margrit smiled. "Yes. Until then. I have to admit though, I could have stayed in the back, but you weren't the only one who was curious."

John smiled at hearing that Margrit was "curious" about him. The chair he leaned against began to slide forward. Trying to regain his balance, John's arms swung wildly in the air as he fell forward. He closed his eyes and expected to crash onto a table and then the floor.

He opened his eyes and found himself face to face with Margrit. Her arms were wrapped around his waist, holding him tightly until he was able to stand.

John's face flushed with embarrassment. "I'm sorry about that. I guess I had too much to drink. I don't usually drink that much. I didn't know what else to do while I waited for you."

Margrit shifted her body so one arm was wrapped around John's waist. "Don't worry about it. Most soldiers drink a lot more. But how are we going to get you home?"

John thought about walking home on his own, but liked the feel of Margrit's arm around his waist. "I'm staying up the block, at the old school. Get me to the door and I'll be fine."

Margrit walked John to the door. "Uncle. I'm taking him to the school. I'll be right back."

As Margrit opened the door, Gautier yelled. "Be careful."

7

John sat in the dining room with Tom at breakfast the following morning. "Tomorrow? Are you kidding? How can they think we're ready?" he said. "This isn't a joke? We're going into the camp after just a few days of training?"

"That's pretty much the size of it." Tom held a spoon of oatmeal temporarily suspended in front of his mouth while he spoke.

John rubbed his temples. "And we're finding out now? Have they known we would be going in this soon since the train?"

"I don't think so. We found out at dinner last night. Since you came back to the room so late, you didn't find out until now."

"That's still pretty short notice." John looked at his bowl of oatmeal and felt nauseous.

Tom shrugged. "Apparently a group of young Germans were captured. The whole company surrendered. The General thought this might be a good opportunity. So in we go, like it or not."

John pushed the oatmeal away with a frown. "How is this going to work?"

"What do you mean?"

"Well, we go in tomorrow, right? What do we need to do to get ready?" John rubbed his temples again, fighting his headache.

"Major Jacobson will meet us at the church sometime today with more details." Tom took a long drink of coffee. "We're supposed to report to training as usual."

John wagged his head. "I hope they know what they're doing. I'm not disappointed to get out of training, but do you think we're ready for this?"

"Don't overthink this." Tom leaned back in his chair with a smile. "With the way they've been 'training' us, we won't get any more ready than we are now. We'll be fine."

Classic Tom, not worried about anything. "I hope you're right."

#

The level of disorganization in the dim monastery concerned John. It wasn't like the trainers scurried around in panic. But they furiously wrote on papers, only stopping to argue about the quality of their work.

"What's going on?" John's voice echoed in the old sanctuary.

The group of four men jumped, practically in unison, at the unexpected voice. "Oh, it's you." The de facto leader of the group was a former college professor named Lieutenant Harry Mason, a tall, gangly man who never seemed to have pants long enough to reach the floor.

Lieutenant Mason, ink stains on all of his fingers, mumbled as he resumed his work. "We need to get your papers ready. Even prisoners have identification papers, but we didn't think you'd need them this soon."

He looked at one of his associates with a frown before adding, "Our expert seemed to think he could take his time to get these done."

The other soldier scowled through glasses balanced on the tip of his nose. "How the hell was I supposed to know we would need papers already."

Mason clenched his jaw. "It shouldn't matter. If you had—"

"Okay." John stepped forward. "What do you want us to do today?"

Mason waved his hands. "I don't care what you do right now. The Major will be here with your uniforms around lunchtime. He wants the papers done by then."

John smiled at Tom who had walked through the side door. Plenty of time for an early visit to Gautier's.

"On second thought, you two better practice your stories. In German, of course. We won't have time to work with you today," Mason said.

John frowned at Tom. "I guess we're working."

Tom winked. "Hey, Lieutenant Mason, how about we practice somewhere else, you know, to stay out of your way here."

Mason didn't bother to look up. "Fine, whatever. Be back by noon."

Walking out the doors, John asked, "Where did you have in mind to practice?"

"The real question is, where did *you* have in mind?"

Without a word, the two men walked straight to Gautier's.

When they passed the corner of the building, the two soldiers stopped and watched Margrit unloading boxes from a wooden handcart into the back of the restaurant.

Tom elbowed John. "Well Casanova, here's your chance."

John's mouth curved into an embarrassed smile. "It's not like that. But it does look like she could use some help."

Tom turned to walk away. "I'll meet you at the school before lunch so we can go back to the monastery together."

John headed toward the back of the inn. He had the thought that, by not working with Tom as ordered, this might be the first time he broke a rule. A minor infraction no one would know about, but he felt guilty nonetheless. The guilt subsided when he saw Margrit's smile.

"What are you doing here?" she blurted.

John caught his breath as Margrit beamed at him. She wore dark red lipstick that matched her crimson dress. As usual, her hair was tied up in the back with a strand hanging down her long, olive colored neck.

Girls back home don't look like this, he thought, trying to suppress his smile.

"I happened to be in the neighborhood and thought you might want help carrying these, uh," John looked at the lone box that remained in the cart, "this box inside."

Margrit gave John a shy smile. "Yes, I think I would like the help."

John carried the wooden crate into the back room of the inn and didn't know where to set it. Shelves overflowed on every wall. He set the box on a small table with a butcher-block top at the center of the room.

"Wow, this is smaller than I expected." John spoke in German.

"It's big enough for me. We only offer a few meal choices a night, so it works." Margrit nodded at the broken stove near the door. "It used to work, anyway."

"So you're cooking at the fireplace again?" John glanced through the door into the dim restaurant. Rays of sunlight peeked through the cracks in the wooden shutters.

Margrit nodded. "Yes, but just for lunch. The blacksmith will be here sometime this morning to fix the stove."

John leaned against the table. "Is there anything I can do to help?"

Margrit gestured to the back door. "There's a pile of wood in back. Could you bring in a load to the fireplace so we can get it started?"

John removed his jacket and carefully folded it before setting in on a shelf. A few minutes later, he lit a roaring fire that brightened the dim room. Shadows danced around the restaurant as the flames popped and jumped. He explained to Margrit how he started many fires growing up in the sometimes harsh winters of Nebraska.

Back in the kitchen, Margrit diced vegetables at the table. "And in Nebraska, you don't have anyone to go back to?"

"My family is there." John looked at the floor. "They are all still on the farm."

"Of course there's family. But when you spoke with my uncle, you mentioned there was someone else. A girl?" Margrit scooped piles of diced vegetables into a pot.

John knew he needed to tell her the truth.

"A few weeks before I left for training, I spent time with someone I've known since I was a boy. It wasn't serious; at least I don't think it was. We both knew I was leaving, but we enjoyed spending time with each other." John watched Margrit as he spoke.

She handed John a vat filled with soup before she ran a metal rod through a slab of beef. "And this person, she feels the same way as you?"

John half shrugged, trying not to spill the contents of the pot. "I think so. I mean, she was the one who insisted we not get serious before I left."

Margrit pursed her lips as she seasoned the meat that would soon be roasting over the fire. "You know, women are hard to

41

understand sometimes. She might have said you shouldn't get serious, but I doubt she meant it."

John knew Margrit was right. He remembered the day he left Nebraska. His brother brought him to the train station and said goodbye on the street. When John walked onto the platform, he found Rose waiting for him with a smile. They said goodbye the day before, but she wanted to surprise him. Deep down, he knew Rose would wait for him.

John set the pot on the counter. "I've thought about that a lot, especially the last few days. I realize she hopes I'll come back home to her. But honestly, I don't know if I'll even live that long. And if I do, I don't know if I will go back to Nebraska."

Margrit peered into John's eyes. "Life has a way of sorting these things out. I want to know you aren't here, passing time with me, when you've made a promise to someone at home."

John spoke gently. "What I told your uncle yesterday is true. I hope you'll learn I am not the kind of man who would lie to you."

"Well, to what do we owe this honor?" John jumped at the loud voice of Gautier. "Another visit already?" John still hadn't gotten used to the booming voice of the boisterous Frenchman.

A grimy man carried a piece of black metal and a leather tool bag that clanked as he walked behind Gautier. John assumed he was the blacksmith. He was shorter than the Gautier, but had a muscular build from years of pounding metal.

John smiled after he realized who shouted across the room. "I got the day off. Well, sort of. I am supposed to be practicing…" He paused and looked at the blacksmith again. "I need to learn French culture. What better place to learn it than here?"

Gautier frowned. "Well, it's nice to see you here again. Now, if you'll excuse me, I have to get my stove fixed."

Gautier added from the back of the room, "Why don't you two go for a walk until we're done."

8

John and Margrit left the restaurant and walked by the river. John hoped he wouldn't be spotted by his superior officers, but decided a few minutes with a beautiful woman was worth the risk. After all, what would they do if they caught him?

"Better not head this way." John nodded in the direction of the old monastery.

Margrit took hold of John's arm as they walked. "Why not?"

"Oh, it's just army stuff. And besides, I've answered all the questions today. I think it's your turn."

Margrit squeezed his arm. "Alright, what do you want to know?"

John thought he was ready to ask questions, but now his mind was blank. After a few seconds, he blurted, "Tell me everything about you."

"Everything?" Margrit raised her eyebrows.

"Well, not everything. At least not yet. Tell me how you came to live here, with your uncle." John slipped his left hand onto Margrit's.

"It's not an interesting story, I'm afraid," Margrit said. "My mother and aunt Joceline were sisters. Every summer I would stay with my aunt and uncle for six weeks. After spring term ended in 1914 I came here like I have since I was five."

"Every year for six weeks?" John asked.

"My aunt and uncle didn't have children. They tried for many years, but couldn't. So they loved to have me come visit. Since my uncle and aunt owned the restaurant, they couldn't get away to come visit us. So I came here."

"Okay," John nodded. "Sorry, go on with your story."

"Well," Margrit resumed. "The war broke out not long after I got here. Back then we could still send letters and telegrams across the border. My mom and dad thought I would be safer here than travelling home. So I stayed."

John craned his head and pretended to look across the river so he could inhale the scent of Margrit's perfume again. "And then what?"

Margrit leaned in toward John. "Everyone expected the war to end soon. I've been here more than four years now. A few years ago, we received word that my parents had to leave our home and stay with my grandparents because our town got shelled. We know they arrived safely, but that's all."

"So," John rubbed the back of his neck with his free hand. "They don't even know about your aunt, about what happened to her?"

Margrit shrugged. "I don't know. We sent a letter with the Red Cross, but I haven't heard from them in a long time."

The two stopped walking at the bank of the river and looked at the ripples on the water. John turned and looked at Margrit. He hadn't noticed until now how much shorter she was than him. She didn't look at him, but watched the water as a duck with her babies struggled through the waves.

"I know this won't mean much. You don't even know me, not really anyway. But I'm sorry about what you have gone through. All of it." John squeezed Margrit's hand.

She looked toward the water and didn't say anything. John took a deep breath and stepped in front of her. He placed one hand on her arm and the other beneath her chin.

"I'm sorry." John nudged her chin so she would look at him.

Without warning, Margrit burst into tears. At first, it startled John. The tears came so forcefully he thought he might have made a mistake in prodding her to talk about such painful memories. He put his arms around her as she huddled into him, her body racked with sobs.

Margrit wept for a few minutes before she tried to speak. The whole time, John held her close.

"I'm sorry." Margrit's cries turned into more of a whimper. "I shouldn't have done that. It's just, well, I haven't cried since my aunt died."

"No, don't be sorry. Don't ever be sorry." John realized the importance of the fact that it was he whom she chose to have this moment with. Not her uncle, not a friend, if she had any friends here. This American whom she barely knew was the man she chose to let down her guard with.

"Before my aunt died, I cried all the time. I missed my parents and couldn't control it. She didn't mind, you know. Joceline was remarkable. She held me and let me cry, every time. I was a schoolgirl when the war broke out, and she understood. When she died, I knew it was time to stop crying. My uncle needed me."

John frowned. He didn't know what to say, so he pulled her closer. Margrit wept again, this time she quietly cried into his chest. The sobs subsided and were replaced with soft tears.

When the tears receded, John looked into her eyes. His mind raced. He thought about how quickly his relationship with Margrit was developing.

"You must think I'm a mess. Crying like this with someone I hardly know." Margrit whimpered.

"No, I think you need a friend."

Friend? John thought to himself. *Is that what I am?* He wanted more, but wouldn't press it.

"I'm glad I was here for you today," John said. "I don't know what you're going through, nor can I imagine. But I'm glad to have been here."

Margrit leaned her head against his chest. "Now what?"

John inhaled the scent of her perfume. "I don't know. I'd like to get to know you better. But I guess that's up to you."

Margrit giggled. She turned to look into John's face. "I meant what do you want to do now? We can't stand here by the river all day."

John's face flushed. "I don't see why not. I kind of like it this way."

Realizing John still had his arms around her, Margrit reached around and squeezed his waist. "I like it too."

"I have to be back before noon, so we still have time. Are you hungry?" John reluctantly loosened his arms, but did not remove them completely.

Turning in the direction of the shops, Margrit grabbed John by the hand and pulled him behind her. "I've already been there once today, but there's a shop nearby with wonderful rolls."

After a quick tour of the town shopping area, John and Margrit stopped at a small bakery to buy sweet rolls. Arriving back at Gautier's, John and Margrit stood at the back door of the restaurant and ate the last bites of their pastries. John had enjoyed himself so much, he hesitated to bring up his upcoming absence. "I have to tell you something. I don't think it's a big deal. But I have to go away tomorrow morning for a while."

Margrit kept smiling. "When will you be back?"

John's eyebrows rose. "I don't know exactly. You aren't upset?"

"You're a soldier. Soldiers leave and then they come back. It's not a surprise to me, I live so close to the front I see it all the time."

John exhaled. "I don't know for sure when I'll be back, but I think I'll be around tonight. Can I see you again?"

"I'd like that," Margrit said.

John hesitated as he turned to leave. "Can I ask you one more question?"

"Of course," Margrit said.

"I'm not sure what's happening, but are we moving too fast?"

Margrit's eyes sparkled. "You know, my aunt used to say 'When you know what you want, grab it today. Tomorrow may never come.' That's how she lived and that's how I will live."

John nodded. "Okay. I'll see you tonight."

# # #

All the way to the school, John felt the squeeze of Margrit's arms around his back. When he entered the building, he still smelled the aroma of her perfume on his jacket. He inhaled the scent as he walked in the direction of his room. Not finding Tom there, John discovered his friend asleep on one of the plush brown leather sofas in the library.

John tapped him on the foot. "Looks like chasing girls wore you out."

"No." Tom yawned. "Playing cards at night wears me out. Chasing girls wakes me up. Speaking of that, how'd it go with your chef?"

John was reluctant to share too much. He didn't want to give the details of his time with Margrit. "It went well. We didn't have much time so I'm going back tonight."

"Of course you are." Tom laughed, stretching himself out of the couch. "Any chance you'll be back early? I arranged another card game with a few of the guys."

John shook his head. "I don't think so. Better plan it without me."

Arriving back at the monastery, John and Tom tried on their German uniforms. John pointed at Tom's legs with a frown. "They're a little short, aren't they?"

Tom looked at his pants that were at least three inches too short and then at John's that were too long. "What gives Major? You couldn't find a corpse our size to steal these uniforms from."

"For god's sake Schlicting, we didn't steal these uniforms off dead men," Major Jacobson retorted with a scowl. "And no one will notice anyway. Half the German army has the wrong size uniform."

Tom laughed. "Okay, Major. Sorry. So what's the plan tomorrow?"

Major Jacobson informed them they would go to the prison camp separately. "When you're in there together, take time to act like you're building a friendship."

John thought he could actually hear Tom's eyes roll as Jacobson pointed out the obvious, but he nodded in agreement.

"One other thing. I guess I should have brought this up before." Jacobson hesitated. John and Tom glanced at each other. "When you're in there, no matter what happens, you have to stay on our side of the line."

Tom's eyes narrowed. "Well of course we do. Who wants to get caught behind enemy lines?"

Jacobson shook his head. "No, that's not what I mean. Listen, there are rules of war, international rules, that we're kind of skirting with this operation."

"What are you getting at, Major?" Tom asked sharply.

"Technically." Jacobson ignored Tom's tone. "You're not supposed to wear the uniform of an enemy combatant in a war zone. That's against international law and there's no protections for it. If you're caught and the Germans figure out who you are, they could shoot you on the spot."

Tom eyes widened. "Are you kidding? You just happened to forget this bit of information. That we're violating international law?"

"I know." Jacobson waved his hands. "But you aren't going into a war zone, since prison camps are excluded. So *technically*, you aren't violating any law. But if the Germans advance and gain ground, you have to stay on this side."

John crossed his arms. "And what are the chances of that happening?"

"Not likely," Jacobson said. "In fact it has never happened before. You don't have to worry."

"Easy for you to say," Tom glared at Jacobson. "You're not the one who won't be given mercy if things go bad."

Major Jacobson glared at Tom. "We all have to do our part, don't we Lieutenant? We need information and, so far, only you two are close enough to being ready to get it. It's up to you whether you will go in or not. We aren't going to force you."

"So we can refuse the assignment?" John asked.

Jacobson's cold stare turned to John. "If you don't want to do this, I'm sure the commanders at the front can find a use for you translating in the trenches."

Tom took a step toward Jacobson. "What is that, a threat?"

"Take it however you want. The reality is, we have plenty of translators. We don't need any more. What we need are soldiers who can go into a prison camp and blend in. I'm sorry I didn't mention it before."

Tom's face grew more red. John patted him on the chest. "We'll do it."

"What do you mean we'll—"

"I said we'll do it." John repeated firmly.

"Good." Jacobson turned to leave. "I knew you'd see it through. Mason has everything you need. Good luck tomorrow."

The Major scurried out the door before they could ask any more questions. After he left, John turned to Tom. "Now it's my turn to tell you to relax. Nothing has changed."

"I'm not sure I agree with you." Tom frowned.

John patted Tom on the shoulder. "We've known all along we have to do this. Rules or no rules. We're pushing the Germans back—we'll be fine."

"I don't like it," Tom said. "It's not that I don't want to do my part, and it certainly sounds fun, but I don't like the way they sprung this on us at the last minute."

"No, neither do I," John said. "But I'm also not surprised this isn't exactly legal. Look at the way they pushed us into it in that hot, smoky, train car. Not that you needed much convincing."

Tom said, "I guess you're right. But Jacobson turned into such a weasel. I really wanted to deck him."

John slapped his friend on the back with a laugh. "That's one way to stay away from the front. A trip to Leavenworth for hitting a superior officer."

"Don't you mean a higher ranking officer?" Tom laughed.

After all the details were offered by Lieutenant Mason, John volunteered to go in to the camp first, which meant he would be taken in at five thirty the following morning. Tom would arrive closer to noon.

Walking out the door of the monastery, Lieutenant Mason stopped them. "One more thing. I guess Major Jacobson forgot to mention it after your, uh, discussion earlier." Mason frowned as the two soldiers glared at him.

"We haven't gotten all of the older prisoners transferred out yet." Mason stared at his feet.

"What do you mean?" John spoke before Tom could respond.

"Well, there's a group of prisoners who have been there a while. They have the respect of the younger prisoners and they help the guards keep order in the camp." Mason shifted from one foot to the other.

"They help keep order? Just being nice guys I suppose?" Tom crossed his arms.

Mason shrugged. "I don't know for sure, but it sounds like the guards give them special privileges for helping out. I'm telling you this as a heads up. Just be aware we haven't been able to get them out yet."

"John leaned against the wall and put his hands in his pockets. "How can you not get them out? The General can do whatever he wants."

Mason wagged his head. "I know. But these mix ups keep happening. We think the guards like to have them around to keep the place quiet, so they purposely lose the transfer orders. It shouldn't matter though, since you will look like all the other new prisoners."

Tom looked toward the door. "Okay, so we need to watch out for those guys. Anything else?"

Mason shook his head. "No. Just be careful in there. Those old timers have been around a while and have a nasty reputation. Oh, and have fun tonight."

9

John squinted as he searched Gautier's for Margrit. It took a moment for his eyes to adjust to the dark room. Seeing only patrons in the restaurant and Gautier behind the bar, John's mouth curved into a smile when the sound of a pan hitting the metal grate of the stove reached his ears. The familiar French voice belted out a tune over the old gramophone, and the flame in the fireplace was almost out. The smell of smoke from the dying fire mixed with the aroma from the kitchen and the sweet smell of pipe tobacco from an old man at the bar.

"Where to sit, sir?" John was getting used to hearing his French hosts speak in broken English when they recognized his American uniform.

He turned and discovered a tall woman with brown hair wrapped in, what looked like, an old green and white headscarf.

"Uh, anywhere is fine," John answered. He scanned the room, hoping for a seat with a view to the kitchen.

Gautier yelled and pointed to a stool near the bar. "Over here, Camille. Have him sit over here." Gautier's English was better than Camille's.

John settled into a seat in the center of the bar while Gautier poured five tall glasses of beer. He nodded to an old man next to him, but got no response.

"Well, Yankee, you came back again." Gautier placed an unordered beer in front of John. "For the food or the company?"

"Both." John took a long drink before he ordered something that sounded similar to a meat pie his mother used to make.

"So." Gautier peered at John. "Tell me about yourself."

"What do you want to know?"

51

"Start with where you're from. Tell me about your family."
Gautier didn't stop working. The old man next to John was now
sound asleep, head teetering on his palm.

"Ok." John nervously tapped the bar top. "I grew up in a small
town in Nebraska called Beatrice. Well, not in town, on a farm
outside of town. My folks were German immigrants. Dad works at
the flour mill in town."

"Wait a minute, I thought you were farmers?" Gautier walked
around the bar with a handful of drinks.

"We are farmers." John spoke loud enough that Gautier could
hear over a loud group of American soldiers near the back. "When
they went to America, my parents didn't have enough money to
buy a farm, so Dad worked at the mill. After he saved enough to
buy a small place, he kept working and buying more land. Now the
farm is big enough for my brother to run it full time."

"Your dad works, your brother farms. What do you do?"
Gautier returned to the bar with an armful of empty glasses.

"I graduated from law school in Lincoln. When the war is over,
I plan on working as a lawyer." John's stomach growled when
Camille set a plate in front of him. The crust on top had a gash
through it, which revealed a light gravy mixed with meat and
vegetables.

"Why not a farmer?" Gautier poured more drinks.

"It didn't suit me, I guess. After high school, Dad said I either
become a farmer or go to college. So I picked college." John took a
bite of the steaming beef, savoring the flavor with his eyes closed.
It reminded him of his mother's cooking.

"It's funny, even though Dad worked at the mill my entire life,
he used to say 'We didn't move to America so our children could
work in a factory. If that were the life we wanted for you, we
would have stayed in Germany.'"

Gautier nodded. "And being German, what do your parents
think of all that is going on here?"

John continued to chew while he spoke. "Well, they aren't
happy about it. We still have family in Germany. But we're
Americans."

"Even your parents?" Gautier asked.

"Yes, especially Dad." John took another bite. "My brother,
Alex, was born two years before they left Germany, but Dad

52

named him Alexander because it was a family name that sounded American. At that time, they were already planning to move. That's why he named me John. He said 'It's the most American name there is.'

"He even calls himself Rudy, instead of Rudolph, to sound more American. It drives Mom crazy. But he says 'If we're gonna live here, we're gonna be Americans.'" John smiled when he talked about his parents.

A commotion from the table of soldiers at the rear of the restaurant drew Gautier's attention, preventing him from asking another question. An American soldier leaned back in his chair, pointing in the direction of the entrance.

"Look at that boys, they have trained monkeys in uniforms over here." The soldier slurred every word with a thick southern accent.

Three black soldiers in French uniforms stood in the entrance of the restaurant. They looked at each other, obviously not understanding what the soldier said.

"I think you boys wanna find somewhere else to eat," the soldier bellowed.

The black soldiers spoke to each other in a language John didn't understand. He knew it wasn't French.

Gautier practically sprinted to the front of the restaurant. The old man moved faster than John thought was possible, considering how he usually shuffled around the restaurant.

"Excuse me." Gautier stretched his arm to shake the hands of the new arrivals. "You're welcome in my place. Where would you like to sit?"

The American soldier struggled to his feet, steadying himself on the shoulders of the men sitting on his right and left. "Are you telling me we're expected to sit here with those blacks? To eat in the same room with them?"

Gautier led the new guests to a table near the front window. "They're members of the French Foreign Legion. They are welcome in my place."

The soldier stared at Gautier and clenched a fist at his side. "If you're saying they can eat here, then you're saying I'm not welcome to eat here. Is that what you're telling me?"

John moved closer to the American soldier before Gautier could reply. "I don't think he's saying anything like that. It looks like

53

everyone is welcome here. But if that's how you want it," John pointed to the front door. "Allow me to help you to the door."

The soldier glared at John. "And who the hell are you?"

John glanced at the soldier's rank and nametape. "Listen, Private Howard, Gautier doesn't want any trouble. Why don't I pay for your meal and you can call it a day."

The private snorted as John spoke. "I'm not getting kicked out of this place. It's bad enough I got drafted to come fight in this lousy country. Now, because you want to serve those blacks, you think I'm gonna leave? And don't give me that *private* crap."

"Okay, if that's how you want it, I guess you'll be eating in the same room as them." John nodded at the new arrivals.

"The hell I am. I'll throw 'em out myself if I have to." Private Howard staggered in the direction of the three soldiers.

John stepped in his way. "No, you won't, *private*."

Fist clinching, Private Howard shouted, "Then I'll throw you out, too, you dirty son of a bitch."

Before he could act, Private Howard's friends grabbed him, one on each side. "Come on Jim, it's not worth it. Let's let the hero pay for our meal. We were gonna leave soon anyway."

Huffing and pulling against his friends, Private Howard snorted. "Ok, fine. Let me go. I don't wanna stay here anyway. Let's get out of here."

As they walked past John, the private's friends loosened their grip on his arms. John turned when he heard one of the female diner's gasp. The last thing he saw, before he collapsed to the floor, was Private Howard's huge fist approach his indefensible face.

John lay on the floor in a daze. He heard the door open and the American soldier laugh. "That'll teach the son of a bitch to mind his own business. Officer or not."

It took Gautier, Camille, and the suddenly alert old man from the bar to get John to his feet. John asked to be taken outside to get away from the gawking eyes of the restaurant patrons.

# # #

For the second time that day, John was alone in the alley with Margrit. His head rested in her lap as she sat on the wooden

54

landing. Tenderly, she took a wet washcloth and dabbed his darkening eye.

"So." Margrit looked at his face. "This is how you get alone with me. Good plan."

John winced when the rag touched his tender eye. "Whatever it takes to spend more time with you."

"You're lucky I was almost done with dinner. My uncle and Camille can handle it for a while." Margrit gently wiped John's forehead.

He realized he would be going into a prison camp the next day. "Oh no, what am I going to do about this eye? I can't go in looking like this."

Margrit raised her eyebrows. "Go in where? Are you confused?"

"Oh, no, it's only work stuff," John said. "Never mind."

He already realized he would tell the other prisoners an American soldier attacked him after he was captured. This might buy him credibility with the Germans, and it was partly true.

"What was that about in there? All I could hear from the kitchen was that big guy yelling. The next thing I know, you're on the floor and he's walking out," Margrit said.

"That." John grimaced. "Is Jim Crow."

"Who?"

"That's how we describe how blacks are treated in America." John laughed. He realized the soldier who hit him was also named Jim.

"A lot of people back home don't like them, black people that is." John reached to feel the growing bump under his eye.

Margrit stroked his hair. "That sounds like Jews in my country. In most of Europe, actually. There aren't laws about it in France, but they aren't treated well either. Many were kicked out of Russia when my mom was a girl. She told me about how they were treated when they traveled west."

"I guess we aren't that different. The same people who don't like blacks in America don't like Jews either." John closed his eyes. He enjoyed the warmth of his head in Margrit's lap.

She was quiet for a moment. "The Africans fight for us in the Foreign Legion. I think that helps people in France accept them."

"Blacks fight for us, too, but that doesn't seem to matter in my country." John looked at Margrit. "And what do you think about it? The blacks and Jews I mean?"

Margrit stopped stroking his hair and leaned her chin on her hand. "Indifferent, I suppose. I know how that sounds, but I haven't thought about it much. Until now, that is."

"And if I told you my grandmother was Jewish? Would that change your opinion of me?" John sort of held his breath and waited for her reply.

"Not at all." Margrit resumed stroking his hair.

"Good." John exhaled. "I must be a strange sight for you. A Lutheran Jewish farm boy from Nebraska, with a broken head, lying in your lap."

Margrit leaned close enough to his face that he could feel her warm breath. "There is no place I would rather have your broken head right now." She gently kissed the growing purplish black mark under his eye. "And no place I would rather be."

John fought the dizziness to force himself into a seated position, facing Margrit at a sideways angle. "And there is no place I would rather be, even if it takes a sock to the face to get here."

John held himself with his hands firmly placed on the wooden landing and leaned forward to kiss Margrit. She didn't pull back or turn away, but closed her eyes.

"I hope that was ok?" John said.

"Yes, it was." Margrit leaned in again.

John looked into her brown eyes. "I don't want you to think I have wrong intentions."

"If I thought you were capable of that, I wouldn't be with you. Camille or Uncle Gautier would be sitting here." Margrit smirked. "Although I doubt Uncle Gautier would let you kiss him."

"That's true." John laughed. "And besides, I am light headed. Maybe you're the one who's taking advantage of me."

As they leaned in for another kiss, Gautier coughed from inside the kitchen. "Margrit, Camille needs your help inside. It'll only take a minute."

Gautier waited for Margrit to leave. "First, I want to thank you for what you did in there. I think I would have gotten the black eye if you hadn't been there."

"Don't mention it." John pulled himself to his feet. He wobbled when he tried to stand. "I get embarrassed by my countrymen sometimes. I'll take a shot or two to make up for it."

Gautier nodded. "The other thing, as you might have guessed, is Margrit. She's young and only finally opening up again after a long time of sadness. I know she is opening up with you. She chose you. I don't mean to offend you, but I don't know why. She has been through so much and I don't want to see her hurt again."

"I'm not going to hurt her."

"I know you won't mean to." Gautier took hold of John's arm as he swayed with dizziness. "But I was once a young man too. Sometimes it happens. Be careful with her. You have earned my respect, mostly because she trusts you. Tonight you showed me your character. Trust is an important thing. Always remember that."

John held the old man's arm for balance and looked him in the eyes. "I will remember and I won't take your trust lightly."

Gautier smiled. "Now go out with her, have fun. After taking a hit like that, you've earned a night out with my niece."

"Go out" implied they would have a nice dinner or an evening of dancing. John and Margrit were content to sit under a tree in the park. They listened to the sound of music floating down the boulevard from orchestra hall. Being only ten miles from the front, the thunder of battle echoed in the background.

Reclining against the tree while Margrit leaned against him, a knot pressed into John's back. He wasn't willing to reposition himself, lest he risk disturbing Margrit. He grimaced when he reached his arms around her waist.

"Tell me." John squeezed her a little tighter. "What did you want to be when you were a child?"

"A fireman." Margrit giggled.

"Okay. I'll be more specific," John said. "What do you want to do when the war is over?"

Margrit rested her warm hands on top of his. "I don't know. I love to cook and thought about staying with my uncle until I get…" She nuzzled her head into John's chest. "Until I get married and have a family."

John inhaled the sweet scent of Margrit's perfume. "Why stop cooking when you have a family. You're a wonderful chef."

Margrit shrugged. "Maybe I won't. I'm sure my uncle wouldn't mind the sound of little feet in the restaurant."

She tilted her head to John. "Now your turn. What do you want to do after the war is over?"

John caressed Margrit's bare arm. "I don't know. I used to think I'd go home and practice law. Now that I'm out of Nebraska, I'm not sure I want to go back."

"Where would you go?"

John leaned his head against the tree. "I liked what I saw of New York before I got on the ship to come here. Or, I could stay in France if I had a reason to stay."

John twirled a blade of grass, waiting for Margrit's reaction. She moved her body so she faced him and placed her hand on his unshaven cheek. "And what kind of reason would that be?"

John leaned forward and kissed Margrit. "A beautiful fireman might keep me around."

Margrit laughed and settled her head back on John's chest. "That settles it. I'll be a fireman and you can cook for my uncle."

10

In the morning, John changed into his German uniform and prepared to go into camp. Lieutenant Mason made him crawl around in the dirt to make it look like he'd been to the front. Between the sweat and dirt, the aroma of Margrit's perfume still lingered. John inhaled with a smile.

Walking toward the camp at daybreak, John didn't think about what awaited him inside the fence. He couldn't stop thinking about Margrit. He still felt the warmth of her lips against his. He felt her body pressing against him.

When the prison gate became visible in the distance, John ignored the soldiers on either side and stopped. His legs wobbled a bit. *I can't believe I'm really going in there,* he thought to himself, the reality setting in.

"Keep moving." The soldier on John's right pushed his shoulder. "We don't have time for this."

John closed his eyes and took another breath. *Just get this over with so you can see her again soon.*

The soldier pushed John again. "Let's go."

John opened his eyes and scowled at the guard. He swallowed hard and resumed walking. Inside the gate, fourteen rows of tents stretched across the soggy enclosure. A narrow muddy walkway lined each row where a few patches of grass hadn't succumbed to the trampling of prisoners.

Pushing him through the gate, the soldier laughed. "Well buddy, welcome to your new home."

John tripped and fell into a shallow puddle. Rising from the mud, he turned to make a comment in German, but the guards were already halfway through the gate. Turning around, he scanned the

59

camp. *Camp*, he thought to himself, *I went to summer camp when I was a kid, and this isn't camp.*

He walked to a group of young German soldiers who watched him fall into the mud. A little nervous, he stuttered as he tested his German. "Hey, c-can you help me?"

"You look like you're doing fine." One of the young Germans laughed and pointed at John's wet, muddy pants.

John looked at his pants and laughed. "It looks like I have more mud than pants."

The German smiled. "So you're wondering what to do next, right?"

"Yes." John nodded. "Among other things."

"The most important thing is to find a place to sleep." The German waved his hand across the field. "Find a tent with room. Each tent has two cots. Start looking until you find an empty one."

John scanned the field. Groups of men milled near the rear of the camp. "How will I know if a cot is taken?"

"If someone is in it, it's taken." The prisoner laughed again.

Great, more jokes. John turned to walk away. "Okay, thanks for the help."

The young German kept laughing. "Hey, Fresh Fish, I'm serious. You won't know where to sleep until sundown. When they blow the whistle and we go to our tents, you'll have a few minutes to find an open cot."

"What if I don't find one?"

"There are always open beds. Prisoners don't stay here long. This isn't a permanent camp."

"Thanks," John said. He scraped the mud accumulating on the bottom of his boots, not knowing what else to do. Feeling his stomach rumble, he asked, "When do we eat?"

The German pointed toward a table at the back of the camp. "See that big bench next to the row of latrines? They bring the food there. You'll know when it's time."

Thinking this answered all of his questions, at least for now, John thanked the soldier again and went for a walk around the camp. He stopped at the edge of the fence when he saw a section of tipped over wooden bleachers outside the enclosure. The prison was once an old soccer field, converted to hold as many prisoners as possible. Before he could continue his stroll, a whistle blew.

John followed the throng of soldiers and lined up in front of a huge table at the rear of the camp. He found himself, again, with the three young German soldiers.

"Looks like you got here just in time, Fresh Fish." One of the young Germans walked beside John. "Don't want to miss breakfast before morning work crew."

"Work crew?" John looked sideways at the young man.

The group of soldiers laughed. "Yeah Fish, work crew. You don't think they'll let us sit in here and do nothing all day, do you? Most of us go on work detail after breakfast, except those ones." The German pointed to a group of older looking soldiers who were already eating their breakfast. "They stay here and *clean up* the camp when everyone is gone."

John thought it was strange the way the kid emphasized the words "clean up," but decided he misunderstood something in translation.

When he reached the table, John received a shallow metal bowl, a spoon, and a metal cup. All three were so dinged, he imagined they could be left over from the Civil War. Arriving at the vat containing breakfast, John grimaced. His meal appeared to be a mixture of runny oatmeal and creamed wheat. He was pleased to discover a cup of hot coffee awaited him at the end of the table.

In training, John was instructed to eat all of his food so he wouldn't stand out. Prisoners are always hungry, Mason explained. John choked down every bite of his food, which tasted better than it looked, but had the texture of soggy sawdust. While the meal wasn't great, John was surprised to discover the coffee was delicious. He even wondered if he was allowed more. His question was answered when he looked toward the serving table, only to find it cleared after all the prisoners were fed.

Still looking over his shoulder, John noticed the young Germans laughing at him. "So Fish, you liked the food?"

"I guess, why? What about it?" John was afraid they were about to reveal a disgusting secret ingredient he had ingested.

"We've never seen anyone eat all their food on the first day. I mean, we've only been here a month, and you're the first Fresh Fish to actually eat all of his food."

Realizing the information he received in training was misguided, John sighed with relief. "Oh, that. I grew up on a small

61

farm near Siegen. We were pretty poor back then. Today's breakfast would have been a feast on the farm."

Looking at his empty coffee cup, John asked, "The coffee was great. How'd we luck out and get it?"

"That's simple, Fish. The French and British have colonies in Africa where they grow coffee. That's the one thing we get in here that's any good."

John was already tired of being called "Fresh Fish" by a kid that couldn't be more than eighteen, but decided to ignore it and change the subject. "About the work detail, how do I know where to go?"

Getting up from his spot in the mud, the young German didn't seem to care that his entire backside was caked in wet dirt. "Just follow the crowd when you hear the whistle. We all go to the same place. And when you're walking, don't go off the road. The Yankees don't like that."

"Thanks," John said, impatiently tapping his cup and plate together.

They were given about fifteen minutes after breakfast before the front gates opened and a loud whistle blew three times. Most of the prisoners plodded toward the gate. On either side of them, American soldiers stood guard and appeared ready to shoot anyone who tried to escape. There didn't seem to be anyone in the group interested in making a run for it.

After exiting camp, John learned the prisoners were broken into work crews of fifteen men. As he peeled off with his group, he watched two American soldiers escorting a ragged looking prisoner toward the gate.

What's he doing here? He's not supposed to be here until noon. John quickly made his way to the group of prisoners Tom was taken to.

One of the escorts announced to the crew leader, "Got another one for you. They found this one hiding in a barn outside of town last night."

The American crew leader looked from his clipboard. "Why didn't they bring him in last night?"

"Interrogation." The escort pushed Tom toward the other prisoners. "Apparently they found him on our side of the line and wanted to find out how he got here."

"Oh, okay." The soldier scratched his head. "How *did* he get across the line?"

"They don't tell me that. I'm just here to deliver him," Tom's escort said, and walked away.

The guard looked at Tom and shrugged. "Sorry buddy, you missed breakfast."

Tom looked at the soldier with his head tilted to the side, not acknowledging that he understood anything. The young German who John recently met spoke up. "He said you missed breakfast. We're going on work crew now."

Shoulders slumping, Tom nodded and followed the other soldiers. John couldn't be sure, but he was fairly certain Tom's disappointment was genuine. The thought of going on a work crew seemed to have taken all the excitement of the mission right out of him.

They walked out of town for what John guessed was about two miles. The entire walk, John tried to get Tom's attention. He wanted to find out what went wrong that led Tom into the camp early. When John finally made eye contact, Tom only shrugged.

John rubbed his neck and mumbled to himself, "It's already going bad. They threw us in here too early."

Arriving at their destination, John discovered he would work on a farm that bore a strong resemblance to the one he grew up on. There was no corn, but he was put to work baling hay.

The young German was on John's work crew and came beside him while he rolled hay into round bales. "You look like an expert at this, Fresh Fish."

John winced when he heard the nickname again. "Like I told you, I grew up on a little farm. I can bale hay with my eyes closed."

"I can see that." The German, who didn't seem to have worked all morning, turned toward Tom. "Maybe you could teach the newest fish something. He looks like he's never seen the working end of a pitchfork."

John resisted the urge to point out that the young man had not yet done any work, and instead decided it was time to be "introduced" to his friend. "Sure, will we get into trouble if we call him over?"

The German shook his head and yelled. "Hey you, Fresh Fish, come here. The farmer here will show you how to do it right."

John worried that shouting would alarm the guards, given the young man's previous warning. They simply stopped talking long enough to make sure everyone resumed their work. John thought it wouldn't be difficult to escape if any prisoner was interested in going free.

After he demonstrated to Tom how to properly roll hay, the German meandered toward another group of prisoners. John stopped him. "Hey, I haven't even introduced myself. My name is Alders Bayer." John decided to use his grandfather's name as his cover.

"Yea, sure, I'm Otto. Otto Fiedler. Nice to meet you."

John and Otto looked at Tom. Tom hesitated before murmuring, "I'm Franz Schlicting."

With the introductions over, Otto succeeded in finding another group to avoid work with. John made small talk with Tom until Otto was away, before whispering, "What are you doing here this early? I thought you weren't coming until noon?"

"Hell if I know." Tom frowned. "All I know is I was sound asleep in my nice warm bed when Mason came pounding on my door. He said something about wanting me on 'the crew' before it goes into the field."

"They got you out of bed so you could make it to work crew?" John blurted out while subduing his laughter. "Like you're gonna get information working in a field all day."

"Laugh all you want buddy. I'm not laughing." Tom looked pale.

"I can't believe how disorganized this operation is." Tom mumbled. "They ruined a perfectly good hangover for this."

Still laughing, John leaned on his wooden pitchfork. "I wouldn't be so sure it wasn't revenge. Jacobson was pretty mad yesterday when we argued with him."

Tom rubbed his forehead for a moment before laughing.

John's eyes widened. "I figured that would get you more upset."

"Ah, what the hell? At least the guy has a sense of humor." Tom shook his head before returning to work. "That'll teach me to get smart with a superior, I mean, higher ranking officer."

John's smile turned down. "I am nervous that you coming in so soon after me will arouse suspicion. Don't get me wrong. I'm glad you aren't here because of a problem. But Jacobson's little revenge might cost us."

Tom shook his head. "Don't worry. Lots of prisoners come into the camp every day. No one will notice us."

11

John and Tom were not used to working in the fields. They looked like two worn-out rag dolls on the walk back to the camp at nightfall. It didn't help that Tom hadn't eaten breakfast, and for lunch, a wagon delivered the same gruel that was served in the morning, this time cold and without coffee.

Walking into camp, John could smell that dinner was more than the slop he had eaten earlier. Once in line, the distinct aroma of fresh bread reminded him of Mondays back on the farm, when his mother and sisters did the weekly baking. Arriving to the table, he was delighted to find that not only was there fresh bread, but a slab of meat smothered in a dark brown gravy awaited him. After the long day of work on two meager meals, John wouldn't even ask what kind of meat he was about to consume.

Unexpectedly, he heard a shout in an eerily familiar southern accent. "What the hell are you doing here?"

Not able to pinpoint why he recognized the voice, but feeling goose bumps on his neck, John glanced over his right shoulder. He couldn't see who'd yelled so he shuffled forward in line.

"Hey, you." A hand pushed John's right shoulder. "I asked you a question, what the hell is going on?"

John's face flushed when he realized who was screaming. He pivoted and came face-to-face with Private Howard, the soldier that gave him the black eye the previous night. Howard's wild eyes examined John from head to toe.

Pretending to not know the private, John glanced over his shoulder. He looked at Howard again and shrugged. John tried to continue shuffling in line, but was stopped.

The private pushed his shoulder again. "I'm talking to you. Why were you wearing an American uniform in town last night?"

John searched for the words "I don't understand" in German. "Ich verstehe nicht," he stammered.

"Don't give me that crap, I know you speak English." Private Howard gripped his rifle.

"What's going on, Jim?" Another American soldier stepped closer.

"This Hun. I swear he's the same guy I decked at the restaurant last night. Look at his eye. I gave that to him." Private Howard pointed his finger so close to John's eye, he tried to back away.

Howard grabbed John by the collar of his sweaty jacket and shouted, "Oh no you don't. You stay right here."

John's eyes flashed wildly to the growing crowd of onlookers. This was not a scenario he prepared for, or even imagined, in training. He turned his head back and forth and watched the other prisoners back away. A circle formed around John, Private Howard, and the other American soldier.

"No English," John stammered, in his best German accent.

Private Howard grabbed John by the collar with both hands, allowing his rifle to dangle from his arm. Howard stood face to face with John and yelled, "You better start talking. I know that was you at the restaurant last night."

John trembled and shook his head more vigorously. "No English, no English."

He knew he could give in and tell Private Howard the truth, but that would ruin the mission in a single day. John's legs began to shake. He thought if the private let him go, he would collapse.

"Ich spreche kein Englischhe." John's voice trembled.

Howard threw John to the ground and paced in a semi-circle. "You better explain this real fast."

Howard drew his rifle and pointed it at John's head. "Or your buddies are gonna be carrying your cold body out of here."

"Jim, relax." The other soldier put his hand on Private Howards shoulder. "Look at this guy. He looks like he's gonna piss his pants. There's no w—"

"Oh, it was him," Private Howard shook the man's hand off his shoulder. "And I'm gonna get to the bottom of it. He wore one of our uniforms yesterday. Probably a spy or something."

You have no idea, John thought. He wasn't going to wait any longer. This was a ridiculous mission that wasn't going to work anyway. *I'm not going to die for this. Not with Margrit waiting for me.*

John pushed himself higher on his knees and opened his mouth to speak. No words exited. All he felt was the choke of a dry mouth. Before he could speak, the young German from breakfast entered the circle with Tom close behind.

"Excuse me." Otto stood in front of Private Howard with wide eyes. "Maybe I can help. I speak English."

"Yeah, so does he." Howard pushed John back into the mud with his boot.

"Let him talk, Jim." The other American soldier stepped in front of Private Howard.

"Fine, go ahead." Howard glared at Otto.

Otto took a deep breath and turned to John. "They think you were in the city last night. Were you?"

"No, no." John shook his head. "I was with the Americans, being interrogated."

Otto translated the answer to the guards, stumbling with a few words.

"Oh yeah, and how did you get this?" Howard pointed to John's bruised eye, this time pressing his finger into the sore black and purple flesh.

"In interrogation. One of the guards hit me." John pulled away from Howard's finger.

Howard pointed his gun at John's head again. "He's lying. Something about this doesn't seem right."

Keeping the gun pointed at John's head, Howard looked at Otto. "Ask him how he can prove it."

John sighed and waited for the translation.

"Him." John pointed to Tom. "He was there when they took me out this morning. He saw me."

After Otto translated, the other American turned to Tom. "Is that true?"

Tom nodded.

"I guess that settles it, Jim." The soldier turned to Private Howard. "You mistook him for someone else. You were pretty drunk last night."

"I don't know." Private Howard peered at John, who was still on his knees in the mud. "I wasn't that out of it. I'm gonna keep my eyes on him."

Otto helped John to his feet. "Wow, only a day in and you already made friends with the guards. That must be a record."

Otto turned to Tom. "It sure didn't look like you knew each other this morning. What was that all about?"

Tom answered before John could speak. "I don't know him. I saw him get hauled out this morning while I waited to get interviewed. I'm not gonna let some cowboy shoot one of us for nothing."

"Sure, I get it." Otto nodded.

"Thank you both." John stretched his arms and squeezed both men's shoulders.

Tom shrugged. "Glad to help."

Tom looked beyond Otto and noticed the group of older prisoners watching them. "What's their story? Why are they staring at us?"

Otto gave an uneasy smile. "Those are the old timers. They've been here a long time. When we leave for work each day, they *clean up* camp."

"What do you mean, saying it like that?" John glanced at the old men.

Otto pivoted his head nervously and whispered, "We call the new guys Fresh Fish. When they come in, they sometimes leave stuff in their tent. You know, so they don't lose it at work. But the old timers *clean up* the camp when we're out on work crew."

Already a little hot under the collar, John scowled. "Why doesn't anyone stop it?"

"Shhh," Otto pleaded. "Listen. Some of them have been here since the beginning. This is supposed to be a short-term camp, you know, before we get sent to the permanent ones away from the front. Why do you suppose the guards keep them off the transfer lists?"

John scratched his head. "Bribes?"

Darting his eyes back and forth, Otto motioned for the two to move closer. "First, it was the French who ran this camp. Now it's the Americans. The old timers have been here the entire time; at least that's the rumor. And they get to leave camp at night and sleep in the infirmary. Get it?"

Otto nodded in the direction of a building outside the fence. The structure appeared to be an old sports clubhouse that now displayed a big red cross on the front.

"Yes, but that doesn't explain why they keep looking at us." Tom glared at the old men.

"Please be quiet," Otto pleaded again. "They know everything that goes on in here. Just keep your heads down. Some prisoners have been sent to dig trenches at the front. You don't last long working at the front."

"And the ones sent to the front happened to have made enemies with those guys, I suppose?" Tom huffed.

Otto shook his head. "That's the rumor. Anyway, the guards mostly let them do what they want. I hear they get a portion what the old timers *clean up.*"

John crossed his arms. "And I suppose they help keep things quiet in here too, don't they?"

Otto backed away from John and Tom. "Yeah, something like that. Listen, I gotta go. I'll see you guys around."

Tom waited until Otto was out of earshot. "I guess he's done talking."

John shrugged. "I don't blame him. Unlike us, he's not untouchable. If we are even safe in here."

"This near the end of the war, I'd keep my head down too. But I think we might have found the group we need to target for information." Tom squinted at the old men.

"Bayer. Alders Bayer. Alders Bayer." One of the guards at the front of the camp shouted into cupped hands.

John turned to the gate. "What now?"

He spotted Major Jacobson standing on the other side of the fence looking very unhappy.

12

"What the hell happened in there?" Major Jacobson slammed the door to his office at the old monastery.

"It was a fluke." John raised his hands, trying to remain calm. "I happened to come across that guard yesterday at the restaurant down the street. He recognized me and completely lost it. How can I help that?"

Jacobson threw his hat on the desk before pointing at John's face. "And do you want to explain *that*?"

John clenched his teeth. "*That*, Major, also happened at the hands of the guard at the restaurant. That's how he knew it was me."

John seethed at Jacobson. "I can't help it if I keep running into that guy. He was drunk and got out of hand. When I tried to calm him down, he decked me."

The major hunched over his desk with his fingers pressed onto the wood so hard his fingernails turned pink. "So an enlisted man strikes an officer, and you didn't think you should report it?"

John's cheek twitched. "No, I didn't. I was busy."

"Busy with the girl at the restaurant, I suppose?" Jacobson snarled.

Heat rose up John's neck. "How, exactly, do you know about her?"

Jacobson laughed. "You know we watched you in training and on the boat coming over here. Didn't you think we might still pay attention to what you're up to?"

John's eyes narrowed. The only sound he heard as he glared at the major was his heart pounding. "No, I didn't think you were still

71

spying on me. Apparently you weren't watching too closely, since you didn't know about this." John pointed at his barely open eye.

The major snorted. "Regardless, you almost blew the mission on your first day. Now what the hell are we supposed to do with you?"

John shook his head, letting go for the moment, the fact that he was still being watched. "I wouldn't say we blew the mission. In fact, I think when I go back, I'll go in as a bit of a celebrity."

The major stood rigid behind the massive oak desk. His hands moved to his hips. "And how will that be of any help to us?"

John's lips curved into a smile. "Easy, give me a few more bumps and bruises and send me back in. I'll tell 'em you guys decided to *interview* me again."

The major looked unconvinced, so John continued, "We learned more about the older prisoners that seem to run the show inside the fence. I think they'll have the information you're hoping for. If they don't have it, no one will."

"Yeah, we know about them." The major crossed his arms. "The guards let them stay because they help keep things quiet. We've interviewed them a hundred times and got nothing. How do you expect to gain their trust now?"

John pointed at Jacobson. "I won't get their trust. You'll get it for me. Nothing earns trust like a soldier who can take a beating and not talk. When I go back in and look like I've taken my lumps, it'll earn the trust I need."

The major smiled. John couldn't tell if it was at the thought of giving him more bruises, or if he liked the new plan. "Okay, say we send you back in? What about that idiot guard? After today, he'll be watching you."

John shrugged. "Best to tell him why I'm there. He still won't like me, but at least I won't get shot."

The Major rubbed his chin before he finally nodded. "I think that might work. We'll find him when he's off duty tonight and talk to him. You can go back in tomorrow morning."

Pausing for a moment, the major smirked. "I suppose it'll be good to have him help keep an eye on you. You seem to have a talent for getting into trouble."

Before John could reply, Jacobson yelled, "Corporal, come in here please."

John frowned when the major's aide entered the room. The corporal stood a little shorter than John, but was about a third as wide with dark brown hair and a massive jaw.

"Yes, sir?" The corporal stood at attention.

Jacobson seemed to relish the moment with a wide grin. "Corporal, you get to have a little fun before Lieutenant Bayer leaves for the night. I need you to rough him up a bit."

"Sir?" the corporal's head tilted to the side.

"That's right, Gary, you get to take a few shots at an officer. He needs some more marks on his face before morning." Jacobson snickered again.

The corporal turned to John with wide eyes.

John shrugged. "He ain't kidding, kid. Just go easy on me, okay?"

The corporal's stunned expression turned to a grin. He stepped toward John, cracking his knuckles along the way.

#

Walking toward his room rubbing the new welts on his face, John decided to get a bath and shave. He frowned when he thought about the last thing Jacobson said before leaving his office. "Stay away from that restaurant tonight. We don't need any more trouble."

John didn't argue.

He remembered he still needed to look the part of a dirty prisoner in the morning, so he decided against shaving. After a quick bath, he returned to his room. On the way, he noticed a soldier sitting on a wooden chair near the stairway.

John shook his head and mumbled, "Still watching me."

When he was dressed, John peeked out his door. The soldier remained at his post down the hall. Quietly, John closed the door and went to the window. His room was on the second floor, but the exterior brickwork had a decorative design. Perfect for climbing. With one leg dangling out the window, John hesitated. *Am I really doing this?*

Not waiting to answer his own question, John pushed himself the rest of the way out the window and shimmied down the wall.

He looked at the window he'd left partially open before hurrying away from the building.

Walking in the direction of the restaurant, John kept to the alleys to avoid getting caught. He laughed as he thought about Tom spending the night in camp while he was at his new favorite place, ready to have a hot meal and a cold beer. Tonight, he didn't care what Major Jacobson ordered him to do.

John approached the back door of Gautier's and peeked in the doorway of the kitchen. He savored the unmistakable aroma of garlic wafting through the air. He watched as Margrit, whose back was to him, crafted what he knew had to be a masterpiece at the old black wood stove.

He leaned against the cracking white doorframe, inhaling the fragrance of Margrit's cooking mixed with her perfume. John thought about how she changed the course of his life. *Is this what love feels like? I really think I could spend my life with this girl.*

He jumped at the boisterous voice of Gautier. "Are you gonna stand there staring or are you coming in?"

A little embarrassed, John stepped into the kitchen. "I'm coming in." He still hadn't gotten used to the booming voice of Margrit's uncle.

Margrit smiled and threw her arms around John's neck, momentarily forgetting about the ingredients on the stove. "What are you doing here?"

"Slight change of plans." John smiled painfully and pointed to his new bruises.

Margrit gasped and caressed the new marks on his face. "What happened?"

"Just another day at the office, I guess." John shrugged with a smile. "But I didn't come here to talk about that."

"You better get him something to eat," Gautier said. "He looks like he could use a little cheering up."

"I would like a good meal. Where I've been, the food has been pretty rotten." John reached for the plate Margrit had already prepared for him.

Looking at the finely cut steak with a garlic-butter glaze and green vegetables, John's stomach rumbled. Knowing he might be eating prison meals into the foreseeable future, John relished his feast. He had that "last meal of a condemned man" feeling as he devoured his food. When Gautier put a glass of beer in front of him, he slurped it down in two gulps.

"Wow, I guess you were hungry," Margrit said, as she refilled his nearly empty plate from the sizzling pan on the stove.

Waiting for Margrit to finish, John spoke in between bites. "Any chance you can get away early tonight? I have to leave in the morning. I think it will be for a while this time."

Margrit looked at a small brass clock on the shelf to the left of the stove. "I think so. Dinner is almost done, and my uncle can handle the small food orders after dinner."

"You don't think he'll mind?" John was still apprehensive about Margrit's protective uncle.

She smiled and shook her head. "He's starting to like you and he knows how I feel about you. He won't mind. Besides, Camille's daughter is here working tonight, so he won't miss me."

While Margrit prepared the dinner orders, John volunteered to help with the dishes to speed things along. He knew this was his only night with Margrit for a while, and he wanted as much time with her as he could get. After his initial experience in camp, John was uneasy about going back in.

Walking out the rear door, Margrit squeezed John's arm with both of hers. "So where do you want to go tonight?"

"Everywhere. But I'm not supposed to be out tonight." John raised his free hand to point to the bruises on his face. "And I'm not exactly easy to miss these days."

Looking puzzled, Margrit nodded in the direction of the stairs. "How about a quiet evening upstairs? Then you can tell me about those marks."

Walking up the stairs, John couldn't keep his eyes off Margrit's slender figure. She wore a black dress with buttons up the back. He hadn't noticed before, because she wore an apron, but he now appreciated the fitting dress. Her hair was braided high on her head, which allowed him to see her smooth neck to her hairline. He could also smell the flowery perfume that reminded him of his first encounter with her in the restaurant. It had only been a few days, but it felt to John like he'd known Margrit much longer.

John stopped when Margrit pushed open the worn out, white paneled door to the spacious apartment. "Gautier won't be angry, you know, that we're here alone?"

Margrit pulled John to the sofa at the side of the room. "Not at all. He's French. They have different ideas about love than Americans. And Germans, too, I guess."

She said "love." John smiled to himself.

He pulled Margrit close to him on the sofa so she lay with her back against his chest. He wrapped his arms gently around her waist.

"What now?" he asked. The muffled sound of voices and the phonograph playing in the restaurant below wafted through the apartment.

"This is all I want," Margrit answered. "Just hold me. Tell me where those bruises came from."

Pulling his hand away from her waist and running his fingers through his hair, John hesitated. "I'm not really supposed to. If anyone found out, I'd go to prison. Especially since you're German."

John laughed out loud as he thought, *I'm already going to prison tomorrow,* before he added, "Ah, why not?"

Margrit pressed her body closer into John, pulling her hair out of the braid and resting her head on his chest. He told her about the camp and his mission, not discussing specific people, other than the soldier who hit him. When he got to the part of the story with the gun to his head, the hand across Margrit's waist started shaking.

Margrit placed both of her hands on John's trembling hand.

"So there I was, on my knees in the mud, and that big monster held a gun to my head. Here I am, an American, and he's standing there ready to shoot me in the head. I couldn't believe this was how I was going to die."

"What did you do?" Margrit stroked his hand.

Pausing, John put his other arm around her again. "Nothing. I mean, I guess I was going to tell him who I really was."

John paused again. He exhaled, and as he did, his entire body shuddered.

"I was going to tell him. I was actually going to tell him," John repeated in disbelief, almost as though he was asking himself a question. "I was going to tell him, just like that. First day in, gun to my head, and I crack."

Shaking his head, he repeated, "I would have told him, too, if..." he trailed off, thinking about how Tom and the young German had intervened.

Margrit tilted her head to look at John. "If what?"

He didn't answer—he just kept talking. "I thought that was it. I sat there, leaning back on my knees, watching his finger. I knew he was going to pull the trigger. I knew it. I could see his finger pulsing with anger. I looked at his red face, veins popping out everywhere. He was so angry. I was going to die."

His eyes closed and his face grimaced as though he was in pain. "I was a dead man. I'd never go home. Never see my family again. Never see you. My brother said I would die here, and he would have been right."

"But you didn't." Margrit turned her body over so she leaned against his. She stared into his brown eyes. "You didn't die. You're alive, here tonight, with me."

John squeezed his eyes tighter, trying to hold everything back. With his eyes closed and jaw clinched, John's chest shook. Tears streamed from his face. "I was going to die."

John breathed deeply with his eyes closed and lips tight. He'd ignored the reality that he could die for so long; trying to convince himself he was safe. Now, he was faced with the reality of life in war. He held his breath before opening his eyes, tears streaked his bruised face. He looked at Margrit, whose body was now pressed firmly against his. Her hands caressed his unshaven cheeks and her forehead rested against his.

"It's all right, you're safe now," she whispered and caressed his face. "You're going to be okay."

John rubbed his eyes with one hand and took a deep breath. "When I first got to France, I saw the trains returning from the front. Trains filled with wounded and dead soldiers. When he pointed the gun at my head, I wondered if I would see the bullet as it flew toward my skull. I wondered if I would feel it. I actually thought about that. Then I imagined my limp, dead body bouncing in the back of one of those train cars. I panicked and was ready to say anything to survive."

Pressing herself tighter against his trembling body, Margrit repeated, "It's all right. You're safe now."

John was silent. He wrapped his arms around Margrit's body. She raised her head to look into his eyes, wiping tear streaks from his cheeks and chin. He held her when she needed him, and now he was the one who needed her.

I do love her. I want her with me forever, John thought, as he stared into her eyes.

He leaned his head forward and kissed her. His wet, stubbly cheeks pressed against hers. Pulling her even tighter against him, John felt every angle of her body. He didn't let go, and she didn't pull away. Margrit placed her arms around his neck, keeping him tight to her.

Hearing the noise below the apartment, John pulled his head back.

"What's the matter?" Margrit asked.

John instinctively turned to look at the door. "What if your uncle comes up? He'll kill me if he sees us like this."

Margrit said nothing. Smiling, she took John by the hand and led him down the hall to a partially opened door. Standing inside the room, Margrit said, "I am in love with you, John Bayer."

"And I am in love with you."

Margrit pulled John into the room and quietly closed the door.

# # #

John awoke earlier than he needed to the following morning. Not sure if Gautier knew he was in the apartment, or what would happen if he found out, John held Margrit's warm body close. He watched her sleep as the dim light of the city shone through the window.

"I love you," he whispered, not loud enough to wake her. "I want to spend my life making you happy."

He held Margrit and dreamed of a future with her. He imagined taking her home to meet his family. It would be hard to face Rose, but his mother would be happy he found a nice German girl. He imagined staying in France after the war, not going home for a while. His American law degree was useless in Europe, but that didn't matter because of how he felt about Margrit. He wouldn't even mind living with Gautier until they figured things out. Maybe they could live in New York. At least he could find work there. It didn't matter to John where they lived, as long as they were together.

When it neared the time he was expected back at the monastery, John gently shook Margrit. He was told to return to the Major's office by five so he could get ready to be marched back into camp. He knew he needed to leave early enough to climb back to his room. He hoped they hadn't checked on him during the night.

"Good morning, my love," he whispered, caressing her dark black hair. "I'm afraid I have to go to work."

"Oh, already?" Margrit responded groggily. "It feels like we just fell asleep."

"I'm sorry. I wish I could stay and hold you forever."

Margrit wrapped her arms around him. "And if I refuse to let you go?"

John held her close and smiled, "Then I would hold on as long as I could. Too bad my commanding officer knows where to look for me."

Margrit didn't look up, but laid her head on John's bare chest. "What now?"

This time, John knew exactly what she meant in asking the same question she asked at the river. "I guess this is goodbye, for now. I'll be back soon."

Margrit tried to smile, but as it faded she asked, "But then what? You live in America. I live four thousand miles away."

"I meant it when I said 'I love you,'" John reassured, kissing Margrit on the forehead.

"I know we haven't known each other a long time, but I hoped you would come with me." John gently stroked Margrit's hair. "It's asking a great deal, I know. To leave everything you have ever known."

Margrit kissed John's hand before holding it to her cheek. "I have lost everything before, only it was because of war. I can give them up again for love if you really mean it."

John exhaled. "I do mean it. I love you. I know this has happened fast, but in these few short days, I have fallen in love with you. I want us to spend our lives together."

Margrit squeezed John's hand and smiled. "I love you and I will spend my life with you. Wherever that leads us."

He held her a little longer, realizing if he didn't leave soon, he would be late. "I have to go, but I promise I will be back soon."

As John slipped out of bed, he froze. "What about Gautier? He's going to hear me leave."

Margrit giggled. "He can sleep through almost anything. When the guns roared only a few kilometers away, he slept through the whole thing. Besides, I usually leave early to go to market. I'll walk you out. Then I get a few more minutes with you."

Walking out the door of the apartment, John sensed the change in the weather. Whereas the last few days were pleasantly mild, this morning was already hot and humid. Sweating before he reached the bottom of the stairs, John dreaded going on a work crew. After waking up with the girl he wanted to spend the rest of his life with, he couldn't stand the thought of being away from her.

Arriving at the end of the street, the two prepared to part ways. Stopping, John gazed into Margrit's dark brown eyes. "I meant it, you know. I want to spend the rest of my life with you. I want to marry you."

"I know." She put her arms around his neck and pulled her lips to his. "I knew, the first time I saw you come into the restaurant, there was something about you I needed to discover. I'm glad I did."

Margrit added, "You come back to me soon."

John smiled. "I'll be back before you know it."

13

For the second time in as many days, John found himself walking between two guards. A faint smile creased his face. His sweat-soaked uniform was already uncomfortable. Walking through the second set of rusty metal gates, John scanned the compound. Prisoners milled around waiting for breakfast. The humidity and lack of a breeze caused the smell from the latrines to hover over the compound like a dense fog.

John moved toward the breakfast table. He stopped to inspect his uniform for the third time to make sure it was sufficiently filthy. He glanced at the blood stains across the front of his shirt and was satisfied with his appearance. Before he resumed walking, the familiar voice of Otto reached his ears.

"Well, Bayer, back for another day in paradise I see." Every word out of Otto's mouth sounded like a joke, even if it wasn't meant to be.

John shrugged and turned, happy Otto wasn't calling him "Fresh Fish" anymore. "I didn't have a choice, did I?"

"Whoa, what happened to your face?" Otto's eyes bulged. "You look like you fell face first off a horse."

The volume of Otto's voice attracted the attention of nearby prisoners. John studied the growing crowd around him. The daily boredom of life in a prison camp made anything out of the ordinary a major spectacle. It would be difficult to do anything discreetly here.

"Oh that." John tried to sound nonchalant about his bruises. "That was their attempt to get information from me."

"What'd you tell them?" asked another familiar voice.

81

With a smirk, Tom waded into the group. Bags under his eyes revealed he hadn't slept much the night before.

John raised his hands, palms up. "What's there to tell? They mistook me for someone else. It's as simple as that."

John pointed to his face. "And for their mistake, I got more of these."

"It got you out of here for a while though, didn't it?" Otto had a hint of envy in his voice.

Lowering his eyebrows, John tried to remember the details of the interrogation center before answering. "You've never been to the cells they hold you for questioning, have you, kid?"

John savored calling Otto "kid."

Otto shook his head. "No, why?"

"It's no holiday, I can tell you that. Other than getting slapped around, I slept on a rock floor last night." John massaged his neck in an exaggerated manner.

Otto raised his eyebrows. "It must have been better than sleeping in this mud hole."

John rolled his eyes. "I would have rather been in here on one of those little muddy cots than on the cold floor with no blanket."

A few of the old timers stood at the edge of the circle and listened. John tried not to smile when he thought about what his night was really like. He already missed Margrit's warm caress.

"They knew they had the wrong guy." John shrugged. "I think they like to beat on someone now and then."

"Who was your interrogation officer?" A raspy voice from the back of the group floated over the crowd. The circle parted, making a path for the voice to approach.

John thought the skinny, balding man didn't make an intimidating impression. He was no more than five-and-a-half feet tall, but all the prisoners in camp showed reverence, or fear, for him.

"Hintz." John nervously cracked his knuckles one at a time, trying to maintain eye contact with the old man.

"Describe him," the voice commanded with authority. He peered at John through hawk like, narrow eyes.

John shifted on his feet and thought, *Who is this guy?*

"What?" John plunged his hands into his pockets trying to hide his nervousness.

82

"Describe him," the voice repeated. He stood close to John, but far enough away that he didn't have to tilt his head to look at the taller, younger man.

John glanced at Tom, who nodded in assent. "Okay. He was maybe the same height as me. He had light hair with a bald spot on the crown of his head. Flat nose. Skinny in the arms, but a little round at the belly, from what I could tell. He always wore his jacket though.

"But," John added. "He didn't do the dirty work. He called in his bulldog. Some blonde haired corporal whose name I can't remember but who had a wide figure and an even wider chin."

"Interesting." The man spoke slowly, his voice almost croaking. "They hardly ever beat us. They starve us, they work us, but they don't beat us. What makes *you* so special?"

John took a step backward. The old man's un-naturally yellow teeth made him shudder. "I don't know. Like I said, they mistook me for someone else and I took a beating for it. Maybe the private pulled some strings to get me beat up. He was pretty angry."

The old man continued to stare at John. John stared back, glancing at the ground occasionally. The old man turned and walked back through the prisoners, pausing to look at John again before re-joining his comrades.

John wiped a bead of sweat from his forehead. "I probably won't like the answer, but what was that all about?"

"It's like I told you yesterday." Otto pivoted his head as he spoke. "Those guys do what they want in here. Information is valuable."

"And intimidation," Tom added.

"Whatever it was, I didn't like it." John looked at Otto. "I don't want to get stuck digging trenches at the front just because *they're* watching me." John tried to play the part of a prisoner as authentically as he could, expressing a fear of working at the front he didn't actually have.

Shaking his head, Otto replied, "I don't think that will happen, at least not yet. They aren't done with you. I've only been here a short time, but I've seen it already. They'll try to get more information from you before they decide anything."

With the small group of Otto's friends still assembled close enough to listen, Tom nodded toward the meal line. "Let's go eat."

Stepping into the food line and out of earshot of other prisoners, John whispered, "Thanks for getting me out of trouble yesterday. I thought I was a dead man."

"So did I." Tom laughed, slapping John on the back. "It was like pulling teeth to get the kid to interpret for you. He was terrified. I thought we would have to give the whole thing up before he finally stepped forward."

Nodding, John agreed, "Me, too. I was about to crack."

"Fill me in on the rest during work crew." Tom scooped a spoonful of food into his mouth before he reached the end of the line. Looking at the pile of food on his plate, John grimaced. He thought about how much better his meal was the night before.

John and Tom stuck close to each other through breakfast and work crew selection. The trainers might have been wrong about many things before entering camp, but John knew they were right to make sure they weren't alone inside the camp.

John and Tom worked at the same location as the previous day. Walking the two miles in the already humid morning, beads of sweat trickled down their cheeks before they arrived at the little farm. Both removed their green wool German army jackets and slung them over their shoulders. It could be another day back home at the farm, as far as John was concerned.

Rolling hay bales a small distance from the other prisoners, John described to Tom his run in with Private Howard at Gautier's and explained how he received the new bruises on his face.

Tom laughed, "You mean you volunteered to get your head cracked up again?"

"It was either that or accept defeat and get sent to the front." John wiped the sweat from his brow with the back of his hand. "I know you don't want to get sent there. Besides, if I hadn't done it, I might not have seen Margrit last night."

With a smirk, Tom said, "I knew you looked a little too comfortable with those bruises. Are you sure you didn't get them doing something else?"

John's face flushed. "Anyway. We decided to tell the guard from yesterday why we're in here. The plan is to infiltrate the old timers. I don't know how we'll do it though."

Watching an American soldier walking in their direction, Tom leaned over with his pitchfork and returned to work. "I think I know the answer to that," he said quietly. "They don't leave for the infirmary until sundown. That gives us plenty of time after supper to talk to them."

John wagged his head. "If they'll talk to *us*. The one this morning didn't seem too friendly. They seem like a closed group."

Tom winked. "We'll figure it out, don't worry about it. That guy seems to be the leader of their little group. The prisoners call him 'die Stimme.'"

"Die Stimme? Doesn't that mean The Voice?"

Tom snorted as he bent over to resume working. "Yeah. Nobody knows his real name, so they call him 'The Voice.' The tall guy with white hair is called Vater Ziet."

"Vater Ziet? Father Time?" John asked. "Nothing but nicknames around here." He grunted and picked up a bale to toss on the wooden cart.

After a full day in the summer humidity, John was happy to return to the muddy camp. On the way, he hoped Jacobson remembered to talk to Private Howard. On the other hand, he smiled to himself at the prospect of getting out of camp for another night if the soldier confronted him again. Looking at his soaked shirt, John laughed and thought he would have to take a longer bath before seeing Margrit again.

Tom spotted Howard first, elbowing John when they entered the camp. "Here we go."

John held his breath and tried to avoid eye contact with the angry soldier. Glancing over, he noticed Private Howard staring at him. Howard mumbled something to the guards nearby and turned his back to John.

John sighed with relief.

As he walked past Private Howard, another American soldier stepped in his way. John tried to sidestep the soldier, but the man moved to block his escape.

"Hey, Jim, isn't this your buddy from yesterday?" The soldier laughed.

Private Howard looked over his shoulder at John. "Yeah, so what?"

"So what?" The other soldier laughed again. "Don't you have something you want to say to him?"

John glanced at Tom, who stood nearby with a growing group of prisoners. Every event turned into a spectacle in camp.

Private Howard clinched his teeth. "It was a mistake. I had the wrong guy."

The soldier pushed John toward Howard and cackled. "You were pretty sure yesterday. How can you be sure he's not your guy?"

John could tell the soldier was having a laugh at someone's expense. He wasn't sure if it was his, Private Howard's, or both.

"I said it was a mistake," Howard said more firmly, this time stepping close to the other soldier. "Now drop it."

"I don't think I will," the soldier sneered. "I think he *was* the guy and you're afraid of him."

Private Howard glared at the soldier. His face turned red and the veins in his neck grew large. John could see Private Howard's heartbeat in the bulging veins.

Howard grabbed John by the collar. *Oh no, not again*, he thought, reaching his hands to brace himself for a fall that didn't come. The private pushed John to the side.

"If you have something to say." Private Howard's upper lip curled. "Then say it."

John's attention turned to Private Howard's hands, clenching and unclenching rapidly. Wanting to move away from the action but also curious of the outcome, John only took a few steps back.

"No," the soldier scoffed. "I ain't got nothing to say. I can't help it if you can't figure out I'm just playing around."

Howard moved toward the other soldier again, his cheek twitching the entire time. Before he reached him, two soldiers stepped in the way.

"Relax," one of the soldiers said. "Just relax. Why don't you two stay away from each other? This is happening too often lately."

"Because," the other soldier scoffed before he turned away. "It's too much fun getting him all worked up."

Realizing there would be no action, the small crowd dispersed. John rejoined Tom and headed in the direction of the dinner table. John noticed one of the old men had watched the scene unfold.

"This camp is too small."

14

John stood in line for what looked like the same meat and gravy meal he didn't taste the night before. He thought about how different this night would be than the last. Sleeping in a warm bed with his beautiful Margrit after a delicious meal was certainly preferable. He consoled himself with the thought that he would be out again soon.

"When you get your meal, come eat with us," the Voice commanded, his voice raspy and unsettling.

John turned to respond, but the old man was already walking back to his group. The old timers watched John and Tom while eating their meal. They were served first, and it looked to John like they received more food than the other prisoners.

"Do you think they meant both of us?" John reached for a metal plate from a prisoner serving dinner.

"Probably not." Tom shrugged. He glanced over his shoulder to see the old timers watching them. "We'll go together anyway."

The conversation stopped when John and Tom reached the circle of older men. John was surprised most of these old timers weren't any older than his father. They appeared younger than his grandfather, yet were given the nickname "old timers."

Not acknowledging Tom's presence, the Voice stared at John. "So, Alders Bayer, tell us about your little holiday last night."

John frowned when the old man use his fake name. "What do you mean? All they did was question me about whether I snuck out of camp the previous night."

"Did you?" the Voice asked tersely.

John shook his head. "No. I was in the same building the night before, and they knew it. But they still asked if I was in the city."

"Then what?"

John gave a half shrug. "What do you mean? That was it. They slapped me around and sent me back in this morning."

"And why," another voice from the group said, "do you think they gave you such a beating?"

John breathed an exasperated sigh. "I don't know. Like I said this morning, maybe the guard from yesterday has a friend at headquarters."

The Voice pointed to Tom. "And your friend here. He was in there with you?"

Tom, who was eating the entire time, spoke with a mouthful of food. "I wasn't *with* him," Tom muttered between chews. "I saw him going out while I waited to go in."

The group turned their attention to Tom, who chewed on his last bite of sinewy meat. Father Time took a turn questioning them. "And you. We heard you were found in a barn somewhere. How did you get on this side of the line?"

"Easy." Tom smiled and took a slow drink of his coffee. "I was captured with the rest of Third Division. They marched us to the train yard, only the train wasn't there. We had to wait all night in an open field. During the night when two guards went to take a piss, I walked away."

"As simple as that?" The Voice asked.

Tom nodded. "Yep. When I was away, I didn't hear any whistles or anything." Lying had become second nature. "I don't think they even kept an accurate prisoner count. They might not have realized anyone was missing."

John could tell the group wasn't convinced of their story when the Voice asked, "How did you get caught?"

"I didn't get caught. I got hungry." Tom seemed completely convinced his story was true. "I hid in a barn for about a week and didn't have much luck finding food. When I heard a patrol of Yankees outside the barn yesterday morning, I yelled out and surrendered."

The Voice crossed his arms, appearing to decide if he believed Tom's story. He squinted as he stared at Tom. "I think that will be all for now."

John turned to go. Before he and Tom could leave, The Voice said, "One more thing before you go."

John shivered at the sound of the old man's voice. Something in the way he spoke made him uneasy. ".Yes."

"You're from Siegen, right? Alders Bayer from Siegen?" The Voice stepped closer.

John swallowed hard. "Yes. How do you know that?"

"We know everything that happens in *our* camp." The Voice smiled with his right lip sort of turned in a snarl. "But I think you knew that already."

John didn't like this. Nothing was going the way he was told it would. He was supposed to be in a camp with young, naïve prisoners. Not these men who seemed to know and control everything, and thought of the place as 'our camp.'

John clenched his teeth. "What's your point?"

"My point?" The Voice sneered and took his time to answer. A few more of the old timers joined the growing circle.

"My friend here, he saw you with the Americans after work crew today. He's been watching you." The Voice spoke slowly.

"And why is that?" John didn't know where this was headed, but he knew it wouldn't be good.

"Well, my friend has a cousin from near Siegen. His cousin died in the first year of the war. When my friend was a younger man, he used to visit his cousin every summer." The Voice seemed to be enjoying himself. "It's funny, when you spend so much time in an area, you learn about the rumors and scandals. Have you ever noticed that? How bad news spreads faster than good news?"

John nodded but couldn't speak. His throat as dry as a desert.

"That's how it is with gossip in small towns. There's one scandal that was one of my friend's favorites. Can you guess what it is?" The old man smirked.

"No." John practically choked on the word, oblivious of what the Voice was about to reveal.

"No? Well, he remembered hearing about a family. They were called Bayer. That's your name right? Alders Bayer from Siegen?"

John hated the old man for toying with him. "Spit it out," he screamed in his head.

"The story goes like this. There was another young man named Alders Bayer, about fifty years ago. Do you know that Alders Bayer? You must, it's a small town and not a common name."

John's legs shook as he stammered, "He, he's my, he was my grandfather."

Still sneering, the Voice said, "Ah yes, I guessed as much. You were named after your grandfather. This man, your grandfather was German. He grew up a good Christian German. And do you know what this Christian boy did?"

The old man allowed the question to sink in.

"That good young German went off and married a Jewess. Can you believe that? A nice German boy shaming his entire family by marrying a Jew?" he mocked.

Realizing where the old man was taking the conversation, John found his resolve. "And what, exactly, does that matter?"

"It matters," the Voice said, "because you're the grandson of a Jewess. And worse, you're the spawn of a German who would marry one. It matters because that means we can't trust you."

John's entire story had fallen apart. The premise on which he was chosen, being the son of a German immigrant, failed. Now he was simply determined to survive. Throughout the conversation, Tom stood behind him.

"And why can't you trust him?" Tom stepped forward. "So what if he's Jewish."

The old man shot Tom a condescending smile. "No, we can't trust the grandson of a Jew lover. In fact, we think he might be giving information to the Americans."

The Voice glanced at his friend before returning his gaze to Tom. "My friend has been watching him since he heard the name Alders Bayer. He saw your friend practically walk right into the same guard from yesterday. That guard nearly got into a fight trying to avoid your Jew friend."

The Voice looked hard at Tom. "And maybe you're in league with him. It's interesting how you *both* came in here around the same time and became friends so quickly."

"This is ridiculous," Tom blurted. "Look at his face."

"Yes, look at it," the Voice said. "It reminds me of a story from when I was a child. Back then, I was a mischievous boy. One day, my mother sent me to the store to buy bread. When I got into town, I noticed a candy cart on the street near the bakery. Being a boy who liked sweets, I decided to buy candy instead of the bread my mother sent me for."

"So what?" Tom huffed.

The Voice ignored Tom. "On my way home, I knew I would get into trouble for buying candy. Before I got home, I stopped and rolled down a hill into the creek near our house. When I arrived home, soaking wet and dirty, my mother believed I had fallen into the creek and lost her money.

"I didn't get into trouble that day," the Voice said. "And I learned that people will go to great lengths to get someone to believe them."

John's eyes narrowed. "What could I have to gain by having you believe I was beaten?"

"You tell me," the old man replied coolly.

"I've had enough of this." John turned from the old man. "Believe what you want."

The Voice was silent when John walked away. Tom stood awkwardly for a moment; first looking at John, who stopped to wait for him, then back at the old timers. Tom pointed at the nameless man next to the Voice. "How do you know your *friend* isn't lying?"

The Voice wagged his head. "I know because we grew up together in Nuremburg. We lived down the street from each other. Raised our families together. Went to Mass together. And when war broke out, signed up to fight together. I know he's telling the truth."

Tom scowled at the Voice before walking away.

# # #

"We're dead," John blurted, as soon as he and Tom were away from the other prisoners. "You've heard what they do to traitors in these places. I wouldn't be surprised if they killed us in our sleep tonight."

"Then we don't sleep," Tom said. "I don't think they are completely sure about us yet. We'll know in the morning, if we get sent to the front for work crew."

"I'm done with this." John rubbed the back of his neck with one hand. "Everything they told us in *training* was wrong and it's going to get us killed. I'd rather be at the front, knowing where the enemy is coming from, than in here expecting to get killed in our sleep."

"Stay calm and we'll be fine." Tom squeezed John's arm. "We just need to keep an eye on each other."

Taking a deep breath, John noticed his hand shaking. He put it in his pocket and took another breath.

"Where are you sleeping? I think I should be in a tent nearby, but not in the same one."

Tom pointed to his left. "I already thought of that. There's an open cot in a tent across the path. Two tents down from mine."

With both hands in his pockets, John nodded and made his way to the tent Tom had selected. Before entering for the night, he looked around camp. Private Howard stood near the fence watching him.

15

John lay motionless on his muddy cot, listening for any movement outside. The rain pounding on the canvas reminded him of the sound of cattle stomping over the wooden bridge across the creek back home. He knew it was morning, but the cloud cover prevented sunlight from penetrating the darkness.

Rolling off the cot onto the ground, John peeked out the front flap to search for any movement. Looking out the small opening got his face and chest wet, so John crawled back into his cot out of the mud. He watched a small trickle of water slowly fill the divots his feet created in the muddy floor.

Laying on the cot, John was surprised his thoughts wandered to Rose. The day before he left home, he and Rose went for a walk around her farm when it started to rain. By the time they made it to the barn, they were soaked. John remembered looking at the way the water caused Rose's dress to rest against her body. He was drawn to her then and wanted to ask her to marry him.

Thinking about that moment, sitting on bales of hay with Rose leaning against him, John wondered if he'd made the right decision with Margrit. He thought he loved Rose and was prepared to marry her before he left. Now he felt the same way about Margrit. He loved her, at least he thought he did, but was it any more real than how he'd felt about Rose a few months earlier? What really worried him was the thought that he was the kind of man who so easily fell in and out of love.

Maybe his brother was right. He had more arguments with Alex in the days before he left for boot camp than he'd had his entire life. Alex thought John should stay on the farm and sit out the war. "We may be Americans," Alex argued, "but we are also German."

For the first time, John wondered if Alex was right. He was bound to hurt at least one person he loved, and with the old timers watching him so closely, he may not survive at all.

He hadn't been lying in his cot for long before he heard the sound of a loud, strange thumping accompanied by a slurping noise. He rolled back into the mud and looked out the flap. Walking up his row was a guard, in full rain gear, slapping each tent with long wooden pole.

"Get up boys. We still have work crew, even in the rain," the American soldier announced in broken German. "If you don't work, you don't eat."

John crept through the flap of his tent and wished Major Jacobson would find an excuse to get him out of camp for the day. To describe the ground beneath his feet as muddy would be an understatement. Every step John took was an act of will, which explained the slurping sound the soldier made when he walked. John's foot sank into the mud and made a sound reminiscent of pigs at the feeding trough at home.

Many prisoners made their way out of their tents and slogged through the mud to line up for breakfast. A fair number remained in their tent, preferring a day without food to working in the rain. *Maybe*, he thought, *the food here isn't worth working in this weather.* Staying in camp meant being close the old timers all day, so John continued his trudge toward the breakfast line.

Without rain gear, it took no time for the prisoners to get soaked. John laughed when another prisoner exited a tent without a shirt and with a bar of soap in his hand. At least the stink of camp was washed away, if only for the day.

Lining up for breakfast, John wondered why no steam billowed from the cook tent. In line, he overheard a guard say the cooks couldn't keep a fire in the stoves. Water from the downpour washed into the metal stovepipes and flooded the stove.

When the gate opened, a group of prisoners carried trays of what quickly became soaked bread. With no fire in the stoves, the usual breakfast gruel couldn't be cooked, so they were served all that was available. There wasn't even coffee, which disappointed John more than the lack of hot food.

After choking down a few pieces of waterlogged bread, John searched the compound for his friend. Finding Tom with Otto and the young Germans, he approached with a small amount of trepidation. He wondered if it was worth the risk to be seen talking to Tom, considering how things went with the old timers the previous night.

"It's about time you found us." Tom didn't seem apprehensive. "We're gonna head out for work crew."

"Back to the fields?" John dreaded working outside in the rain.

Otto laughed. "Worse. When it rains they send us to haul coal at the train yard."

"Don't they have machines for that?" John grimaced.

Otto shook his head. "You really don't get it, do you? They don't make us haul coal because they need our help. They just want to keep us busy."

"Better than digging at the front, I suppose." John turned to follow the crowd.

Otto was right when he described the task for the day as simply made up work. When each prisoner passed through the gates at the coal yard, they were assigned to either shovel coal into a wooden handcart or push the cart across the yard, dump it, and return for another load. There weren't enough carts or shovels, so two soldiers were assigned to each cart. Even then, there weren't enough jobs for everyone. A line of prisoners stood on the side of the station, out of the rain. John and Tom made sure they were assigned to the same cart.

Pushing the empty cart toward the huge mounds of coal across the rail yard, John steered a short distance from the other prisoners.

"What are we doing here?" John gasped for breath. "After yesterday, no one will trust us."

Tom pushed on his side of the cart, trying to keep it stable on the uneven ground. "I have a feeling something's going to happen soon. We need to try to figure out what it is."

John slowed the cart to a crawl. "How will we do that? The old timers aren't even here and they're the ones we need to talk to."

"But they are here, sort of." Tom nodded in the direction of a group of younger soldiers leaning against the wall of the train station.

John glanced over his shoulder. "Who are they?"

"Otto and the boys call them the 'enforcers'" Tom stopped and tied the boot on his right foot. "If a new prisoner makes trouble about the old timers, those guys take care of it."

"Make trouble?"

Tom took his time with his shoelace before switching to the other boot. "Yeah, make trouble. Like complaining when the old timers steal their stuff."

"But will they trust us?" John put his shoulder against the cart and grunted.

"We'll find out soon enough." Tom stood and steadied his side of the cart. "I think you better let me do the talking though."

The two friends took turns pushing and pulling the cart through the ever-increasing mud until the lunch truck arrived. The stoves still did not work for lunch. John found more soggy bread along with salted pork on his metal plate.

After eating their meal and washing it down with cold coffee, John and Tom made their way in the direction of the enforcers, trying to make it look like they were attempting to get out of the rain. Tom pretended to watch an army airplane in the distance.

"Where do you suppose he's going?" Tom asked, loud enough for the entire line of men to hear. "In this rain, I can't believe he's even up there."

John shrugged, looking down the line of prisoners.

Not getting the response he expected, Tom continued, "I can't tell, is it an American or French plane?"

John turned to watch the airplane but remained quiet.

One of the prisoners leaning against the wall took a bite of meat before pointing in the direction of the airplane. "You see the circle on the bottom of the wing. The one that looks like a target?"

Tom nodded.

"That's the symbol on French and British planes. The American's have a star on their wings." The soldier stuffed the rest of the meat into his already filled mouth. "It's probably a French scout plane."

"Why do you suppose they have him flying in this weather?" Tom asked.

The soldier spit small bits of food out as he spoke. "I guess they want to keep an eye on things. Watch for signs of an attack."

Tom scratched his chin. "Do they expect there to be another attack?"

The soldier picked up a soaked piece of bread. After rolling it into a ball and squeezing the water out, he popped it into his mouth. "Why do you want to know?"

Tom gave a half shrug. "What do you mean 'why do I want to know?' I'd like it if our boys would get us out of here before we get sent to a permanent camp."

"Permanent?"

"Well, not permanent, but until the war ends," Tom said.

The soldier glanced at John before looking at Tom. "And when do you think the war will be over?"

Tom leaned against the brick wall. "I don't know, but I don't like all the mud here. Maybe our boys will win it soon."

The soldier pushed himself off the wall and crossed his arms. "And do you think it's possible with the Americans in the war now?"

Tom forced a smile. "Sure. They're young and soft, from what I hear. No match for battle hardened Germans."

The soldier pointed at John's face with a sneer. "And would your friend agree that they are soft?"

John tried to laugh. "It's easy for them to get the better of you with shackles on. I'd like my chances in a fair fight."

"An offensive may be coming. When that happens, those loyal to the Kaiser will be rewarded." The soldier glared at John. "Those disloyal will also be *rewarded*."

Goose bumps pricked John's neck. "I hope so."

Before he could add anything, a guard announced, "Lunch is over. Back to work."

The enforcers did not move into the rain for work, and the guard ignored them. John and Tom returned to their cart. John dreaded an afternoon pushing and pulling the cart, but didn't like the idea of spending the rest of the afternoon near the station with the enforcers either.

Tired and disheartened, he worked as slowly as he thought he could get away with. He wished he were in the trenches. At least he wouldn't be slaving away all day, even if he were in greater danger. If it was more dangerous for him at the front, at least he might be in a bunker where it was dry.

Away from the other prisoners, John whispered to Tom. "It sounds like they think something's going to happen, doesn't it? We need to tell Jacobson."

Tom nodded and casually looked over his shoulder. "Yeah, but what do we tell him? We think an attack might happen but don't know when or where?"

"I don't know," John said. "What do you suggest?"

Tom took over pushing the cart for John and groaned against the weight. "We need to get real information first. The new prisoners in camp would have a better idea since they recently arrived from the front. The old timers get their information the same way as us, from the newcomers."

John stopped and looked at his friend. "So we just wait?"

Tom shrugged. "What else can we do? Besides, they wouldn't have a scout plane up there in this weather if they didn't suspect something. They already know as much as we do."

John wagged his head and returned to work.

After struggling to push and pull the wooden cart for a few more hours, one of the enforcers approached John and Tom. It was the first time John had seen any of them move out from the shelter of the building.

"You two." The German pointed at them and nodded to his left. "Lighter coal over here."

John lowered his eyebrows and squinted at Tom. "Lighter coal? Something isn't right."

"Keep your eyes open. We can't let them separate us." Tom glanced over his shoulder.

John shook his head. "I'm telling you we shouldn't go with him. I'd feel better if we at least had a shovel."

Tom pushed the cart in the direction of the German. "This is what we're in here to do. Let's see what we can find out."

John said, "I hope you know what you're doing."

Rounding the last massive mound of coal in the row, they discovered the German waiting for them alone. Tom looked around before turning back at the German. "What do you want?"

The German smirked. "You know who we are, right?"

Tom nodded. "We've heard rumors."

The German walked toward John and Tom. "We like to keep our camp nice and calm. If it stays quiet, the guards take care of us. And we take care of them."

The German took his hat off. After ringing the water out of the soaked cap, he said, "Sometimes, prisoners come into our camp and cause trouble. When that happens, the guards get nervous. Then we can't work together."

John's lip curled down. "Yeah, I get it. I made trouble with the guard and you're warning me. I'll consider myself warned. Now we're going back to work."

As soon as John finished the word "work", footsteps splashed in the wet ground behind him. He held his breath and turned. Three more prisoners approached with unpleasant expressions on their faces. John and Tom stepped away from the cart and stood back to back.

"Relax." The German raised his hands. "If we planned to hurt you, you wouldn't have heard us coming."

Tom pointed at the surrounding men. "What's all this about then?"

The German returned his hat to his head. "We just want to show you something."

He pointed across the yard. "Look over there."

John turned in the direction the man pointed. A lone prisoner struggled to push a cart toward a massive pile. "So?"

"We believe he's been giving information to the Yankees." The German spoke coolly. "We're willing to work with the Americans to keep the camp quiet in exchange for things we want. We are not willing to give them anything extra."

Tom crossed his arms. "Why are you telling us this?"

"Just watch."

The man with the cart stopped at a pile of coal. Another man John recognized as one of the enforcers appeared with a shovel from behind the pile of coal. Without warning, the enforcer swung the shovel into the face of the defenseless man.

A loud thud echoed across the yard and a splatter of blood, like crimson fireworks, exploded from the man's nose. Without so much as a whimper, he slumped to the ground. The enforcer turned and calmly walked away, tossing his weapon to the side.

Tom's face was red. "What the hell was that?"

The German sneered. "Keep watching."

John and Tom returned their gaze to the scene, where the enforcer and two guards appeared. Because of the distance, John couldn't hear what the man said. The enforcer waved his arms and made shoveling gestures. The guards simply shrugged and walked away.

"Accidents happen, you know?" The German spoke in a growl, having moved right behind John. "There's no telling what can happen if you don't follow the rules. And as you can see, the guards don't care."

John's eyes narrowed. "Is that a threat?"

"Just a reminder. In case you were thinking of getting friendly with the Americans."

John said, "I don't know how I'm gonna get you to believe—"

"Get back to work. This isn't playtime." Private Howard stepped into view and gripped his rifle.

No one moved.

"I said get back to work," Howard repeated.

The four Germans smirked and shuffled past the private. When John walked by, Howard mumbled, "Watch your step from now on."

John turned toward Private Howard. Before he could speak, Tom took hold of his arm. "Just keep walking."

As they pushed their cart across the yard, two prisoners moved another cart toward the soldier who'd been hit. John stopped and watched them load the lifeless body into the cart. His left arm dangled over the side and his legs hung off the end of the short cart.

"I can't believe the guards aren't going to do anything about this." John spoke more to himself than to Tom.

Tom shook his head. "They don't care about another dead Kraut."

John sighed. "I think it's time to get out of here."

16

The next morning, John again silently lay on the tiny green cot looking at the dirty canvas above. The rain stopped sometime in the night, and the sound of prisoners exiting their tents for breakfast reached his ears. His scratchy eyes felt swollen in his head and he realized he'd hardly slept the past four nights.

Lying alone and awake most of the night, John periodically slipped out of his cot onto the muddy ground to peek through the tent flap, only to discover no one approached. He would crawl back into bed and try to fight off sleep. Each time he nodded off, a noise outside startled him awake.

No one came for him.

Emerging from the tent, John's first sight was Private Howard standing against the fence near the end of his row. *Has he been there all night?*

Next, he noticed the flap of Tom's tent tied shut. Not wanting to show his concern, he walked down the pathway in front of Tom's temporary dwelling. Stopping to tie his left boot directly in front of his friend's tent, John peeked between the flaps. It was empty.

"Looking for someone?" Tom spoke nonchalantly from a couple rows over.

John jumped at the boisterous sound of his friend. Not sure who was in nearby tents or why Tom wasn't being more cautious, John answered carefully. "No, just tying my boots."

John nodded in the direction of the breakfast table. Tom didn't appear concerned about secrecy when he smiled and walked in that direction.

Moving toward the breakfast line, the other prisoners avoided John. Seeing Otto a few feet away, he waved. "Good morning Otto, how are you today?"

The young German stepped backwards. "Good, thank you." He nearly tripped over a tent spike when he turned in the other direction.

"Looks like I have the plague or something," John commented when he approached Tom.

"We're the camp lepers." Tom laughed.

John scanned the compound. The old men hadn't entered camp. Enforcers loitered near the fence watching him. He hated the way they leered, occasionally making comments to each other.

"What time is it?" John kept his eyes on the enforcers.

Tom cupped his hand over his eyes and looked toward the cook tent. "I'd say close to six. The tent's been steaming and smoking since I got up."

John nodded toward the area the group of old men usually assembled. "Where do you suppose they are? Aren't they typically up by now?"

"I wondered that myself. No one will talk to us, so I don't know whom to ask." Tom yawned, raising one arm over his head and the other toward the ground in an exaggerated stretch. "It's time to give it up and come back after *all* the prisoners have been replaced. What do you say?"

"The sooner the better. I was afraid we wouldn't even survive the night." John looked in the direction Private Howard had been standing. Not seeing him, he surveyed the camp.

"Look over at the medical building." John elbowed Tom.

They watched three American soldiers exit the Red Cross building. Each soldier carried a small bag. They looked over their shoulders, not talking to each other even though they walked together.

John watched until they disappeared around a shed outside the fence. "What do you suppose is in those bags?"

"I don't know for sure," Tom answered. "I'd guess it's the reason the old timers have the run of the place."

After breakfast, John and Tom followed the same routine they had the last two mornings, this time without the company of Otto and the other young Germans. After they finished eating, they walked in the direction of the front gate for work crew.

Prior to getting sent off into groups, John whispered, "Maybe it's time to get out of here. Something strange is going on."

Before Tom could reply, the group of old timers appeared outside the gate. They stood next to one of the soldiers John and Tom had watched leave the medical building.

"Let's see what this is about first," Tom said. "Something's going on, they don't usually come out for work crew."

"You two." A soldier who stood with the old timers pointed to John and Tom. "You're on my work crew today."

"Stick together," John whispered. "We'll ask for Major Jacobson and get out of here as soon as we can."

"Absolutely," Tom nodded. "Let's see what we can find out first. That *is* why we're in here."

"How do we even know which guard to trust?" John asked quietly. "I don't see Howard anywhere."

"We'll figure it out," Tom said.

Trying to hide his uneasiness, John ignored the disdainful expressions on the faces of the old men and asked the soldier where they would work that day. "Wo stehen wir heute gehen?"

The soldier shook his head. "Sorry, buddy, I don't speak German."

Tom smiled at the old men. "I bet *you* know where we're going?"

The Voice smiled. "How would we know that? We don't know any more than you do."

Tom stepped closer to the Voice. "Why are you outside the fence then? We thought you never leave the camp."

The Voice waved Tom away dismissively. "We decided we want to get out of the camp today. You know, get some fresh air."

"And they just happened to oblige your request?" Tom nodded at the American soldiers. "And include us on your work crew."

"We asked them nicely," the Voice replied with a sneer.

"I bet." Tom's voice hardened. "And the bags they carried out of your building had nothing to do with it."

The Voice ignored Tom's reference to their bribe. "When we heard how efficient your friend is at bailing hay, we wanted him on our crew."

103

He eyed John from head to toe with a curled upper lip before adding, "We also enjoy your company and would like to talk with you some more."

John exhaled and shook his head. "I've already told you everything. There's nothing left to tell."

"We'll see about that."

17

John and Tom found themselves walking to the northeast with eleven old timers and enforcers, and two younger prisoners. They travelled in a different direction than the other days on work crew. The temperature grew hotter by the minute, unlike the previous day of nonstop rain. All the water from the day before caused the humidity to return, making the walk nearly unbearable.

"Why are we walking toward the front?" John tried to whisper to Tom over the sound of explosions that grew louder with every step. "If they got us sent to work in the trenches, why are they coming with?"

Tom spoke with a raspy tone and imitated the Voice. "Maybe it's because we like your company, eh Fresh Fish?"

John laughed at his friend's mocking behavior, but still wasn't at ease. Every step toward the trenches reminded him of the terrible effect of armed conflict. Each stride was taken in an atmosphere that echoed with explosions and gunfire. It wasn't deafening, but sounded like a distant thunder growing louder.

The landscape was devastated from advances and retreats across the no longer farmed fields. Some homes along the dirt road were completely intact; others totally destroyed, while the rest were scarred with shrapnel and bullet holes.

The land did not escape the impact of modern warfare. Left unfarmed due to their proximity to the front, the fields reverted to a mix of mud and weeds, with bright red poppies sprouting wherever they were allowed to grow.

There was something new John had not experienced. Breathing heavily on the humid day, he noticed the unmistakable odor of war. He smelled death at the train depot, but this was different. It was the same stench of rotting flesh, but mixed with the smell of exploded artillery, vehicle exhaust, and a sour odor he didn't recognize, but reminded him of the smoke his father used to extinguish bee hives and hornets' nests on the farm.

The American guards stopped in the middle of the road. One of the soldiers waved his arm to call over one of the old timers. The prisoner they called Father Time, who spoke broken English, approached the Americans and joined the conversation. Talking for a few minutes, he returned to the work crew.

"We're here to load dead bodies into wagons and take them to the train station," the old man announced. "Just over that hill is the train station. A half mile beyond is the medical tent."

John's color flushed. "We can't do this," he whispered close enough to Tom's ear to be heard over the explosions. "It was bad enough thinking we had to watch our back at a farm where we could hear them approaching. But they will have nothing but opportunity to kill us out here."

"Never mind that." Tom ignored John's protests and didn't even try to whisper. "I don't get it. Why in the hell would those old men, who could have been on any work crew, have chosen this detail?"

Shaking his head, John leaned into Tom's ear again. "I don't care what they're up to. I'm not doing it. We'll get one of the guards alone and explain everything to him."

"I'm not sure that's a good idea. They picked this crew for a reason and obviously paid the guards." Tom tried to whisper this time. "We should try to figure out why. I doubt they'd believe us anyway."

"That's easy for you to say." John didn't hide his trepidation. "You haven't had a gun to your head. You're not the one with a target on his back. We have to get out of here."

John looked over his shoulder at the men around him and winced with every explosion. He considered making a run for it before observing a vehicle with two soldiers in the front and an empty flatbed slowly navigating the muddy, rut filled road.

Recognizing the soldier in the passenger seat, John mumbled, "I never thought I'd be glad to see *him*."

Private Howard exited the vehicle and shook the driver's hand. He waved to the other American soldiers and yelled over the explosions. "Sorry I'm late fellas. Took a nap and overslept." Then added with a laugh. "At least I made it before lunch."

"Why are you here?" The lead American soldier asked. "You were on guard duty last night."

Howard pointed at the German prisoners. "Command wanted another guard with this many prisoners working so close to the front. So here I am."

The arrival of Howard calmed John's nerves. At least one person, other than Tom, knew who he was and why he was there. Walking over the hill in the direction of the medical tent, John was almost overcome by the odor. One of the younger prisoners vomited on his shoes before reaching the bottom of the hill. An entire field of dead men lay beyond the train station.

John eyed the small station that had one purpose: to transport troops to and from the battle. Tracks skirted the side of the hill to the south, with a turnaround beyond the station. The station was little more than a shelter with a metal roof and no walls. A short train with twelve cars sat empty, waiting to be loaded. John remembered looking into the empty train car in Bordeaux, thinking he couldn't survive a trip in something so uncomfortable. Now he would load the dead for their final journey to a foreign grave.

"You two." Private Howard pointed to John and Tom. "Get one of those carts. We'll start at the far end of the field and work our way forward."

They took hold of the cart, which was slightly larger than the one they used to haul coal at the train yard. Listening to the squeak of the wheels as they pushed the old wooden farm cart across the uneven field, John was reminded of a similar, horse drawn cart, which he used at home on the farm. If he ignored the smell and sounds around him, this could be like home.

"You two caused a hell of a lot of trouble this morning." Private Howard scowled at John and Tom.

Stopping the cart, the two friends exchanged confused looks before turning to Howard with the same bemused expression.

"What are you talking about?" John shielded his eyes from the sun.

"Major Jacobson sent someone to get you from the farm where the other crews were. When you weren't there, all hell broke loose at headquarters." Howard glanced over his shoulder before continuing. "They finally figured out you were here, and sent me to get you."

Howard paused. "One of you bend over and tie your boot so it looks like we stopped for a reason."

John crouched to obey Howard's command and Tom asked, "If you were supposed to get us, shouldn't we be on our way?"

Howard wiped the sweat accumulating on his brow. "Major Jacobson said not to cause suspicion. I thought this was best. We'll load the cart and push it toward the train. On the way, one of you fake an injury and I'll offer to take you back to camp for medical attention."

John furrowed his brow. "Won't that just get one of us out of here?"

Private Howard rolled his eyes. "I can't carry one of you by myself, now can I? I'll say I need the other to help me. The fella that gave me a ride earlier will be going back soon and is going to give us a ride."

Tom pulled at his sweat-soaked collar. "I'm glad to hear that. I couldn't make the walk in this heat again." He thought for a second before adding, "Why, exactly, did they want *you* to come get us?"

The private pulled the cart close to a row of corpses, "I'm the only one on the inside who knew about this little operation."

"The only one?" John asked. "The General told us there would be a few guards who knew about us."

Private Howard shook his head. "Guess not. Now you two get this thing loaded so we can get the hell out of here."

John and Tom loaded the cart. The corpses, only dead a few days, were already bloated and sticky. The two friends worked together to lift each body as gently as possible. Every corpse had an open wound or sore that emanated the foul odor of death. Private Howard assisted them, saying, "The sooner we get this cart loaded, the sooner we can leave."

With the cart full, or as full at John and Tom could handle, they pushed it toward the train station. Seeing that the other prisoners had already loaded their carts and moved to the train cars, John slowed his pace and glanced at Private Howard.

"Why the rush to get us this morning anyway?"

"I don't know for sure." Howard shook his head. "They have informants in camp. They reported the old timers were up to something. Given the trouble with you the last few days, Jacobson figured you might have become a target."

"Well, thanks for coming out here. You know, considering what happened." John pointed to his face.

"We're still on the same side, over here at least. And I get pretty stupid when I've had too much to drink," Private Howard said. "Now, who's gonna fake an injury?"

Tom agreed to pretend his side hurt near his appendix. The fake pain would render him incapable of walking alone, and require the assistance of John in order to get him back to camp.

Leaving the cart about fifty yards from the station, Private Howard yelled to the other soldiers while he and John supported Tom on either side. "Hey, this one's hurt or something. He keeps holding his side and groaning."

One of the guards frowned and replied loudly. "What do you want me to do about it? We can't go back until the job is done."

"I guess I'll have to take him myself." Private Howard put his arm around Tom's waist to support him and nodded in John's direction. "I'll have to take this one too. I can't carry him myself."

The other soldier shook his head with a frown. "Whatever you have to do. Now I have mostly old men to do this job."

While they talked, the explosions increased and the sound of gunfire became louder and closer. Howard's attention turned to the direction of the front. The rest of the group, including the prisoners, turned as well.

Running across the field, at a dead sprint, was a lone American soldier. When he neared the group, it was clear he had no intention of stopping. The soldier's arms flailed and he kept looking over his shoulder. One of the guards raised his hands and stepped in his way.

"Whoa, kid. What's the rush?"

Eyes darting backwards and sweat dripping from his face, the panicked young man slapped the soldier's hands out of his face and tried to push his way through.

"Get out of my way," he screamed. "They've broken through. The Germans broke through the line."

18

"We have to get out of here." John grabbed Tom's elbow and pulled him away from the group.

Tom's face was white. "We'll get shot in these German uniforms."

"It's better than the German's overtaking us and finding out who we really are," John said.

Before Tom could reply, the terrified soldier screamed again. "They've broken through, get out of my way."

He broke free of the grip of Private Howard, who'd let go of Tom and grabbed him by the arm. The soldier ran wildly over the hill. The ashen faces of the guards looked towards the front. When John pivoted in that direction, he witnessed what made their faces grow pale.

About four hundred yards away, where they first saw the lone soldier sprinting across the field, an entire army of American and French soldiers retreated in their direction.

"We gotta get out of here." One of the American guards edged away from the group.

"Wait," Private Howard commanded. "We have to get these prisoners somewhere safe. If we don't, they'll get killed in the confusion."

"The hell with that." The soldier turned in the direction the young man had run, and along with the three original guards, took flight. Private Howard remained.

"Get in this train car." Howard sprinted to the train and opened the door of the nearest car. Realizing most of the prisoners could not understand him, he pointed in the direction of the open door and waved his other arm.

Tom, still trying to maintain his German identity, pushed the other prisoners in the direction of the train. "I think he wants us to get in the train car."

"I'm not getting in there with those bodies." The Voice crossed his arms.

"Fine." Tom shook his head. "Stay out here and you can become a corpse. When those panicking Yankees see your German uniform, they won't know you're a prisoner. They'll just shoot you."

Tom paused with a smile, "Or run you though with a bayonet."

Relenting, the old German climbed into the train car. After all the prisoners were in, Private Howard closed the door and stood outside. The only light inside the car came from sunlight shining through slits in the door.

John turned to Tom and nodded in the direction of the door.

Tom whispered in German, "I think he's protecting us."

"We'll be fine in here. He needs to get out of here." John tried to push himself to his feet to tell Private Howard to leave, but the Voice grabbed his arm and held him down.

"Let me go." John jerked his arm. "Get your hands off me."

The old man snarled. "You sit down and shut up. If those Yankees hear German voices in here, we'll all be dead."

"If we don't do something, the man who saved our lives will die."

The old man tightened his grip on John's arm. "That's his problem."

John pulled harder to free himself from the old man's grip. Two enforcers seized him and pulled him to the floor. John tried to scream, but a sweaty, dirty hand covered his mouth. John jerked and bit the hand.

Before he could scream again, the cold forearm of the Voice reached across his neck. The old man's arm tightened on John's windpipe, closing off his airway. John's eyes bulged. He gasped for a breath of air that did not come.

"Grab him, too." The Voice nodded toward Tom. "They'll get us all killed."

John saw stars and wondered if these were the last things he would ever see. The old man loosened his grip allowing John to gasp. "Don't you realize he saved our lives? They'll kill him when they get near."

"Better him than us," the Voice rasped before tightening his grip again.

John again thought of his first day in France, looking into the empty cars. On that day, the odor was intolerable. Today, the stench of rotting corpses was worse. This is not what he expected when he volunteered back in Nebraska. *I wouldn't be in this mess if I were still home on the farm.*

Voices screamed outside the train car.

"On your knees. Throw down your gun," the booming voice commanded in German.

Watching through the slits, Private Howard lowered himself to his knees so all that was visible was the top of his helmet. Soon, three German soldiers appeared around Private Howard, all pointing their guns at him. The Voice finally loosened his arm from around John's neck.

John yelled in German, "Don't shoot. German soldiers in here. He protected us. Don't shoot him."

The door to the car slid open and two of the three soldiers pointed their guns into the train car. One of the soldiers commanded, "Come out slowly. No quick movements."

One by one, the prisoners emerged from the train car, each shielding his eyes from the bright summer sun. John hadn't realized how hot it was in the car until he exited. His entire uniform was soaked.

The Voice explained to the German soldiers their situation. The soldier took his turn, explaining that the German army launched their summer offensive. They had gained ground against the American and French forces in the area. He proudly declared Germany would soon win the war.

"Congratulations, my friends," he announced to the prisoners. "You are now free. We will return you to your units to resume the fight for the fatherland."

The old man smiled. "It is good to be free, my friend."

The solder nodded in the direction of the trenches. "Walk that way and look for the big green tent. That's the communication tent. They'll figure out what to do with you. It's only a few kilometers."

John looked at Tom, who sat at the door of the train car, legs dangling. A blank expression on his face, Tom didn't return John's gaze.

"That one, up there," John pointed at Tom. "He got sick or something. I think he should wait here for medical attention."

Tom shook himself out of his fog. "No, I'm fine. I can go with you."

John's eyes narrowed. "You could hardly walk fifteen minutes ago. I think you should wait for medical treatment."

The German soldier intervened. "He will stay here. The medical unit is working this way to take care of the wounded."

Tom winced, giving John the "I know what you're up to" look, but didn't protest again.

"And what about him?" The Voice pointed at Private Howard, who still knelt in the grass with his hands clenched behind his head.

The German sneered at the private. "We'll take care of him. Those who hold captive our comrades get *special* treatm—"

"Wait a minute," John interrupted. "He could have run away with the rest of the Yankees, but he stayed to make sure they didn't kill us."

"That one likes the Yankees." The Voice pointed to John. "In the camp, he seemed quite cozy with them."

"That's a lie." John yelled, pointing to his face. "Who do you think did this to me?"

"Exactly," the Voice answered. "Why would you defend the people who did that to you?"

John lunged at the old man, knocking him to the ground. He swung his fists wildly. "He saved our lives, you son of a bitch. I don't care who he is. I'm not gonna let you kill someone who saved us."

The German laughed and pulled John off the old man. "You start walking back to our side of the line. I can see the stress of prison life has gotten to you. I'll catch up and escort you after we take care of this cowboy."

The Voice smiled and pushed himself from the ground. "If I may, I'd like to take care of this one myself. I've been under their thumb in the camp for many years."

113

The German removed a sidearm from his belt. "Yes, I think we can let you take care of that."

John stepped in front of the Voice. "You're not going to do this. He saved our lives."

The Voice took the gun from the German and raised it to John's face, pressing it into his forehead. "Then I will be using two bullets today. One for my oppressor and one for a traitor."

Before John could object again, he glanced at Private Howard. Howard gave him a hard stare and shook his head firmly.

John muttered, "No, I can't let you do this."

Private Howard shook his head again, this time raising his posture into what could only be described as kneeling at attention. John sensed if it wouldn't have raised suspicion, Private Howard, who hated him only a few days ago, would have saluted. Remembering the previous two nights when Private Howard stood near the head of his row, John was unable to talk.

He stood guard over me at night and he did it again today. And I'm going to let him die.

John glanced at Tom, who gave him the same look Private Howard had. There was nothing he could do that wouldn't get all three Americans killed.

"Get going now, boys," the German commanded, patting one of the old timers on the back. "Enjoy your freedom."

John gave Tom one more look before stepping back from the Voice and turning to Private Howard. "Thank you for saving us." Although he spoke the words in German, John knew he understood. Howard raised his chin a little higher when John stepped away.

Walking with the freed Germans, who were exuberant at their rescue, John rubbed the imprint the pistol made when the Voice pressed it into his forehead. He squeezed his eyes shut as he heard a single gunshot, followed by the sound of a body crumpling to the ground.

19

John trudged among the old men and their German "rescuer", trying to keep them in his sight. He glared at the Voice, who didn't take long to catch up after he executed Private Howard. John muttered to himself, "I'm not gonna let you get away with this."

John desperately assessed his situation. They didn't know anything about him for sure. All they could claim was they thought he passed information to the Americans. They had no proof. But what would happen when they contacted Third Division and found out he didn't exist. John dreaded crossing the line into German territory where he would be discovered as a spy.

He searched for any opportunity to escape. The problem he faced, every time he saw a chance, was the old timers had more or less surrounded him. They weren't completely around him like he was their prisoner. It was more like they walked, as group, and he was in the middle. He had no allies and wished Tom were with him.

The close up view of the battlefield was staggering. The semi-flat fields John observed in the morning no longer existed. They were replaced by a crater and mud-filled landscape where no living thing could survive.

The first trench they crossed was shallow. John and the Germans were able to jump across without having to climb. The group kept walking until they reached the next trench, which was both deeper and wider than the previous trench. John counted steps and guessed it was about a half a mile from the previous trench.

They would have to hop into this one before climbing out the other side. This trench was only up to John's chest, but he couldn't

115

climb out without assistance. The muddy walls caused anyone who tried to scramble out to slide back down. There were wooden crates placed every fifty feet that allowed soldiers to crawl out when needed. After exiting the second trench, they travelled about the same distance to the front line trench.

This trench was the largest of the three. Not only was this crevasse cut deeper, but the dirt was piled in front of the trench in a huge berm that provided a place to build underground bunkers. Strung across the top of the berm, barbed wire ran the entire length of the trench. John craned his head in both directions looking for a way back, but the trench ran as far as he could see.

The German soldier led John and the old timers to an opening about two feet wide with a wooden ladder encased in the berm. The ladder allowed soldiers enough support to crawl out. Looking down the line, he saw many such openings. John wondered how many soldiers died to make these openings in the wire before the German attackers broke through.

He crawled into the trench, which was well over his head. Hopping into the deep channel, John expected to sink into mud at the bottom. A thud echoed in the trench when he landed on a wooden plank covered with about an inch of dirt. Crawling up the other side, with one old man in front and another behind, John stopped.

This is it. When I cross the line, the rules for prisoners of war won't apply to me.

"What are you waiting for?" The old man they called Father Time stomped his foot on the wooden plank, commanding John forward. "You act like you don't want to go home."

The Voice yelled, "Maybe he doesn't want to be rescued. Better keep an eye on him, Erick."

"Erick. Father Time's name is Erick," John mumbled to himself.

Walking through the area between the trenches in the early afternoon sun, John grew tired. With each step, his feet became heavier and heavier. He stopped at regular intervals to scrape the growing load of mud off his boots and rest from the exhausting march.

On one such stop, John noticed something he thought looked out of place. There, in the middle of the desolate landscape, was a bright red poppy. "Would you look at that, a flower out here?"

Erick walked beside him. "You haven't been in the war long, have you, kid? Not more than a month or two I'm guessing."

John thought for a second to remember the story he'd practiced in training. "No. Less than four weeks before I was captured. I never even made it to the front."

"I thought so," Erick said.

John raised his eyebrows. "I can tell you're getting at something."

The old man stared into the distance. "I've been here for this whole war. Since the first shot. Every winter, the fighting mostly stops, and this dead land gets a rest. In the spring, when the rains come, the red poppies always grow the fastest.

"And then the war resumes." Erick's shoulders slumped. "It doesn't take long before everything out here is black and brown and crimson, but sometimes one of them survives. In the middle of all this death, one or two little red flowers ignore the world and reach to heaven."

"I thought you guys," John pointed at the men nearby who had also stopped, "had been prisoners the whole war? That's the rumor in the camp, anyway."

"Not me," the old man replied. "I was captured this spring."

John's curiosity took hold. That and the possibility of an ally. "Is it as bad as they say, in the trenches I mean?"

The old man rubbed his forehead. "Imagine the worst place you can think of. Imagine hell, if you believe in that sort of thing. Instead of fire, this has mud and rats and poison and rain and disease. It has noise. The loudest noise you've ever heard."

Erick frowned. "This hell has your friends and family getting blown to pieces, their blood spraying on you. It's a place where you wish the next bullet was for you. If you didn't believe in hell before, you believe in it now.

"Only, this is worse than the real hell." The old man stared at John. "How can there be anything worse than holding your own son's hand, while his heart pumps all his blood out of the stump that, two minutes before, was a leg?"

John dropped his head and stared at the poppy. He didn't understand how the old man could talk with so little emotion. A muddy brown boot entered his field of vision and stepped on the flower. The boot didn't simply step on it and keep moving, it twisted and turned the poppy into the mud.

The Voice scowled at John and Erick. "Get moving. We don't have all day for you to admire the scenery."

John stared at the old man before he resumed trudging. "If I ever get a chance, I'll kill you," he mumbled.

Reaching the other side of the barren middle ground, John studied the German trenches. They were much the same as the American and French ones he had just crossed. It was the same routine. Crawl over the berm, scamper down, and crawl back out. After crossing the first German trench, he was officially behind enemy lines.

"How much further to the communications tent?" John wanted to know how much time he had to make his escape.

"About four kilometers." The German soldier yelled back, before the Voice spoke into his ear. They both looked at John and leered.

John guessed it would take about forty-five minutes to reach their destination, assuming the gap between the trenches was similar to the first ones they crossed. Forty-five minutes to figure it out. Having left his watch at the old school with the rest of his belongings, John started counting to himself. When he reached sixty, he started over.

Almost right when he began counting, the distant rumble of artillery resumed. The low rumble shook the ground under John's feet. He ignored the battle in the distance and kept counting. "One, two, three, four…"

At the seventeen-minute mark, John estimated it had been more than an hour and a half since the German army pushed through the line and "rescued" he and the others.

With the rumble of artillery now continuous, soldiers ran in the direction of the front line.

The German who led the group stopped one of the runners. "Where are you all going in such a hurry?"

"There's a counter attack. The Americans are trying to take their line back." The soldier barely stopped to answer before he resumed moving toward the front.

John knew the confusion would be his only opportunity. Amidst the chaos, the old timers seemed to have forgotten about him.

The German pointed in the direction they had been walking. "Keep going that way. You can't miss it. It's a huge green tent."

The German pointed at the Voice. "You. Get these men to the communications tent safely."

This is it. This is my chance. John looked around before sprinting to a group of wounded soldiers resting on a grassy area nearby.

"Hey." The Voice screamed. "Where do you think you are going?"

John ignored the Voice and crouched to the wounded men. "I need your gun. Our fellow soldiers need me at the front."

One of the wounded soldiers lifted his rifle and handed it to John. He turned toward the front line. The Voice blocked his way and pointed at the gun.

"Where do you think you're going with that?"

John shouldered past the Voice. "I'm going to the line to fight."

The Voice stared at John before Erick stepped between them. "We all need to find a gun and head to the front line."

"All?" John's eyes widened.

"The trench was my home for years." Erick smiled at John. "Did you think I was afraid to go back?"

"No, I just didn't know," John stammered. Stunned, his opportunity to escape was shaping up to have him fighting his own countrymen.

Pushing by John, three of the other old men, including the Voice, reached for guns from the wounded.

"Better take this, too." Erick handed John a gas mask. "Don't want to get caught in the trench without it."

John slung the mask over his shoulder by the strap, allowing it to bounce against his back.

The Voice snarled at the two young Germans who made no effort to find a weapon. "You cowards. Even this one," he pointed at John, "is going to fight."

The young men stood silent and stared at the ground.

"We'll see you when we get back." He glared at the men before walking in the direction of the line. "Let's go."

It occurred to John he had never used a German gun. Finding it similar to the guns he'd practiced with during basic training, he made sure it was loaded and ready.

The sound of battle grew deafening the nearer to the front line they advanced. Gunfire and artillery thundered, even as far as a kilometer away. Artillery exploded closer and closer, as shells overshot the trenches and landed behind the lines.

A new sound, the sound of ear piercing whistling reached John's ears. Having never been in battle, he didn't understand what the noise meant. He watched soldiers nearby take cover, jumping behind wagons, trucks, and into holes.

He stood motionless. Two powerful hands grabbed his shoulders and pushed him into an artillery crater. "Get the hell out of the way before you get us blown up."

The ground shook like an earthquake just as he ducked below the rim of the crater. A shower of dirt and mud rained on John's head.

He bent in the hole, hands covering his head. "You almost bought it that time kid. You really are green, aren't you?"

Erick patted John on the back and stretched to extricate himself from the hole. "Next time, find cover. The shell probably won't hit you directly. It's the shrapnel you need to stay away from."

John and the other soldiers marched toward the front line again. Explosions continued in the distance. John prayed for another close explosion. "One more God, please?"

The explosions became more rapid. Another whistle tore through the air. Not as loud as the last one, but loud enough. Close enough.

John hugged his rifle and ran as fast as he could. He moved away from the old men, parallel to the trench. He knew they would not chase him until after the shell landed. All he heard was the wind in his ears. He didn't hear the explosion at first, but he felt the ground quake. He lost his balance and fell into the dirt.

John struggled to get to his feet. He had only travelled about fifty yards. Erick yelled, "What the hell are you doing over there, kid?"

The Voice talked to the other old men, gesturing at John. John pushed himself to his feet and tried to shake off the dizziness. *I have to run; this is my only chance.*

He looked over his shoulder to the south. A gently sloping field rolled behind him. At the far end of the field, a shallow rock wall. Beyond that, John didn't know.

"Let's go." Erick waved for him to come. "The war's gonna be over before we get there."

The other old timers watched him.

Run.

He took a deep breath and grasped his rifle, pulling it close to his chest. Turning away, he ran for the rock wall. The gas mask bounced on his back as he sprinted across the field.

A loud whizzing zipped to the right of him, followed by the delayed echo of a gunshot.

"They're shooting at me."

Another whizzing, another echo. John dared not turn back. They were old and he was young. He could outrun them as long as their bullets missed.

"Keep running."

John approached the rock wall, which stood shorter than he had thought. He jumped over the wall, but it would not provide the protection he hoped for. The land in front of him sloped downward. A grove of trees that had not been destroyed stood about two hundred yards to his left.

John veered left and reached the grove. He ducked between two trees that grew close together. He bent over, gasping for air. Between breaths, he looked out the corner of his eye for any sign of movement. The heads of the old men bounced above the wall as they drew near.

John struggled for breath on the humid afternoon. He swiveled his head in the other direction. An old barn at the edge of a larger woodland stood a few hundred yards away. If he were still in Nebraska, the grove in the distance would be considered a forest.

John took another breath and sprinted toward the barn. He followed a path that kept the smaller grove between himself and his pursuers. He reached the old white barn and slammed into it with his hands.

Skirting the side of the barn, he got around the corner and discovered an entryway with the door removed. He stepped inside and made his way through the stalls to a window facing the direction of the smaller grove. The glass in the window was broken and bullet holes peppered the frame.

Leaning against the wall with one hand, John studied the ground. He gasped for air. At his feet, a black pool of dried blood mixed with broken glass startled John. Someone else had been in the same spot. He took a step away from window.

Searching the area, John crouched to peek through one of the bullet holes. Not seeing the old men advancing across the field, he found another hole with a better view of the grove.

Behind the trees, two of the old men pointed their guns at the barn. The Voice and Erick were nowhere in sight.

"Where are the others?"

John looked through more bullet holes on that side of the barn.

"Maybe they're already outside the barn."

John bolted to another wall, looking through more bullet holes. After spying holes in all four walls, he returned to the window. The same two old men waited in the grove. He leaned against the clapboard of the wall and thought about the barn at home. He remembered playing hide and seek with his brother, peeking through the slats in the wood wall. This wall didn't have gaps, it had bullet holes.

John peeked through the hole one last time. The two soldiers waited, guns pointed at the broken window. John exited the barn through the same door he had entered, which was not visible to the two men in the grove. He turned to the back corner of the barn, ready to sprint toward the trees.

Around the corner, John came face to face with Erick. His gun raised to John's chest. Time stood still. He saw images of those he loved. Rose and Margrit flashed through his mind. He turned his head to the side, closed his eyes, and waited for the bullet that would tear through his chest.

"Run."

20

John opened his eyes and exhaled.

"Go." Erick lowered his weapon and jerked his head toward the woods. "I will not watch another young man die. Especially not at my hand."

John sprinted into the grove. He crouched behind a small shrub when he was deep in the woods but could still see the barn. The sound of battle echoed loud enough to camouflage his movements.

The Voice appeared around the corner and talked with Erick. John thought he should have gone deeper into the forest and searched for a place of cover. Finding a small crevice in the ground where the roots of a fallen tree had been pulled from the dirt, he was able to back completely into the uprooted tree. The web of roots concealed his presence.

John couldn't see the old men through the hanging roots and shrubs, but could see the top of the barn. He was amazed the barn, like the poppy in the field, survived this close to the brutal war.

A thick root dug into John's back, reminding him of the night with Margrit in the park. Would he ever see her again? He thought about the night they spent together in her apartment.

"Was it a mistake?" he wondered aloud to himself.

He rubbed his eyes and pinched the bridge of his nose. Considering his survival was not guaranteed, how could he be so selfish? And what about Rose? He still had feelings for her. The sound of gunfire faded with the growing darkness. John relaxed in the little shelter and allowed himself to drift off to sleep.

# # #

A movement in the woods nearby jolted John awake. He clutched his rifle and stared into the darkness. He didn't know how long he'd slept, but the fog of sleep wore off quickly.

In the moonlight, he crept to the edge of his shelter. He squinted into the darkness, searching for the source of the sound. A porcupine rustled in a tree branch nearby. John crawled out of the crevice. He watched the silhouette of the barn, wondering if the old timers still lingered there. He decided to move deeper into the forest.

With only the light of the moon to navigate by, John struggled to traverse the dense woods. He stumbled over bushes, roots, and fallen trees. He froze every time he stepped on a twig, afraid of revealing his location.

John didn't know how long he walked before seeing lights through the trees in the distance. He stepped out of the forest and looked in either direction. By the light of the moon and the glow of lights in the distance, he knew he was at the edge of the forest near the front line. With trepidation, John crossed the clearing between the forest and the trench.

John's attention was drawn to movement on the trench. It looked like ants rebuilding their hill after a storm. Soldiers climbed to the top of the berm and disappeared over the side.

"You lost, buddy?" A middle-aged soldier with a thick black mustache tapped John on the shoulder.

"Um," John paused. "Yeah, I am lost. Do you know where Third Division is?"

John knew Third Division was nowhere near this location, or at least he had been told in training it wasn't.

The soldier gave John a puzzled expression. "You are *really* lost. Third Division is at least thirty kilometers north. How did you get all the way down here?"

John took a slow breath, his mind racing to think of a believable story. "Our communications tent was blown up during the attack. I was sent with paper dispatches and got lost. I don't even know how I got to the front line without crossing the rear lines."

The soldier pointed to the forest. "The rear trenches stop at the border of the woods. If you came through there, you would have missed them."

John nodded. "That's where I came."

The soldier furrowed his brow. "If you came with dispatches, where is your satchel?"

John looked toward his hip, acting as if he didn't know the fictional pack was missing. "I must have lost it in the attack. I have to find it or I'm in trouble."

"You aren't gonna find it tonight, not in the dark. Stay here until morning and we'll see what we can do," the soldier said. "We have a bunker nearby you can stay in. Should be a quiet night with the fighting over for now."

John followed the soldier into the trench. He squinted in both directions looking for the Voice. He wasn't sure how he would get back across the line, but for now he was only worried about the old timers.

The soldier led John to the entrance of a bunker dug into the trench. A sloping ramp of dirt with sandbag lined walls led John inside the bunker. He ducked as he entered the bunker, which was only about eight feet in diameter. The place smelled like wet dirt mixed with body odor and smoke from the oil lamp burning in the middle. Six men huddled around the lantern, their shadows dancing on the walls. One of the soldiers held a newspaper near the light.

"Who's your friend, Karl?" An unidentified voice asked John's companion.

The soldier shook his head. "I don't even know. I found him outside, like a lost puppy. He's a dispatch runner from third. Got lost in the shelling."

The soldiers in the bunker didn't seem concerned about John. They were more interested in the newspaper. Seeing that no one asked for his name, John didn't offer it after what happened the last time someone heard the name "Alders Bayer."

John sat near the wall and listened to the soldiers read the German newspaper. It reported the German military neared "complete victory" and the war would soon be over. John laughed to himself. He thought about how American newspapers were reporting the exact same thing.

I wonder what the truth is? Maybe the war will go on forever.

John did not fight the weariness. He rested his head on the sandbags. For the second time that night, he fell asleep sitting up. This time, he leaned against the sandbag wall clutching his rifle.

#

John awoke to the sound of voices outside the bunker. The rhythmic breathing nearby indicated the other soldiers were asleep. He wasn't sure what time it was or how long he had slept, but the lantern was out. The room was dark, with the exception of a dim light from a lantern outside the doorway.

He listened to the voices, but couldn't make out what they said. It sounded like one of the voices said, "He went in there." John wasn't sure.

Tingling shot up John's neck when heard a familiar raspy voice outside the entrance. For a moment, he couldn't move. Feeling around at his feet, John grabbed his gun and gas mask, which had slid off his lap while he slept. He tried to feel his way in the dark bunker toward the entrance.

"Hey, watch it." A voice groaned from the ground beneath him.

"Sorry." John whispered in German.

The voices outside stopped as John crept up the entrance. A group of soldiers stood nearby, not directly in front of the opening. John lowered his helmet to conceal his face and glanced down the trench. A lantern, about fifty feet from the group, slowly moved up the hill. One of the soldiers was climbing.

"Who's there?" the Voice barked.

A tall soldier stepped between John and his escape. John recognized him as Erick. The Voice repeated, "Who's there?"

John clutched his rifle and bent low before he ran straight at Erick. Two powerful hands grabbed John's arms and swung him around to face the group.

"We've got you now, coward," the Voice yelled triumphantly.

Sleepy soldiers peeked out of their bunkers down the line.

John struggled against Erick's firm grip. "I'm no coward. Let me go."

The Voice shook his head. "I don't think so, *boy*. We're going to turn you in for desertion. Or maybe we should take care of you right now."

John thrashed against Erick's grip. "I didn't desert. I'm at the front ready to fight."

The Voice inched his face so close to John, their noses almost touched. John felt the old man's hot breath when he spoke. "Then why did you run from us?"

John took a deep breath. "I didn't want to make it to the front only to have you shoot me in the back."

The Voice threw his head back and laughed. "If I wanted you dead, *boy*, you would be dead." He looked at those around him, some of whom were not old timers or enforcers, and raised his rifle. "I say we take care of this coward right now."

Another soldier stepped between John and the Voice. "That's not how we do things here. If he deserted, it will be found out by the—"

"Get out of my way and let me deal with him." The Voice snarled and tried to push past the soldier.

Erick turned his body away from the rest of the soldiers. To John's surprise, the firm grip of the old man loosened. Erick whispered into John's ear. "Run now or you're dead."

John pulled the rifle to his chest and sprinted away from the group. He ran toward the ascending lanterns.

"Get him," The Voice screamed. "He's getting away."

At a full sprint, John darted past curious soldiers who emerged from their bunkers. He made it to where the soldiers crawled up the high side of the trench. Having rained all of the previous day, the dirt was wet and slimy, making climbing difficult.

"Somebody stop him." The Voice sounded insane as he shrieked.

John scrambled, arms and legs flailing, as he tried to get to the top. His left hand found a wooden rod, a ladder wedged into the ground. Reaching the top, he faced a row of barbed wire running the length of the trench.

John ran along the top of the trench, parallel with the barbed wire. His eyes searched for an opening. He spotted a dark circle ahead and sprinted toward it.

"He's a deserter." The Voice reached the top of the berm with three of the old timers. "Stop him!"

John neared the circle. A wooden spool, unrolling new barbed wire. Two soldiers crouched, pulling the spool.

"Get down, you idiot," one of the soldiers shouted. "The Americans retook their trench and are shooting at anything that moves."

John's eyes flashed. "Americans?"

"Yes. Now get down before you get us shot." The soldier reached for John's leg.

John jumped through the opening in the barbed wire that the two soldiers hadn't yet repaired.

The Voice screamed in rage. "Shoot him. Shoot the deserter."

A bullet ricocheted off the spool after a gunshot came from the American side of the field. The two soldiers unwinding the spool scurried over the berm into the trench. The old timers who followed John to the top slid down behind the berm. Their heads peeked over the top.

The single shot ignited gunfire on both sides. John crawled low to the ground. He was alone in no man's land.

A gunshot thumped into a dirt mound near John's head. The Voice roared behind him. "He's deserting. Don't let him get away."

John crawled between two small mounds that protected him from both sides. A flare shot into the sky. Watching it fall, John knew he wouldn't have much time to run to the next mound. Freedom was only a short distance away. But it might as well be a mile.

He took off his jacket and shirt. He still wore his German army pants, but knew he couldn't get close to the American lines wearing the gray German uniform. He rolled in the mud to hide his white skin. Groping in the mud, John felt something hard beneath him. He pressed his hand in the shallow mud and discovered a dirt-covered corpse.

Pulling his hand away with a gasp, John's lungs burned from gas lingering low in the atmosphere. He reached over his shoulder for the mask, fastening the mud-covered apparatus onto his face. The lenses fogged as he labored to take a breath.

Another flare shot into the sky, illuminating the entire area. In the shadowy pre-dawn of battle, the Voice screamed, "We will get you, traitor."

John looked around before jumping to his feet. He darted from one mound and mud hole to the next. Heart pounding. Sweat dripping. Hands shaking. Mask fogging. Rifle bouncing. Darting.

21

John fought to open his eyes. He didn't know where he was or how he had gotten there. He remembered running, screaming, and falling. His eyes opened slowly, hesitantly. Crusted over and blurry, they barely drew in light.

He lay face down on a narrow cot, his cheek pressed against a flat pillow. Something held him at the legs and waist. His arms were secured to the cot, too. He tried to roll over but couldn't. He was moving. Not fast, but rocking back and forth.

Eyes foggy, head dizzy, he was nauseous. His back throbbed and head pounded. He was soaked. Why was he wet? He fought to keep his eyes open. He studied round rivets in the painted metal floor.

"I'm on a ship," he mumbled into his pillow.

John raised his head and looked around. Not throbbing now, piercing. A sharp pain stabbed his back. Someone nearby moaned. Lying his head back on the pillow, the moaning stopped. The sound of his heartbeat pounded in his ears. He fell back into darkness.

Voices. Who is talking? A woman. What is she saying? He listened, trying to raise his head again. A hand wiped his brow with a damp washcloth. He slowly opened his eyes. Everything was gray, still gray. Foggy. Still nauseous. Whose soft hand wiped his forehead?

"Margrit?" John tried to push himself up.

"Lay your head down, Lieutenant. Get some rest. You're almost home," a calming said.

"Home, I can't be home. This is a dream." John's voice echoed in his head. Back into empty sleep. Darkness. Rocking back and forth, back and forth.

He was awake again. The moving had stopped. He tried to open his eyes. There was light. A white sheet surrounded him. He was still on his stomach.

"Hello?" John's throat burned. "Is someone there?"

The sound of footsteps reverberated around him.

The curtain opened and white shoes walked next to his bed. A bed, he was in a bed. Not a cot. A soft bed.

"Can you help me roll over?" John lifted his head.

"I'm sorry Lieutenant, you need to stay on your stomach."

John twisted to look at the woman. She wore a white outfit with a matching hat. Dark curls of hair dangled onto her neck. A nurse.

"Where am I?" John's voice was hoarse and his cracked lips burned.

"You're in the hospital, Lieutenant Bayer." The nurse held a glass of water to John's lips. "Here, take a sip of water, it will help your throat."

Water dribbled off John's chin onto his pillow. "What hospital?"

"Walter Reed Army Hospital," she said.

"I'm in Washington?"

22

John laid his head on his damp pillow and squirmed in pain. "How did I get to Washington?"

"Please lay still, Lieutenant." The nurse unwrapped the bandage from his back. "All I know is you were shot in the back and got an infection. You've been here three days."

John tried to think, but the short conversation took its toll. He closed his eyes and fell back to sleep. Sleep this time wasn't empty and dreamless. His dreams were filled with images of war. Running, hiding, falling, and screaming.

"Lieutenant Bayer, wake up. Lieutenant, you're going to wake up the other patients." A nurse shook John's foot. "You're only dreaming, Lieutenant."

John opened his eyes and pulled at the straps holding him down. Remembering where he was, he laid his head back on the pillow. "How long have I been asleep?"

"Not long this time." The nurse checked John's bandages. "Mary, the nurse you met earlier, said you woke up for a while this afternoon. That was about three hours ago."

John's leg twitched when the nurse changed his bandage. "Can you tell me what happened? I think I got shot. But why did I get sent here?"

"Your friend said you'd want to know what happened." The nurse pulled a chair next to his bed after she finished examining his wounds. She took a cotton ball and dabbed petroleum jelly on it before rubbing it on John's dry lips.

"My friend?" John asked.

The nurse smiled. "Tom. He's been here every day."

He squeezed his eyes shut. "Tom's here?"

She patted John on the arm. "He's in the waiting room. Only wives are allowed in patient rooms past visiting hours."

John nodded. "Okay, you were telling me how I got here."

"There isn't much more to tell, I'm afraid," she said. "The army doesn't keep good records when they send soldiers from the field hospitals. All I know is you were shot in your back, below the shoulder. You're lucky. It barely missed your lungs."

John reached to feel for the wound, but pulled against the straps. "Why do I have these on?"

"A lot of soldiers have trouble sleeping. The last thing you need is to fall out of bed." The nurse twirled a long strand of blond hair that had fallen loose from her hat.

She reached over to readjust John's bandage before she resumed. "The records from the field hospital indicated they removed the bullet before shipping you here."

"Anything else?"

"I'm afraid not."

John was dizzy. "Why did they send me here? Lots of guys get shot and don't come home?"

The nurse shook her head and stood. "I'm sorry, Lieutenant. I don't know."

Before she left, she turned to John. "My name's Francine, by the way. In case you need anything."

# # #

John awoke the following morning to the blurry figure of a uniformed man in the gray armchair next to him. The man's legs stretched in front of him and his head rested against the chair back with his hat pulled over his eyes.

"Tom?" John squinted, slightly raising his head.

Tom stretched. "It's about time you woke up."

"How did we get here?"

"By boat, how else?" Tom winked.

John shook his head. "You know what I mean."

"We can talk about it later. You need to rest."

John found his voice. "I want to know what happened."

Tom raised is hands. "Okay, okay. Calm down." He took a deep breath. "Do you remember the last time you saw me sitting in the train car after the German offensive?"

"Yes."

"After you left, I waited at the train for the German medics to come fix my phony ailment." Tom leaned in and spoke quietly. "I had no idea how I would get back to our side. Fortunately, the American army launched a counter attack before the German medics reached me."

Tom paused and poured a glass of water from the pitcher on the side table. "At first, they took me prisoner. I explained to a sergeant why I was wearing a German uniform. He took me to Major Jacobson to verify my story. We didn't really know what to do about you, though."

John frowned. "What do you mean, *what to do* about me?"

"You were behind enemy lines and we didn't know how to get you back," Tom answered.

John groaned. "There wasn't much you could do."

"True." Tom took a sip of John's water. "All we could think was to tell the commanders at the front not to shoot any lone German in no man's land."

"That's why they didn't shoot me when I came across?"

Tom leaned back in his chair and laughed. "The way I heard it, the guys in the trench were dumbfounded to see a half-naked German running across the field, getting shot at by his own people."

John laughed a little, but stopped when his gunshot wound throbbed. "That still doesn't answer how I got *here*."

"I'm getting to that," Tom reassured with a smile. "After you made it across no man's land, a company of soldiers from Australia took you to the medical tent. It didn't take long for us to hear about the crazy German who ran across the line screaming in English. When we got to the forward aid station, Jacobson pulled a few strings and got you transported to a hospital in Paris."

"That still doesn't explain how I got *here*," John repeated, with gritted teeth.

"That bullet didn't give you any extra patience, did it?" Tom shook his head. "On the way to Paris, you still hadn't woken up.

The doctor said the shock put you into a coma. After a few days in Paris, we were able to make a deal to get you sent home."

"A deal?" John's eyes narrowed. "What kind of deal?"

"Let's just say those poker games I was in finally paid off." Tom shrugged. "Even if I came home broke."

John stared at Tom. "And?"

Tom ran his fingers through his hair. "You don't miss anything, do you? Even with the medicine they've got you on."

John pushed himself up again. "And?"

"Now that the war is almost over, the army is nervous about keeping enough officers for peacetime. Jacobson is especially worried about keeping guys in his unit, since most will go back to their teaching jobs after the war," Tom said. "He agreed to ask the General for permission to send you home if I remain in the army for a while."

"A while?"

Tom half shrugged. "A three-year enlistment."

John laid his head down. "You agreed to stay in the army for three more years to get me home?"

"Not just for that. I kind of like it in the army." Tom winked. "Free clothes, food, and a warm bed. Besides, after you marched off with those Germans to save me, what else could I do? You'd have done the same thing."

23

John lay in bed, staring at the pile of envelopes Tom placed on the bedside table. "What about Margrit. She must think I'm dead."

Tom stood and peeked out the gap in the curtain where two panels met.

"What's the matter?"

Tom turned to John, his face drained of color. "When we arranged to get you shipped to Paris, I had a few hours before your transport left. You were at the same medical tent we loaded bodies before the attack." Tom took a breath, avoiding eye contact. "I got a ride into town so I could pack our things. I also wanted to stop by and tell Margrit what happened."

John raised his head. "What are you trying to tell me?"

"I made it to Gautier's," Tom said. "Well, what was left of it."

"What do you mean, what was left?"

"German artillery overshot the trenches and landed in the city." Tom shook his head. "Gautier's and three buildings nearby were destroyed. Most of the block was on fire."

"Did you find her? Did you find Margrit?" John pushed himself onto his forearms.

Tom looked John in the eyes. "She and Gautier were both inside when the building exploded."

"How can you be sure?"

Tom squeezed his eyes shut. His face contorted into a grimace. "I saw them. They had been pulled from the building and were on the street with a sheet draped over their bodies. Camille stood on the street screaming. She told me who they were."

"No." John collapsed into the mattress. "I don't believe it."

"I'm sorry." Tom pulled a chair close to the side of John's bed. "I didn't want to tell you while you were still in such bad shape."

John closed his eyes. He thought about his conversation with Margrit when she told him about her aunt, how she decided it was time to stop crying. In this moment, John was unable to cry. He was unable to feel anything.

He turned and faced the wall. He couldn't take the look of pity on Tom's face. John stared at the wall, trying to force himself back to sleep. He hoped he would awaken and find it was all a dream. That he was back in a simpler time, in Nebraska.

John slept off and on for another three days while he recovered. He was able to roll onto his back when the infection subsided. The bullet lodged into the meaty muscle in his back, but the doctor expected a full recovery. Although he said, John would always feel it a little.

Throughout this time, Tom remained with him. He would arrive right away in the morning and stay until the nurses kicked him out. Early one morning, Tom arrived with a paper bag under one arm.

John eyed the bag with suspicion. "What do you have in there?"

"I picked up some goodies at the bakery down the street." Tom reached into the bag and handed John a cookie. "I figured you must be sick of hospital food."

"Thanks." John took a bite. "Don't let the nurses see. They won't let you back in if you get caught."

Tom laughed. "That's why I didn't bring booze."

John smiled and asked for another.

Tom pulled a chair close to John's bed. "I know you've had a tough time, but we need to talk."

"What now?" John asked. Conversations that started like this were never good.

"It's your folks," Tom said. "We sent them a telegram."

"What did you tell them?"

"We told them you're okay." Tom twirled his cap in his hands. "I knew they might be worried not hearing from you, so I told them where you are."

John could tell Tom had more to say. "Is there something else?"

Tom said, "You know the girl you told me about? Rose?"

"Is something wrong?"

137

"No, it's nothing like that." Tom shook his head. "It's just that we got word she's coming here. I don't know all the details, but she'll be here tonight."

All John could muster was, "Oh."

Tom motioned toward the bundle of letters on the table. "Do you want me to put those away?"

John shook his head. "No, keep them there. Maybe I'll let her read them."

Tom sat back in his chair. "Did you ever write her about Margrit? About any of it?"

"No. I didn't know what to say," John said. "When I left, I thought I was in love with her. Now I don't know what to think."

"Well, pal." Tom winked. "You better start figuring it out."

"It's funny," John said, almost thinking out loud. "When you told me about Margrit, my first thought was that I wished I was back home and this was all a dream. If it was a dream, that would mean I was back with Rose. That must mean something."

Tom rubbed his chin. "It means you've been through a lot and you're confused."

"So what do I do?" John asked.

Tom smiled. "Sneak out of here and get as far away as you can before she arrives. It might be safer for you."

#

John fought to stay awake and wait for Rose, but fell asleep before Tom left for the evening. Early the following morning, he awoke to find Rose sitting in the armchair next to the bed. She was wide-awake and sat with her hands in her lap. He tried to smile and inhaled the strong odor of bleach used to wash the floors during the night.

"How long have you been here?" John noticed Rose wore the same green dress she had worn at the train station when he left Nebraska. Her hair was slightly shorter and curlier, but she looked mostly the same.

"They let me in when I arrived last night." She rubbed her hands on her dress to press out the wrinkles.

John stretched with a wince. "Tom's not going to like that. He's been trying to stay late every night. How'd you manage to get them to let you in?"

Rose smiled. "They told me only wives are allowed past visiting hours, but they would make an exception for me."

"I'm glad they did." John looked away. "I can't believe you came all the way here."

"How could I not?"

"I haven't sent you a letter since boot camp." John turned back to Rose. "I wouldn't have expected you to come."

"I want to be here," Rose said.

John nodded. He wondered if she would be here if she knew about France. How would he tell her?

"So." The curtain swished open and Tom glided into the room. "You must be Rose? I've heard a lot about you. I'm Tom."

Rose stood and shook Tom's hand. "It's a pleasure to meet you. Thank you for taking such good care of John. The nurses told me you've barely left his side since he got here."

"He still owes me money." Tom winked. "I've got to get it somehow."

John smiled, glad his friend was here. "Where did you come from?"

Tom winked again. "The nurses station. Keeping myself occupied until you woke up. So Rose, how long are you staying?"

"As long as it takes to get him well." Rose reached over and adjusted John's blanket to cover his exposed toes.

"What about the farm?" John asked, unable to hide his surprise. "Who's taking care of your mother?"

"Your sisters," Rose said. "When I told your mom I wanted to come, she offered to help my parents any way she could."

John wasn't surprised. He knew his mother wanted him and Rose together. She always wanted her children and grandchildren nearby. But his mother would have loved Margrit too. John didn't know what he wanted and was grateful when Tom offered to help Rose find a place to stay. Now that he had seen Rose, he needed time to think.

John decided Rose deserved the truth. After she returned with Tom, she sat quietly beside John's bed. It was lunchtime, but John wasn't hungry. His food sat on the tray, uneaten. When he nodded to Tom, his friend excused himself.

Alone with Rose, John told her the story from his time in France. He didn't keep anything from her, even telling her of his night with Margrit. Part of him hoped she would storm out. When he reached the end of the story, John closed his eyes. "I'm sorry I did this."

Rose sat quietly, fidgeting with the strap of her handbag. She wiped a tear away from her cheek. "So how are you doing?"

John's forehead creased. "You're not angry?"

Rose wiped away another tear. "I have no right to be angry. We made no promises and I knew what could happen when you left. I won't pretend it doesn't hurt, but that won't stop me from caring about you."

John couldn't talk.

Rose repeated her question. "So how are you?"

John wouldn't force Rose to watch him grieve for another woman. When he spoke, he ignored his feelings about Margrit.

"I'm feeling better. My shoulder aches, but I'm getting better."

Rose squeezed his hand. "But how are you *really* doing?"

John squeezed his eyes shut. "Not good.".

Rose held John's hand and sat silently with him. For the next week, she spent most of the day sitting with him. Sometimes they talked. Sometimes they didn't.

The day John left the hospital, he walked out with Tom on one side and Rose on the other. He inhaled the outside air that didn't smell of bleach.

"What now?" Tom held John's elbow.

John looked at Rose. "I'm not sure."

24

John stood in the office of his commanding officer in the Judge Advocates Corps. The year was 1947, two years after World War II ended. The General ignored John and shuffled papers on his desk. John had served under the old man for nearly ten years and was used to waiting for the General.

"John," the General said slowly. "We have to go to Germany for the war crimes trials."

John slouched. He'd managed to avoid overseas deployment for the entire war, and hoped to finish his final enlistment near his home in Washington D.C.

"I thought we didn't have to go." John rotated his hat in his hand. "The main trials in Nuremburg are over."

The General shook his head. "I have my orders from the Chief of Staff. Now that the big trials for folks like Goring are done, they want us to clean up the rest of the little fish."

"But Sir," John hesitated. He didn't want to set off the old man's legendary temper. "This is all routine. We know the Germans are guilty. Any one of the young guys in the office can handle this."

The old man clenched his teeth. "Listen. I know what happened to you over there when you were a kid. And I know you've avoided overseas deployment the last twenty-nine years. But you are going. Everyone in our office is going."

John stepped forward. "But Sir, if I may—"

"No you may not," the General yelled. "I'm not going to Germany to prosecute a bunch of murderers without my only German speaking lawyer."

John eyes narrowed. "So I have no choice?"

141

"No, you don't." The General sighed. "None of us have a choice. Orders are orders."

"When do I leave?" John spoke through gritted teeth. "And when can Rose expect me home?"

The General frowned. "Listen. I'm sorry I lost my temper. I know you're close to retiring and have another grandchild on the way. But I need you over there."

John said nothing.

The General removed his glasses. "It shouldn't be more than a few months. The Krauts have their own lawyers. All we'll do is interview and investigate. When the reports are submitted to the court, we come home."

John took a step away from the General's desk. "Who, exactly, will we be investigating?"

The General leaned back in his black leather chair. "A group of nasty SS officers in an organization called the Einsatzgruppen. They operated mobile death squads."

"I've heard of them?" John's expression darkened.

"Some dirty stuff, I'll tell you." The old man pinched the bridge of his nose. "Apparently, the Krauts couldn't kill them fast enough in the camps. They created this group to go around the countryside killing even more on death marches."

John rubbed his forehead. "When do we leave?"

The General reached for a file on his desk and handed it to John. "You and the other lawyers in the office leave in two weeks. The office clerks leave tomorrow to get everything set up. I am assigning Chamberlain and Cummins to your staff."

#

That evening, John recounted his conversation with the General to Tom.

"What, exactly, is a death march?" Tom asked, reclining in a brown leather chair in John's den.

John shrugged. "As I understand it, German soldiers were ordered to force the prisoners to leave the camps and trudge all over the countryside. Most prisoners either died of exhaustion or got shot along the way."

John took a slow sip of the scotch in his right hand, before continuing. "If the marchers didn't die along the way, the Germans forced them into the woods and shot whoever was left. The ones who survived were lucky to have been abandoned by the Germans at the end of the war."

Tom went to the dining room where the liquor cabinet was open. He refilled his glass before asking, "If they know all this really happened, why do they need to send you?"

"Window dressing, I suppose." John stretched one leg onto a footstool. "They want to make it look like there's a real trial. Even though they already know these guys are guilty. Heck, some of them are even proud of what they did."

"That's not what I mean. Of course they have to send someone. But why *you*?" Tom returned to his chair.

John nodded. "Last year, during the trials for the most notorious ones, a lot of guys volunteered to go. You know, up and comers who wanted to make a name for themselves. Now, those trials are over and the cameras are gone. The army still needs people to help with the rest of the investigations."

Tom took a long drink. "Well I wouldn't want to go. How does Rose feel about it?"

John swirled the ice in his glass. "I think she was as surprised as I was that I didn't get sent earlier. She understands the life of a soldier."

"Well try and stay out of trouble." Tom winked. "I won't be there to watch your back this time."

Two weeks later, Tom and John boarded a plane for their second trip to Europe. When John asked Tom how he arranged to get assigned to his staff, Tom laughed. "I guess you're lucky. You get good company on your trip."

25

John rested his graying hair against the dark blue vinyl seat. He marveled at how much faster the journey to France was on an airplane. Twenty-nine years ago, he spent a long, nauseating week on a crowded ship with the man who would become his best friend. Across the aisle, Tom was sound asleep before takeoff.

The flight lasted thirteen hours, with one stop in Greenland for fuel. Every time John closed his eyes he dreamed, not about this journey to Europe, but about the circumstances related to his last, agonizing trip home. Those memories caused an ache in his stomach.

John rubbed his eyes after turbulence jarred him from his dreams. The plane circled Paris and descended in the direction of an airfield outside the city. John steadied himself to face memories he had long ago buried. He reached across the aisle and tapped Tom's leg.

"I'm awake." Tom's arm stretched across his face. "Just pretending I'm at home taking a nap."

John laughed. "You know the grandkids don't let you nap. And Francine would have a project for you anyway."

"I am the king of my castle." Tom yawned. "I don't need permission to sleep. Besides, with six kids and thirteen grandkids, I've earned a little rest."

John smiled and thought about his friend, who he had expected to grow into an old bachelor. As it turned out, Tom settled into family life before John. Two months after John was discharged from the hospital, Tom married the nurse he met there.

John and Rose married a year after his hospitalization. Rose worked in the secretary pool at the War Department until their first child was born. They raised their family in Washington D.C., three blocks from Tom and Francine.

Tom kept his word and stayed in the army. He worked in the linguistics department for the past twenty-nine years. John suspected Tom had something to do with their lack of deployment during the war. Although Tom had only risen to the rank of captain in all that time, John knew he could still call in favors when he needed to. That, at least, hadn't changed.

Now they traveled together to Europe again. Emerging from the silver army air corps plane on a windy day, Tom pulled his collar up. "Here we go. Once more into the breach."

John, now a colonel, adjusted his tie and made sure his long black coat was buttoned before carefully walking down the wet metal stairway. "As I recall, it was a lot warmer the last time we were here."

Tom's jacket, only partly buttoned, flapped in the breeze. "I suppose there will be many things different this time. I hope we can find some good food though, like the last time."

John winced at the implied reference to Gautier's, a place he tried not to think about over the years. "I hoped we could do some sightseeing before we go on our tour."

"I thought you might say that. I'm your personal assistant on this trip. We have two days in the city before boarding a train for Germany." Tom slapped John on the shoulder and laughed.

John cringed when Tom's hand landed on his shoulder. He arched his back and stretched his right arm, circling it back and forth.

Tom pulled his hand back. "Sorry buddy. I forgot about the back."

"It usually only hurts in the cold and rain."

Tom shook his head. "Nice reminder of our last time here, isn't it?"

John frowned. "A nice reminder of the bastard who shot me."

"I bet you'd love to get your hands around his neck."

John smiled and arched his back again. "I think about it with great pleasure every time it rains. I'm sure he's been dead a long time by now."

"Maybe we'll find his grave." Tom laughed. "We could dance on it."

John chuckled. "I'm sure we'll be too busy for that after we start the tour."

Tom gave an exaggerated grimace. "I almost forgot we actually have to work on this trip."

Getting sent out on a "tour" meant John and Tom would visit a concentration camp and some of the mass graves uncovered after the war. The General wanted all of his lawyers to witness, first hand, Nazi atrocities. Every time John thought about what he would witness, his stomach tightened. He didn't look forward to this tour, but accepted it as part of the job.

With his hands in his pockets, John waited on the wet tarmac for their suitcases. He squinted in the direction of the city. "Do you think we'll have time to go to Verdun?"

Tom nodded. "Yes. I'm surprised you didn't come back here before now."

"I thought about coming back. I wrote letters to the shopkeepers near the restaurant, to see if she was really..." John paused. "I never got a response though. After Rose and I were married, I didn't see the point."

Tom reached for his suitcase from a soldier crouching in the cargo bay. "I already made the arrangements. In the morning, you, or we, if you want some company, will leave first thing."

"We. I'd like the company."

In the morning, John walked out of the hotel into drizzling rain. He pulled his overcoat tight, expecting the usual open-air jeep most soldiers used for travel. The driver, a young corporal name Wilcox, stood next to a green four-door Chevrolet Deluxe. A single white star was painted on the front door.

"What's this?" John asked, as the corporal opened the passenger door.

Corporal Wilcox shook his head. "I don't know. The General has never volunteered his car before."

"Really?"

Wilcox nodded toward the backseat. "Maybe he knows."

John peeked into the back of the car. Tom, already reclining with his hat over his eyes, smiled. "Maybe the General realized how important we are."

John shook his head. "What did this cost you?"

"I heard a rumor the old man was so happy after getting an old bottle of brandy, he offered us his car," Tom said. "It's our lucky day, I guess."

"I suppose your suitcase is a little lighter this morning?"

Tom mumbled from under his hat. "I don't know what you're talking about. Now if you don't mind, I'd like to take a nap."

The journey to Verdun was quiet. Tom spent most of the four hours asleep. John stared out the window and prepared himself for the emotions he would encounter. Every so often, Corporal Wilcox attempted to find a station on the radio. When unsuccessful, he swore under his breath and turned the dial back to the off position.

Approaching Verdun, Corporal Wilcox pointed to a sign along the road. "We're getting close. Where to first, Sir?"

Tom sat up in the backseat, squinting, but alert. "What do you think? The old school first?"

John shook his head. "No, not yet. Do you think we can find where the front was? You know the part I'm talking about."

Before Tom could reply, the corporal answered. "Most of the trenches from the first war are still there. They kept them as memorials. My company crossed them a few times during the war."

Tom pulled a brown piece of paper from his inside jacket pocket and pointed to a spot he'd circled. "I have a map of the trenches. I think we can find what we're looking for. It's right here."

"Where did you get the map?" John asked.

Tom smiled. "I borrowed it from the library back home."

John looked at the jagged edge of the map Tom had torn out of an old textbook. "Borrowed it, huh?"

Tom winked. "It's not like they were using it anyway."

Corporal Wilcox looked to the spot on the map. "I can find it. We're pretty close already."

Driving through the city, John recognized many of the buildings. "I remember when we got here last time, I wanted to

147

visit all these places. Funny I only ate at one restaurant the entire time we were here."

They crossed the bridge near the riverbank where John first held Margrit. He'd kept that memory to himself, not even sharing it with his friend as an excited young man. "We stood in the grass over there." John pointed. "That day we were supposed to be practicing. Do you remember?"

Tom nodded. "I remember."

They passed the soccer field that served as a prison camp, but Wilcox didn't stop. John recalled walking with the old timers in the same direction, although on a different road. He experienced the same dread he had so long ago. "It took about two hours to walk to the front. I thought we were dead."

. "So did I," Tom said.

John shook his head. "I guess we—"

"There." Tom pointed to a hill in the distance. "Sorry to interrupt, but that's the hill we're looking for. Next to the tracks."

John exhaled, his mind returning to distant thoughts.

Wilcox slowed the car at the side of the dirt road and parked next to the hill. "What now, sirs?"

Tom opened the back door and jumped out. "We'll get out. You can stay dry in the car or come along if you want. It's up to you."

Wilcox remained in the car and fiddled with the radio tuner. The crackle of the speakers echoed over the empty field. John surveyed the area. The train tracks had not been removed after the war and were entrenched in the earth, brown and orange from rust. John pictured where the twelve train cars once rested. The foundation of the old depot remained, cracked and heaved, but the wood structure and metal roof were gone.

John stopped at the edge of the depot and swallowed hard. "That's it. Over there is where Private Howard was killed."

John took another step forward.

"He saved us," Tom said. "We were dead and he stood guard for us."

John nodded. He'd replayed the scene in his mind a thousand times. Private Howard on his knees in the hot sun. He took a few steps closer to the spot Howard was shot. "Were we helpless?"

Tom put his hands in the pocket of his black overcoat. "What do you mean?"

"We stood there and let him die. There must have been something we could have done."

Tom slouched. "I don't know. I've thought about it every day since that day. I knew at the time we didn't have a choice. But I wish I had tried something. It's not an easy thing to live with."

"I remember when he decked me at the restaurant. I hated him." John dropped his head. "He was just a kid. I don't even know where they buried him."

Tom's voice cracked. "A lot of kids died back then. At least he knew he was saving us when he died."

John was silent for a moment before he pulled a folded piece of paper from his pocket. He stared at the paper for a long moment before he read in little more than a whisper.

"In Flanders fields the poppies blow
Between the crosses, row on row,
That mark our place; and in the sky
The larks, still bravely singing, fly
Scarce heard amid the guns below.
We are the Dead. Short days ago
We lived, felt dawn, saw sunset glow,
Loved and were loved, and now we lie
In Flanders fields."

John paused, his throat tightening. As he finished, his tears mixed with raindrops falling on the paper.

"Take up our quarrel with the foe,
To you from failing hands we throw
The torch; be yours to hold it high.
If ye break faith with us who die
We shall not sleep, though poppies grow
In Flanders fields."

John folded the paper and placed it on one of the iron rails. He picked up a rock and set it on the paper. "I'm sorry I let you die," he whispered.

#

Corporal Wilcox followed the road back to town and parked on the street directly in front of where the restaurant once stood. Most of the buildings on the block were gone, except for the tailor shop that remained at the far corner.

John exited the car and took a deep breath. He looked up the street toward the old Catholic school before turning back to the site of the restaurant. "It really is gone."

John glanced at Tom. "Not that I didn't believe you. I guess it was finally time to see for myself."

He walked into the abandoned block, overgrown with weeds and shrubs. He stopped at the place he guessed the kitchen had been. Although unused for years, the imprint of the alley behind the building remained. Four divots in the old concrete floor revealed where the stove rested. John imagined Margrit standing in front of the divots, cooking at the old stove.

He closed his eyes and remembered lying on the cot in the prison camp, dreaming about Margrit. They would bring their children to visit Uncle Gautier, he thought back then. Maybe he would have stayed in France.

But Rose. They had a good life and three wonderful children. He would not replay the "what if's" because that would diminish what he had with his wife. Life did not allow John and Margrit to be together. And now, he knew it was okay. Standing where he first kissed her, John expected a flood of regrets. They did not come.

"I'm ready to go." John turned toward the car.

Tom stood with his face buried in his coat and his hands deep in the pockets. "Already. Are you sure?"

John smiled. "Yes. I should have come here a long time ago."

26

Two days later, John and Tom prepared to board a train for their tour. John noted this was the same station they had arrived when they travelled to France during the first war. He smiled and thought he probably spent more time on trains in France than anywhere else.

They stood on the platform with nine soldiers from John's office. The group was ordered to tour Germany's first concentration camp at Dachau, near the city of Munich. Following Dachau, they would travel along the route of the last death march before reaching Nuremburg, the location of the war crimes trials.

John settled into his seat after boarding the train. He inhaled the familiar smell of old leather and cigarette smoke. The train was so much like the one he had taken when he arrived to France in 1918, John thought if he closed his eyes hard enough, he might be back as a twenty-three-year old kid headed to war on the same tracks. *Some things don't change.*

Before Tom could pull his hat over his eyes, John tapped him on the arm. "Thanks for coming on this trip. I know you'd rather be home with Fran and the kids."

Tom swung his left leg onto the chair across the aisle. "I don't know what you mean. I had to come. Orders are orders."

John shook his head. "I'm not doing that today. I know, somehow, you worked it out to be here. Thank you."

Tom smiled. "You're welcome."

John knew he was lucky, but not only to have Tom on the trip. It seemed like he had been keeping an eye on John ever since training camp twenty-nine years ago. He appreciated how Tom took care of the little things, like arranging for the General's car.

Tom, whom John didn't expect to grow up, always had everything under control, even if he looked like a ragged mess.

Houses and buildings outside John's window slowly turned into fields and barns as the train entered the French countryside. John smiled at the sight of farmers working their fields. He imagined somewhere in Nebraska his brother out doors, laboring on the farm. It was mid-summer and he knew there was work to do in the fields. He had few regrets about the life he chose, but he missed the freedom of spending summer days outside.

He did regret that he had only been home about a dozen times in the last twenty-nine years, mostly for weddings and funerals. The most recent trip home was when his father died. John remembered riding a train that time, feeling guilty he hadn't followed his father's dream of becoming a farmer.

While he daydreamed about life on the farm, John nodded off to sleep. He awoke to the squealing brakes when the train slowed to a halt at the border of Germany. The idea of crossing into Germany made him uneasy. The war was over and he knew it was safe, but the emotions he felt walking toward the front with the old timers returned. He knew this feeling wouldn't ever completely go away. Even so many years later, he sometimes awoke thinking he had fallen asleep under the tree by the old white barn.

John and Tom moved to another train and went to the dining car. After ordering his meal, John took a piece of bread from a bowl on the table and smeared it with butter. "What do you think we'll see at Dachau?"

Tom took his own piece of bread. "I saw a newsreel about some of the camps a while back. It looked awful."

"I'm not looking forward to it."

Tom took a bite of his bread. "You've already done the hardest part, going back to Verdun. This won't be fun, but it shouldn't be that bad."

"It's different for me," John said. "My grandmother was Jewish. I never met my grandparents before they died, but I had family over here."

"Has your mom heard anything from the family since the war?"

John shook his head. "They all seem to have vanished. I mean, they were older than my dad and might have died of old age. And they were Lutheran. Grandma converted when they got married.

152

So they might not have even been taken to the camps. But we haven't heard a thing."

"Are you going to look for them while we are there?" Tom reached for another piece of bread.

John shrugged. "I don't know what good it would do. If they're gone, I can't change it."

After their food arrived, Tom said, "This might be your only chance to find out. To see the city your parents grew up in. Why wouldn't you go?"

John took a bite of food. "When we came here as young men, all I wanted to do was visit Siegen. Back then I didn't know part of the reason my folks left was because they were Jewish."

John paused to take another bite. "You know, I never asked Dad about it before he died."

"Why not?"

John shook his head. "I don't know. I guess I figured they would have told us if they wanted us to know. Maybe if I'd moved home after the war, I would have found the chance to bring it up."

Tom, who had already devoured most of his meal, pushed his plate to the side and rested his elbows on the table. "What do you know about what happened to your family anyway?"

"Not much." John shrugged again. "All I know is what the Voice said in the prison camp. I know more about that story from someone who tried to kill me than from my own father."

Tom slid his chair away from the table and leaned back with his legs crossed. "I think you should go. When my folks went to America, it was with the whole family. Grandparents, aunts, uncles, everyone. I don't have anyone to look for, but I'd still like to go check it out if it wasn't on the Soviet side of the country."

John smiled. "I bet you, of all people, could find a way to get into the Russian side if you wanted."

Tom laughed. "I think even that is beyond my realm of influence."

27

The train ride from the border to Munich lasted about four hours. John's stomach churned as he exited the train. Four jeeps awaited them to transport the men on the tour. A young private, named Bob Pratt, was their guide and would take them to Nuremburg. After staying the night in the barracks of an American army base, John, Tom, and the nine men from the office left for Dachau.

When they arrived at the camp, the group walked up a quiet dirt road lined with young poplar trees. John thought this could be any country road in America. At the end of the road, a driveway led to a brick building with a huge metal gate in the center. A tall chain link fence topped with barbed wire extended from both sides of the building and ran for hundreds of yards in each direction.

The German words "Arbeit Macht Frei" were built into the frame of the gate. John remembered this saying, which means "Work will make you free", had been on the front gates of other camps across Europe.

None of the men had spoken since they exited the Jeeps. A ghostly silence permeated the atmosphere. The only sound, other than water running under a small wooden bridge, was the cawing of blackbirds resting precariously on the fence.

An American soldier stood guard at the entrance and pushed open the gate. Loud creaking from the metal caused the blackbirds to fly away. John experienced the same view thousands of prisoners witnessed when they marched into camp. Taking a deep breath, he detected the odor of old soot. The smell reminded him of cleaning the woodstove back home.

Directly in front of the group, an open field about seventy feet wide ran to the far end of the camp. This, Private Pratt explained, is where roll call took place every morning and evening. To the left, two rows of well-maintained green barracks were separated by a narrow street. On the right, various administrative buildings.

Private Pratt pointed to the barracks. "Each of the eighteen buildings was designed to hold about a hundred and seventy-five people. By the end of the war, they crammed eight hundred in each one."

The group entered the barracks. Rows of wooden beds, built three high, lined the room. One of the soldiers asked, "Where's the mattresses?"

The private shook his head. "There weren't any mattresses. They slept directly on wooden planks. The ones in this camp were lucky, sort of. Some of the camps had barbed wire wrapped around the wood they slept on."

The group was silent. John stepped to the back of the tour.

Pratt walked toward the door. "If there are no other questions, we can go to the showers."

The group crossed the field and moved toward a small white and gray building near the front of the complex. They entered the building into a mostly wide-open room with huge concrete pillars. On the right and left were long rows of benches attached to the wall. Showerheads hung at various locations throughout the room.

"When prisoners first arrived in camp," Private Pratt said, "they were processed through here. Their heads were shaved and they were deloused with lye powder before taking a shower. When it was first opened, prisoners took one shower a week. Toward the end of the war, the water to the camp didn't work so there were no showers. Those who survived until liberation were covered in sores and they all had lice and scabies."

Tom pointed to eight large hooks on the far wall of the room. "What are those for?"

Pratt said, "The SS tied the prisoners' hands behind their backs and latched the tied hands over the hook. After kicking the chair out, the prisoner hung with their hands tied behind their back. Most died while they dangled there. Those who didn't were killed because they could no longer use their arms to work."

Private Pratt moved toward the door on the far side of the shower building. "Two more buildings to see before we go to the furnaces."

They walked out the door and almost immediately encountered another building, about ten feet from the showers. "This is the *infirmary*." The soldier opened the door allowing the group to enter.

John looked around. The room looked like a typical medical facility, with hospital beds and metal examination tables. "Why did you say it like that?"

Pratt shook his head. "Sick prisoners didn't come here. This was a different kind of hospital. Nazi doctors were allowed to do any experiment they could imagine in here."

Private Pratt pointed to a metal tube at the side of the room. "You see that long cylinder?"

The group turned to the strange device.

"That's a decompression chamber. They put prisoners in there to see how much pressure they could withstand before dying. Imagine being bound inside that thing while the pressure blows your eardrums." Pratt tapped his chest. "And disintegrates your lungs?"

Tom pointed to a small room in the corner. "What's that?"

"That's a freezer," Pratt answered.

"A freezer?" John asked. He wasn't sure he even wanted to know what it was used for.

"They did cold weather experiments outside in the winter and wanted to keep doing them in summer," Pratt said. "They tested everything on the prisoners, from tuberculosis to malaria to hypothermia. Even when they were losing the war, they wasted money on things like this."

John leaned against a wall.

"Do you need to take a break, Sir?" Pratt asked John. "Lots of guys get sick on this tour."

"No." John stood straight up and took a deep breath. "Let's keep going."

The private led the group through the front door of the infirmary to a concrete building with few windows. "This is called 'the bunker.'" He reached for the door and explained, "This is the solitary confinement building. It's where the Gestapo and SS

156

performed most of their interrogation and torture. Few people made it out of here alive."

The group entered a long corridor. Metal doors lined the hallway on either side. Tom asked, "So it was like a prison?"

"Basically." Pratt led the group down the hallway. "The lucky ones were left alone in the dark in those rooms. Most of them were tortured and killed in there. The Gestapo liked to torture people inside the cells so other prisoners could hear their screams."

Private Pratt pushed open the door to a cell, revealing a low room with nothing but concrete floors and walls. Blood stains lined the walls around the little room.

Tom whispered to John, "I won't have any trouble sending these guys to the gallows after seeing this."

John nodded. "I think that's why the General insisted on this tour."

Private Pratt turned to the group. "There isn't much else to tell about this building. This is different from other camps because it was the first one used for political prisoners. They didn't bother to interrogate prisoners at other camps, just killed them." He moved toward the door. "Unless you want to see something else on this side of the camp, we can go to the side with the ovens."

John marveled at how matter of fact the young man appeared. He could have been giving a tour of Yankee Stadium and would have shown as much emotion.

The group walked toward a small entrance at the rear of the camp where another guard pushed open the unlocked gate, revealing two small buildings. One was similar to the shower building. The other, a small brick structure with three tall smoke stacks. The top of the stacks stained black from smoke emitted over the years.

"This is the gas chamber." Private Pratt grunted as he opened the huge metal door. The sound of squeaking from the hinges bounced around the white tiled walls in the empty room. "They designed it to look like it was another shower building."

Pratt pointed to the ceiling. "You see those shower heads?"

John looked up.

"They aren't real. The Nazis made this gas chamber to look exactly like showers so the prisoners wouldn't panic when they came in."

Pratt pointed to a table at the side of the room. "They were given towels and soap to complete the deception. Those towels were there, just like that, when we liberated the camp. The General ordered them left like that."

John wanted the tour to end. All he could think about was his unknown relatives who might have been in this room. "Can we move on?"

Pratt nodded and stepped toward a side door. The group exited the building through a wide metal double door and walked across a narrow alley into the smaller building.

Tom pushed the door open. "I assume this is the crematoria?"

"Yes," Pratt answered. "These buildings were constructed close enough to each other to make it easy to move the bodies from one to the other. That's why they have the wide doors." He pointed to three huge brick ovens with massive black metal doors. "The ovens could fit two bodies each."

John had seen and smelled enough. The odor of old smoke, along with the emotions, made him nauseous. "I'll be outside getting some air when you're ready."

John hardly made it out the door before he vomited, barely missing his shoes. He had witnessed war and death, but this was something different. He had seen the pictures from the camps in the official reports, but he almost didn't believe it was possible. Now that he was here, he couldn't deny what happened. He knew he would go to Siegen before he returned home.

28

The following morning, John, Tom, and the nine other lawyers loaded into their Jeeps for the second leg of the tour. Private Pratt pointed down the road as their convoy pulled out of the gate. "We're going to follow the path of the last death march today."

Tom shouted from the back seat, over the roar of the engine. "What do you know about the marches?"

Pratt glanced over his shoulder. "I was with the army when we got to this area. I saw it first-hand. That's why I get the job of giving tours. I'm the only one from my unit left who's still in the country. We found dead bodies along the roadside the entire way."

"I thought they got shot in fields or in the woods?" John said.

The private shook his head. "No, Sir. About half of those that started out died along the road. If someone tripped or fell out of line, they got shot." He pointed to a road emerging out of a grove of trees from the left. "That's where the march began. From here, fatigue and exhaustion took hold of the prisoners who had already been starved and abused for months."

"So where are we headed?" John looked around, trying to get his bearings.

"We're going to head east a few miles to get on the highway where the march started." Pratt pointed to his right. "Then we'll zigzag across the country a bit."

"Zigzag?" Tom leaned forward.

"Yes, Sir. That's how they did it." Pratt said. "The German's didn't march the prisoners straight from Dachau to Tegernsee. That would have been about fifty-five miles, and most of the prisoners

159

would have survived that distance. They marched back and forth across the countryside to kill as many as possible along the way."

John squeezed the handle on the door of the Jeep. "Wouldn't that have wasted a lot of resources, going back and forth like that?"

Pratt turned onto another road. "Probably. I suppose it made it easier to dispose of the bodies at the end if only a few made it."

Tom said, "Those Nazis were so damn crazy, they probably didn't care what they wasted."

Pratt turned down another road and pointed to places where he remembered a body had been found. The day was cloudy, so after a few turns, John struggled to figure out which direction they were travelling. Finally, the private pulled the vehicle to the side of the road and climbed out. The other Jeeps in the convoy parked in line behind him.

"We'll have to walk this trail for a few hundred yards." Pratt pointed to a narrow, overgrown path in the woods.

The path was well-worn by foot traffic and widened into a mowed field. A large marble stone sat in the center of the field, with a little white farmhouse and a brick barn visible in the distance.

"I have a pretty good idea what happened here, but what is that?" John nodded to the stone with Hebrew engraving.

"Basically, it's one big gravestone for everyone that's buried here." Pratt walked the perimeter of the field, but didn't tread onto the middle. "When we got here, there were several hundred bodies. The engineers came in with a bulldozer and dug a big grave for everyone."

John's eyes widened. "Together? Why not bury them separately?"

Pratt frowned. "There were too many bodies. And this was the tip of the iceberg. We had to bury them, and we needed to do it quickly. A colonel in the engineer's corps said 'Better buried together than left for the birds.'"

This, John thought, was the first time the private showed any emotion. "What does the marker say?"

"I don't know. I heard some rich guy from New York paid for it. I only know it's a verse from the Old Testament," Pratt said.

"What was it like?" John asked. "I mean, did you have to help bury them?"

Pratt shrugged. "I was here with the patrol that first came across the site. But we made the locals do the dirty work." A slight smile flashed across his face. "You should have seen these German men in suits and women in their Sunday best marching out here to bury dead bodies."

Another soldier asked, "How many were here?"

Pratt walked back to the trail opening. "Seven thousand left the camp, give or take a few. We found a little less than a thousand here. There is one more big site like this. No one knows how many died along the way or how many made it to Tegernsee."

Before he walked back up the trail, Pratt turned to the field and made the sign of the cross. Without a word, he turned in the direction of the Jeep. John lowered his head and followed the private, stopping halfway up the trail to look back at the marker. *Could this be where my family ended up?*

# # #

The group ate lunch at a restaurant in the small town of Greding, a few hours from Nuremburg. The exterior of the two-story stucco building was unremarkable. The inside layout was almost identical to Gautier's, with the bar to the left, fireplace to the right, and tables set up in the middle. The walls were painted plaster rather than the wood paneled walls found at Gautier's. German music blared on an old gramophone. It was so eerily similar, it made John's neck tingle.

John and Tom sat at the huge marble bar. The rest of their group ate together at a large table in the rear of the restaurant. After the tour of the death march sites, John didn't feel like eating with the others.

A young man with dark hair washed glasses at a little sink behind the bar.

"What's the most German thing you have on the menu?" Tom asked.

The bartender dried a glass with his apron and smiled. "Well, usually when Americans come in here, they want sausage with sauerkraut."

John thought for a moment, not looking at the one-page menu in front of him. "My mom used to make a dish, roast pork, I think. It came with braised cabbage. Do you have anything like that?"

The man's eyes brightened. "Oh, you are real Germans, no? I should have known by how well you speak our language. It's called sauerbraten. It's one of the most popular dishes in my country. Most Yankees don't like it though. Too sour."

"I'll have that, too, and a beer for both of us." Tom reached into his pocket. "I hope you'll take American greenbacks."

The bartender collected the bills. "Yes. American dollars are better in my country than German Marks."

The man watched John and Tom as he poured thick German ale. "How is it you two speak such good German?"

John smiled, thinking about his family in Nebraska. "My folks grew up in Germany." He nodded at Tom, who was already drinking a beer. "His, too."

The bartender released the lever on John's beer. "And what do you think of your homeland?"

John sort of frowned. "It's not our homeland. We're Americans. So far it seems nice, although we have only been in this country a few days."

"Only a few days? Were you not here for the war?"

John took a long drink of his beer. "We aren't young fighting men anymore."

"Then may I ask what you are doing here?" The man paused. "I'm sorry if my questions bother you, but most GIs who come in here don't speak German."

John waved his hands. "It's no problem. I wanted to talk to you anyway."

The man's countenance dulled. "Talk to me, why?"

Finishing his beer, Tom pushed it toward the German. "We're here to investigate certain activities of people in your country."

As he refilled Tom's drink, the German asked, "What kind of activities?"

"Activities, like what happened at Dachau," Tom said.

The man's shoulders slumped when he heard the name "Dachau." He pushed the beer across the marble bar top to Tom. "I see."

John said, "Mind if I ask how long you've worked here?"

162

The bartender's eyes narrowed. He eyed the two Americans with suspicion. "My father-in-law owned the place before the war. I worked here when I was a teenager. That's how I met my wife. My father-in-law died in the war and we kept it running the best we could until the war ended. Now it's ours."

Tom rubbed his chin. "Why weren't *you* in the war. I thought all the young men went off to fight, unless they worked in the camps killing prisoners?"

The German swept his leg onto the bar top. With his foot resting on the bar, the man pulled back his pant leg to reveal a wooden leg with metal joints secured to his knee. "I *was* in the war. I got this in Russia in forty-one and came home after I got out of the hospital. I wasn't sent back to fight. Not much use for a one legged soldier at the front."

Tom rubbed his forehead. "I'm sorry, I didn't mean to…Well, you know. I'm sorry about the leg."

The German smiled again. "That's okay, I'm used to it. Every day during the war someone asked the same thing."

John rubbed the graying stubble on his unshaven cheeks. "So you were here since forty-one. Most of the war?"

"Yes. We weren't exactly busy back then and had a hard time getting supplies most of the time. But we tried to stay open. Mostly old men came in back then." The man peered at John. "Why do you ask?"

"You must have heard a lot of talk," John said. "About what was going on in the camps."

The man looked around the room before leaning in. "I'm not sure I understand what you're getting at."

John lowered his voice to a near whisper. "We keep hearing, in America, how most people over here didn't know what was happening. If anyone would have known about what went on in the camps, it seems to me it would be a bartender, right? No one hears more news and gossip than a barkeep."

The man pivoted his head again before whispering. "Some don't like to hear people talking about this sort of thing."

"What do you mean?" John looked over his shoulder for an enemy he would not recognize.

The man tapped his fingers on the bar and kept looking around the room. "I have a business to run, you know? Some people have

163

had their homes burned after they talked to the Americans. I can't afford that."

Tom said, "It's not like we don't know what happened over here."

The German spoke cautiously. "Of course, everyone knows *what* happened. It's the *who* they don't want to talk about. Some important people who were too old to fight worked in the camps."

John raised his hand. "I'm not here to put anyone in danger. I'm curious about what the German people knew. From what I read, everyone over here claims to have known nothing about what happened."

"There's a railway less than a mile from here." The bartender pointed out the window. "When I was a kid, I used to sit next to the tracks with my friends and throw rocks at the train cars. We would try to get them to bounce off and hit each other. It was kind of a game."

John leaned back on his stool. "What are you getting at?"

"We knew what was in those cars back when we were kids. You could tell if it was cattle or coal or something else." The young man looked around again. "I remember telling my papa what we had seen over dinner at night."

"And?" John asked.

"Those trains never stopped running, for the whole war. When the Americans or British bombed the bridge, the army made sure the railroad was fixed. Even when the Americans were almost here, they made sure the trains ran on time. Day and night. And you know what was in the trains?"

John and Tom shook their heads.

"People. We were losing the war, and they kept filling trains with people. Not guns or food or fuel. People."

"And then what?"

"What do you mean 'And then what?' And then nothing. That's it." The man whispered so loud it sounded like a hiss. "Full trains one way, empty trains the other. And kids like me still throwing rocks at them."

"You're saying people knew what happened in the camps?" John asked.

The man nodded. "How can anyone pretend they didn't know what happened? Trains crossed every little town in Germany filled

164

with people. We knew what the ashes were that fell on the city like snow. People don't just disappear."

Tom leaned forward, his face red. "So you knew what was happening, everyone knew, and no one did anything about it?"

The German looked at the floor. "People who said something ended up on those trains. They ended up behind the fence. They disappeared."

Tom huffed, "Come on? You're telling me the—"

"Please. I don't want trouble." The man raised his hands.

John interjected. "We're not here to cause trouble." John glanced at Tom and back at the bartender. "Thank you for talking to us."

Tom glared at the bartender as he walked away. "What do you make of that? The kid pretends he's helpless while trainloads of people chug by every day."

John shook his head. "He's a one-legged kid with a young wife and probably kids at home. I can't blame him. I remember walking away from a soldier on his knees who saved my life, and letting him get murdered because I wasn't going to risk getting us all killed." John paused for a second. "And I'll tell you this, if I thought Rose and the kids would end up on one of those trains, I would have kept my head down, too."

Tom rubbed his neck. "Still gets me hot under the collar."

"It doesn't matter now," John said. "Besides, he answered the question I wanted to know."

"Which was what?"

John looked around the room. "Who knew what was happening in the camps? And the answer is that everyone knew."

Tom gave a half shrug. "And why is that such an important question?"

"Because," John said, as he took a bite of the steaming food on his plate. "The men we will interview claim they didn't know what was happening. They claim they were a cog in the machine, ignorant of what was happening down the line. If some bartender in Greding knew, officers in the German military had to know what was happening to people in the camps." He stood and threw extra money on the bar. "It makes our job much easier."

165

29

The convoy of Jeeps entered Nuremburg in the early afternoon. John marveled at the damage the war had done to the city, once the center of Nazi pride. On every block, structures showed signs of battle. In some sections, entire buildings were reduced to piles of debris. Other sections contained only empty lots where buildings once stood. Boarded up windows and unrepaired holes dotted the walls of most structures still standing.

John remembered newsreels before the war of huge Nazi propaganda events in Nuremburg. Now it was reduced to rubble. Symbolically, the allies chose the city as the location for the war crimes trials.

The news cameras were gone and most of the international press dispersed when the main trials ended. Now, John arrived to help with the trials of lesser-known war criminals, the men who actually got their hands dirty for Hitler's Final Solution.

"Cummins and Chamberlain should have the office and housing arranged." Tom spoke loudly from the rear of the Jeep. "We need to find them. Might as well start at the Palace of Justice."

Private Pratt led the convoy in front of the enormous building, which is where the trials would be held. An American soldier jogged over to their vehicle. "I'm sorry, Sirs. No parking in front of this building."

John glanced up the block. Three more soldiers stood guard along the front of the complex. He reached into the back seat for his suitcase and climbed out of the vehicle. "We'll get out here and let Private Pratt go on his way. It's a long drive back to Munich."

After thanking Private Pratt and exiting the Jeep, John, Tom and the rest of the lawyers made their way across a small courtyard in front of the huge complex. The structure reminded John of the pictures he had seen of large universities back home. The five-story building, constructed with huge limestone blocks, had the traditional red tile roof John became used to seeing in Germany.

The palace, unlike most of the other buildings in Nuremburg, had no noticeable damage from the war. Even the trees in the courtyard survived the years of bombing, although shrapnel scarred the bark of some. Strolling through the arch supporting columns, they arrived at two large oak doors guarded by another soldier. After presenting their credentials, the group was allowed entry.

John expected to find the inside of the palace dark and shadowy, given the exterior's bleak appearance. He was surprised to find a glass roof that made the enormous interior nearly as bright as it was outside. The warm summer sun shone through the roof and lit up the white marble floors.

Stairs on the right and left reminded John of an accordion, which zigzagged back and forth, finally reaching the top floor. At the far end of the room, a large statue of a woman with a set of scales watched over the hall. The sound of footsteps in the enormous room reverberated on the stone floor and walls. After surveying the impressive architecture, another soldier directed the lawyers to the office of the Army Judge Advocate on the third floor.

John and Tom hauled their luggage up the stairs to the offices designated for their staff. Out of breath, they found Private Cummins, surrounded by a smoky haze, working at a table in an open room bordered by five wood paneled doors.

"You're late." Private Cummins stood with a cigarette hanging from his lips and saluted the two officers. "The General was in here looking for you this morning. He wants you to start interviewing prisoners."

Tom elbowed John. "It's going to be nothing but work from here on out."

John surveyed the room. "Which door goes to my office? And where will we be staying while we're here?"

Private Cummins pointed to an open door to his left. "Your office is right there. Me and Chamberlain are working here in the open. No room for us anywhere else."

John peeked into the tiny office. Two wooden desks were pushed against opposite walls that seemed gloomier because of the gray paint. "I assume Captain Schlicting and myself are sharing this office?"

"Yes, Sir. Kind of cramped around here." Private Cummins returned to his seat. "We fought to get you that room and to get a table out here in the hallway. Every day when we go to lunch, we take bets that someone will have taken our table before we get back."

"Who are we interviewing?" Tom stepped around John to look into the small office.

"All of them." Private Cummins pulled a package of cigarettes from his pocket and lit another with the end of the cigarette he had been smoking.

"All of them?" John asked.

Cummins nodded. "Well, only the Einsatzgruppen, for now at least. That's who we've been assigned to. There are twenty-four. Mostly commanding officers of the mobile units."

"The death squads, you mean?" Tom's eyes narrowed. "We got to tour some of their work over the last few days."

"They won't admit they did anything wrong." Private Cummins handed a notebook across the table. "Here's the list."

"I guess I'll start at the top. Any idea what we're supposed to find out?" John grabbed the notebook and pushed his suitcase into his tiny office with his foot. "And where's Chamberlain?"

Cummins glanced at the window. "He's out looking for a place for you to stay. There's no room on the army base and most of the hotels in town were destroyed. We've been staying in the office since we arrived, sleeping on the floor."

Cummins dug into one of his piles of papers. "As to what you need to find out, mostly get their side of the story. Where they came from. What they did in the war. That sort of stuff. The General expects a full report for each defendant."

"Don't we already know all that stuff?" Tom studied the list over John's shoulder. "What new information is there to find?"

"We mostly know what they did. But what we have in those files," Cummins pointed to a stack of boxes in the corner, "are eye witness testimonies. We need to get the prisoner's side of the story, written up by an attorney."

168

"By when?" John pulled a small notebook from his pocket and made a note.

"As soon as possible." Cummins rummaged through his papers. "We have all the forms you need to complete."

John decided he and Tom would divide the interviews. The sooner they could get this done, the sooner they would get home. After what he saw during the tours, he decided the prisoners were guilty.

As they walked to the interview rooms, Tom shook his head. "I don't get it. Why do they need us here? Cummins and Chamberlain could handle these interviews. Everything they want is in these forms. All we have to do is fill in the blanks."

John shrugged. "They want a lawyer's name on everything and they want it done quickly. That's where I come in. Even though their guilt is unquestioned, the army is going to make sure everything is done by the book."

"What about me, I'm not a lawyer?"

John smiled. "I will look over your notes and sign off on the final report. If you hadn't come, Chamberlain or Cummins would have done it. But since you managed to tag along, you're my helper."

"Lucky me." Tom laughed.

# # #

The Palace of Justice was chosen for the trials, in part, because a prison was attached to the complex. John and Tom made their way back down three flights of stairs, through a corridor that connected the two buildings, and entered the prison. Tom interviewed a prisoner named Erwin Blobel first, while John interviewed Martin Blume. Both prisoners were commanders of mobile death units for the duration of the war.

John entered the interview room with a small amount of trepidation. An overweight man with a few strands of black hair pasted on top of his head sat in a metal chair at a table in the center of the room. The walls were painted the same dark gray as John's office, and barely any light penetrated the dirt-caked window. John sat across from the prisoner, who tried to sit upright but still had a

169

slump in his posture. "Mr. Blume, my name is Colonel John Bayer. I'm here—"

"I know what you're here for." Blume snorted. "Why are you wasting my time?"

John scribbled on his notepad. He responded coolly, "I'm here to get your side of the story for the record. Can we proceed?"

Blume exhaled. "It won't do any good."

"All the same, Mr. Blume, it's my job."

John struggled to hide his anger at the large man. He imagined the obese soldier riding in a car while he forced thousands of emaciated prisoners to run through the countryside. He went through the checklist of easy questions such as birthday, work history, and family before he moved to the more difficult ones.

"The charges claim you were the commanding officer of a mobile SS unit responsible for the deaths of thousands of unarmed civilians. What is your response?" John asked.

"How should I respond?"

John glared at Blume. "Is it true?"

The prisoner tilted his head and stared at John. "I was in charge of a mobile SS unit. But we did not kill *innocent* civilians."

John wrote in his notepad. "Then what is it that your unit did?"

"Transportation." Blume said. He reached his chained hands across the table. "Do you have a cigarette?"

"I don't smoke." John kept his eyes on his notepad. "What kind of transportation?"

Blume left his fat hands outstretched on the table. "We transported spies, insurgents, and enemy soldiers. We were responsible for taking them to the prisons."

John's hand started to shake as his anger increased. "Your unit never killed anyone?"

The prisoner shook his head. "I'm not saying that. Sometimes prisoners were killed trying to escape."

John squeezed his pencil to stop the shaking. "How many people would you estimate your unit killed?"

"Maybe ten." Blume sneered. "I didn't keep count."

John's heart raced. He grabbed a stack of folders with his left hand. "I have eighteen eye witness interviews who claim they saw you personally kill more than ten people."

"It's not true." Blume stared at John without blinking.

"For the record," John said. "You want me to include in my report that you deny killing prisoners without cause?"

Blume nodded.

John dug through his pile of papers and pulled out a black and white photograph. "Mr. Blume, do you recognize these women?"

"Should I?"

John took a deep breath. "We have testimony that you ordered their execution."

"So?" Blume said.

John shook his head. "Is it true?"

Blume hesitated. "I do not think, well… no, it's not true."

John pushed the photograph of the dead women across the table. "You claim to have only transported spies, insurgents, and enemy soldiers. What category did these women fall under?"

Blume's eyes narrowed. "Spies, I suppose."

"You suppose?" John's voice rose. "Why were they killed?"

Blume shrugged. "Attempted escape. I really don't remember. We transported many prisoners. I can't be expected to remember them all."

John scowled. "They were found two feet from the side of the road, shot in the back of the head. Can you explain that?"

Blume gave John a wry smile. "My men had good aim?"

John clenched his jaw. He completed the interview as quickly as he could and left the room. When he got into the hallway, he found Tom leaning against the wall tossing his pen into the air and catching it.

"What took you so long?" Tom smiled with a bit of sadness in his eyes. "And why do you look so pale?"

John leaned against the wall. "I don't know what I expected? All he did was claim he was ignorant of what happened in the camps and denied committing any crimes."

Tom nodded. "Mine was about the same. We might as well get used to it. It's not like they're going to admit to what they did. Are you ready for round two?"

John half shrugged. "I guess."

They each completed three more interviews before concluding for the day. Returning to their office, John and Tom found Cummins and Chamberlain smoking at the table, not really working. With all the windows closed, John wondered if the blue

171

haze of cigarette smoke ever left the room. "Any luck finding us a place to stay?"

Private Chamberlain took a long drag of his cigarette. "Yes, Sir," Chamberlain answered. "We found you a room. Although, I don't think I had much to do with it."

John looked sideways at the young man. "What do you mean?"

"All week I've been checking with every hotel in town." He paused for another drag. "Every day they were full. Today, at the Maritim Hotel, they happened to have a suite open up and allowed us to take it."

"What's so strange about that?" John asked. "It's a hotel, don't people check out all the time."

"A suite?" Chamberlain waved his hands causing ashes from the cigarette in his left hand to float to the floor. "Generals and politicians get suites. Not colonels and captains. Certainly not privates."

John turned to Tom. "I don't suppose you know anything about this?"

"Not a clue," Tom said with a grin.

30

The following morning, John and Tom divided the list of SS officers they would interview. John's first interview of the morning was a twenty-nine-year old SS officer named Dedrich Haussman. The prisoner slouched in his chair and stared at a glass of water on the table. His dark black hair was cut short on the sides and slightly longer on top. John couldn't tell how tall he was, but given that his legs stretched beyond the table, guessed he was at least six feet. This prisoner looked familiar. John figured it was because he had seen Haussman's picture clipped to the file he studied before going to bed the night before.

John introduced himself to the young man and gave him the same information about the process he had given the previous prisoners he interviewed.

Haussman stared at his hands chained together in his lap. "There's nothing to tell that you don't have in your file."

Do I have to go over this with every one of them, John thought.

He raised the file, repeating what he had said to each prisoner the day before. "Mr. Haussman, what I have here are eye witness testimonies of your actions. I do not have *your* side of the story. That is what I am here for."

Haussman looked up with a blank expression. John paused for a moment and studied the man's familiar dark brown eyes.

"Very well, what would you like to know?" Haussman said.

John was surprised the prisoner complied so quickly. He tried to ignore that even the way the man spoke sounded familiar. "Start from the beginning. We need as complete a history as we can get."

Haussman rubbed his forehead. "I grew up in Berlin after the last war. My father was an officer and was one of the few allowed to remain in the army after the war."

As John took notes, he kept stealing glances of the prisoner.

"It was expected I would follow in my father's footsteps, so when I was old enough, I entered the service," Haussman said. "In 1937, I was in the first class of students at Junkerschule."

"Junkerschule?"

He nodded. "The SS training school south of Munich."

The prisoner reached for the glass of water. John stopped taking notes and stared at him.

"How did you go from there to getting your own command at such a young age?" John asked.

Haussman took a drink of water. "The war mostly. Other officers were re-assigned or killed. I was promoted quickly after I graduated from Junkerschule."

John half stood and re-filled the prisoner's glass. "What were your duties as the commanding officer?"

The young man frowned. "We transported prisoners to the labor camps."

"Anything else." John sat back in his seat.

"I don't know what you mean."

John crossed his arms. He was already losing patience with the prisoners playing dumb. "Yes, you do. You know you've been charged with war crimes. Do you deny these charges?"

Haussman leaned back and held his hands to his chest. The chains rattled. "I committed no war crimes."

John reached for his notepad. "Then you deny murdering prisoners?"

"Yes, I deny *murder*."

Something about the way Haussman said murder made John pause. "In your entire time commanding a mobile unit, you never killed anyone or ordered anyone to be killed?"

Haussman shook his head. "Well, that is another subject entirely, now isn't it?"

"What do you mean?" John asked. "Did you or did you not kill prisoners? You said you didn't commit murder."

"I did not commit murder." Haussman leaned forward, resting his elbows on the table with his hands under his chin. "We did, as part of our duty, end the lives of some."

John remained quiet and allowed Haussman to continue.

"You see, Colonel, there was an element in Germany which required special consideration." Haussman looked John in the eyes. "My father taught me about it. These people are the reason we lost the first war. They needed to be dealt with."

"So you killed them?" John asked.

"At first we tried to get them to leave, but no country would take them. So we dealt with them." Haussman said.

John's heartbeat pounded in his ears. "So you did commit murder? Or at least ordered your soldiers to do so?"

The prisoner shook his head. "No, Colonel, we did not commit murder."

"Get to the point, Mr. Haussman. You either murdered or you didn't," John said.

"First, let me ask you a question, Colonel." Haussman leaned back in his chair. "When you set a trap for a rat or a mouse, do you consider it murder?"

John's voice rose. "We are not talking about rats, Commander Haussman."

"Oh, but we are. And they needed to be dealt with." Haussman's eyes bored into John. "It was no more murder than catching a rat in your basement and smashing its head with a broom."

John took a deep breath before he spoke, squeezing his knee with his shaking hand. "You do not admit to committing murder. You do, however, admit to taking the lives of prisoners in your charge?"

"Yes."

John's leg ached from the pressure of his hand. "And how many, of those in your charge, would you say you killed or died in the camps?"

Haussman's eyes narrowed. "All of them."

John stood. He couldn't get out of the room fast enough. "I think that's all I need, commander."

In the hallway, John took a deep breath and leaned against the wall with his right hand while his shaking left hand barely held onto his folders.

A guard approached. "Are you okay, Sir?"

John raised his hand. "I'm fine. Just not feeling well today."

The folders dropped from his hand.

The soldier stepped back. "A lot of you guys get that way in those rooms. Let me know if you need anything Sir."

John leaned against the wall for a few minutes before sitting on a wooden bench. He closed his eyes and couldn't escape the images from the photographs in Haussman's file. "Why am I here? All these people deserve to die."

When Tom exited his room, he sat next to John. "How many have you done so far?"

John's forehead creased. "What do you mean? One. How many have you interviewed?"

Tom laughed. "Two. We'll never get done if you keep going at this pace."

John shook his head. "That last prisoner was different from the ones yesterday. He seemed proud of his actions. I couldn't even finish the interview. I knew some were proud of it all, but I wasn't really prepared for it."

Tom patted John on the shoulder. "We've got about ten done. Only fourteen or so to go. Then we get to submit our reports for the trial. Maybe they'll let us go when the reports are done."

"I hope so."

# # #

After interviewing two more prisoners, John went for a walk rather than to lunch with Tom. He ambled around the courtyard with no purpose or destination in mind. He could not stop thinking about the young prisoner named Haussman.

"John?" The soft sound of a vaguely familiar voice jarred him from his thoughts.

He stood still. He didn't turn his head to look for the voice. His mind was playing tricks on him after the stress of the morning. He began to walk again.

The familiar German accent spoke again. "John Bayer?"

His mind was not playing tricks on him. He had heard a voice. It was real. John turned slowly. A woman about his age, in a black dress with graying black hair tied up in the back stood before him.

"Margrit?"

31

John stared into the face of the woman he once loved. She stared back. It was a long, stressful journey. He was tired. Maybe this was his imagination.

"Yes." She whispered. "It's me."

John broke into a cold sweat, his neck felt like ice. "How can that be? You're dead."

Tears streamed down her face as she stepped toward John. He stood in place, as though his legs were anchored into the concrete of the sidewalk. He told himself he was dreaming. He had to be dreaming. He was back home in bed. He tried to wake himself by force of will.

"How can that be?" John repeated, more to himself than to Margrit.

Margrit trembled, tears falling from her cheeks.

John rocked back on his heels. "I need to sit down."

He stretched and grabbed the corner of a bench, practically pulling himself into it. He left his briefcase in the middle of the walkway.

John took a deep breath and leaned over, exhaling between his legs. All the while, Margrit watched silently. He pressed his eyes closed and took another breath, exhaling through his mouth. His breath blew pieces of dried grass between his feet.

He looked up. "I don't know if I believe what I'm seeing right now."

Margrit took a step towards the bench. John clutched the metal armrest on one side. Margrit sat on the other end, leaving a strange gap between them. "It is me."

John's eyes widened. "It's really you."

Margrit nodded. "And it's really *you*."

John rubbed the back of his damp neck. "Tom told me you died."

"And Camille told me you were dead." Margrit rested her hands in her lap.

John shook his head. "I don't understand. Why would she tell you I was dead?"

Tears streaked Margrit's face. "That day, when the restaurant was destroyed, Tom talked to Camille. He told her you'd been shot and they sent your body home."

"I was shot." John's throat tightened with every word. "And they sent me home. But they sent me to recover, not be buried."

"All this time I thought you were dead." Margrit looked toward the Palace of Justice. "And you were alive."

John thought about how painful it was when he found out Margrit was dead. He knew it must have been as painful for her to lose him and her uncle on the same day.

"Camille told Tom you were in the building when it was hit by the shelling. Tom saw your body on the street with a sheet over it." John blinked rapidly, expecting to wake up.

Margrit turned toward John. "Two people were in the restaurant that day. Uncle Gautier and Margot, Camille's daughter. That must be what she told Tom, that Margot was dead."

John nodded silently.

"She was hysterical when I got there after the shelling. That's when she told me you were dead. All these years, and we could have..." Margrit looked into his eyes. "What *did* happen to you?"

"It's a long story." He closed his eyes and thought for a moment, accepting that he was awake. When he opened them, he explained what happened to him after their night together above Gautier's. He told her about Rose and the kids, quickly describing the last twenty-nine years.

After he finished, John took a deep breath. "And you? What happened to you?"

Margrit bit her lip. "After my uncle died, I stayed with Camille. I went home after the armistice. That wasn't long after we..." Margrit wiped a tear off her cheek. "When I got home, I too got married." Her expression dulled. "My husband was in the German

179

army. Like you, he stayed in the army after the war. He died in Russia in 1941."

Margrit spoke of her husband's death so matter of factly, it caught John by surprise.

"I'm sorry." John didn't know what to say. He had never been good at this so he changed the subject again. "What brings you to Nuremburg? Is this where you settled when you got married?"

Margrit shook her head. "No. We lived in Berlin since the end of the first war. Emil and I only had one child, a son. After he was born, I wasn't able to have any more children." She stared at the ring on her hand. "When he was a little boy, he wanted to be like his father. All he ever wanted to do was be in the army. When he finished school, Emil was able to get him into the army."

A dark understanding dawned upon John.

"Emil was able to get him into the SS officer school near Munich," she said, without the pride you would expect from a mother.

"Oh my God." John didn't mean to speak out loud.

Margrit turned to John. "What?"

John took a deep breath. "Was your husband's last name Haussman?"

Margrit nodded. "How could you have known that?"

John's head tilted back as he took another deep breath. He looked into the sky, refusing to look at Margrit. "I met your son this morning."

Margrit gasped. "How did you meet him?"

John swallowed hard. "I work in the office of the Army Judge Advocate. We're investigating crimes that happened during the war." John closed his eyes and repeated, "Oh my God."

Tears streamed down Margrit's face again. "They won't tell me how much trouble he's in. He won't tell me anything either."

"Oh, Margrit." John forgot the distance between them and slid closer. "I'm sorry. Do you know what his job was during the war?"

Margrit's lip quivered. "He was some kind of commander. That's all he'll tell me."

John leaned forward, rubbing his temples. He didn't know how to tell Margrit what her son had done. "That's true, he was a commander." He paused and took a breath. "Margrit, have you heard the term 'death march?'"

She frowned when John said the last two words. "No."

"Well, your son. He was the commander of a group that led prisoners on those marches."

Margrit's asked, "What does that mean?"

John felt nauseous again. "I don't know how to tell you."

"Please tell me," Margrit pleaded. "Not knowing has to be worse."

Without thinking, John took her hand. "It means he is accused of killing innocent prisoners."

Margrit either didn't understand, or refused to accept, what John said. "But when can he come home?"

"It's not that simple." John couldn't look at Margrit when he spoke. "He's being charged with war crimes."

"You mean like Goring and Hess?" Margrit gasped. "They were executed. Is it serious like that?"

"It could be," John said. "Remember, not all those who were on trial last year were executed."

"But," Margrit said. "Are they sure he did the things the others did. How can they be sure with all that happened in the war?"

John closed his eyes, replaying the interview from the morning in his mind. "I'm involved in the investigation. He admitted to all of it."

Margrit stood. "No. That can't be. He was in the army and it was war. He was only an ordinary soldier." She turned from John. "I have to go. I'm sorry. I have to go."

Before John could respond, Margrit was halfway across the courtyard. He didn't attempt to stop her. Stunned, he could only watch her leave.

#

When he finally made his way to his office, John's head was so foggy he wasn't sure what was real. Entering the main office, private Cummins barely looked up from his work. "That was a short lunch."

John muttered "yeah" and went into his office. He closed the door before collapsing into his chair. Sitting at his desk, he stared at a picture of his children and tried to imagine the fear Margrit felt. His first thought was that if things had turned out differently with him, she would not be going through all of this. He buried the thought as his children looked back at him through the glass frame.

"Boy, did you miss a great lunch." Tom burst through the office door before frowning. "What's the matter with you?"

John stared at the picture. He wished Rose was in it. "I saw her today. At least I think I did."

Tom asked, "Saw who?"

"Margrit."

Tom's voice lowered. "That's not possible."

John looked away from the picture. "I've been sitting here thinking about it, wondering if I'm going crazy."

Tom scratched his stubbly cheek. "Are you feeling okay?"

John shook his head. "No, I am not feeling okay. But that doesn't change the fact that I saw her."

Tom glanced out the door at Cummins and Chamberlain, who had stopped working and were looking into the office. He pushed the door, allowing it to slam shut. "I saw her body in the street. I think you need to take the rest of the day off and get some sleep."

John shook his head again. "I probably do need some rest. But you didn't see Margrit that day in Verdun. Camille's daughter Margot was killed in the shelling. Her body is what you saw."

Tom rubbed his forehead. "You're telling me you were out for a walk today, right?"

John nodded.

"And while you were out, you saw Margrit." Tom lowered himself into a chair.

"That's what I'm telling you."

Tom took a deep breath. "And you're sure about this?"

John slammed his hand on the wooden desk. "Yes, I'm sure. As sure as you're sitting here right now. I saw her."

Tom raised his hands. "Okay, you're sure. Margrit is alive?"

"I'm sorry." John spoke quietly. "I didn't mean to yell at you. I'm just—"

Tom shook his head. "No. Don't be sorry. I'm the one who should be sorry. I don't know what to say."

"There is nothing to say." John felt numb.

Tom wagged his head. "This is my fault."

"I've been sitting here thinking about it for a while," John said. "I don't blame you. It was a hard day for you."

Tom rubbed his forehead. "I think I'm gonna throw up."

When he heard this, John sort of smiled. He had never known Tom to vomit, even when he drank too much. Without trying, Tom was able to lighten the mood, slightly.

Tom pulled his chair closer to John. "What are you going to do?"

John thought for a few moments. "It's not as simple as finding out Margrit is alive."

"What do you mean?"

John reached for a file on his desk and held it up. "The prisoner I interviewed this morning, Haussman. He's her son."

Tom exhaled. "That's why she's here? I really am going to throw up."

John slouched in his chair. "When I told her about the trial, she practically ran away. She knew nothing about why he is here."

"I am so sorry," Tom said. "If I had gotten it right back then, this would never have—"

"I'm not going to do that." John spoke firmly. "No 'what ifs.' I married Rose and we have a beautiful family. I won't allow myself, or you, to wonder how different things might be."

"Yeah, but you were in love with her," Tom protested. "I mean, now you're always going to wonder."

John glanced at the picture of his children. "No, I won't. I was young back then and thought I was in love. But what does a twenty-year-old kid know about love? What Rose and I have is much better than anything I thought I had as a kid."

"I understand." Tom patted his friend on the back. "But it's such a shock."

John nodded. "I suppose the best thing to do is get to work and get my mind off it. I only wish I knew where to find her."

Tom smiled. "I have a feeling she'll find you."

"Then what?"

Tom patted John on the back again. "I wish I knew."

32

John and Tom walked out the huge oak doors of the Palace of Justice after work. A dark silhouette sat on a bench in the courtyard. It was late and the sun had started to set, but there was enough light for John to recognize Margrit.

"I'll catch up with you at the hotel," Tom said. "You need some time to talk."

Margrit stood and smiled as John approached. "Was that Tom?"

John nodded. "After all these years, we're back in Europe together."

Margrit watched Tom walk away before asking, "Can we go somewhere to talk? I'm sorry I ran away earlier, but—"

"Don't be sorry. I understand. Are you hungry?" John tried to smile.

They found a small restaurant near the Palace of Justice. After they ordered their meals, John poured two glasses of wine. "Tell me more about your life since we last saw each other in Verdun."

Margrit untied a black scarf from around her neck. "Where should I start?"

"Start with the day your uncle…" John hesitated. "I mean, why weren't you at the restaurant when Tom went there?"

Margrit had a faraway smile. "It was simple. We needed bread, so my uncle sent me to the bakery. I had forgotten to go there that morning. My uncle laughed and said 'Young love is the most forgetful kind.'"

John smiled when he heard Margrit say "young love."

"I went to the bakery." Margrit took a sip of wine. "While I was there, the shelling began. I stayed at the bakery until it was over.

By the time I got back, the restaurant was gone. Camille told me you were dead when I arrived."

"I'm so sorry," John said. "After all you had already been through, to find out your uncle was dead and then me. I'm just... I'm sorry."

Margrit reached across the table and squeezed John's hand. "That was a long time ago. There's nothing either of us could have done."

John smiled, not pulling his hand away. "Please, go on with your story."

"Well, as I told you earlier, I stayed with Camille until the war ended. That was only about four months. Then I was allowed to go home." Margrit paused when their food arrived, leaving her hand on John's as she took a bite with her other hand. "I knew I couldn't go home because our town was destroyed. I found my mother at my grandparents'. My father died of Spanish Influenza during the winter."

How much does this woman have to suffer, John thought.

"Well, there isn't much else to the story," Margrit said. "I got married soon after that. We had a quiet wedding and Dedrich arrived later."

Margrit paused at the mention of her son. John thought she might start crying again. When she resumed, he sensed a resolve on her part to finish the story.

"We moved to Berlin and have lived there ever since." Margrit took another bite. "When the war was over, my building was one of the few left standing. In that sense, I guess I was lucky."

Margrit smiled before squeezing John's hand again. "That's my story. Now it's your turn."

John took a drink of wine. "There's not much to tell. After I recovered from my wound, I decided to stay in the army." He pulled his hand from Margrit and pretended to readjust the napkin on his lap. "About a year later, Rose and I got married. We stayed in Washington and raised our family there."

Margrit's lips pursed in thought. "A year? Why did you wait so long?

John sort of chuckled. "I asked Rose to marry me a few months after I got out of the hospital, but she turned me down."

"Why?" Margrit raised her eyebrows.

John's smile widened. "She said she had to know I wasn't settling for her after I lost the one I really loved. She told me 'I can live without you, but I can't live with you knowing you're thinking about someone else.'"

Margrit nodded. "She sounds like a smart woman."

"After a few more months, I asked again. She said no again. I kept asking until I convinced her to say yes," John said. "And it's been a happy twenty-eight years since."

John paused for a moment. He didn't want Margrit to feel worse than she already did by making it sound like he was happier with Rose than he would have been with her. "And you, I know you can't be happy today. But have you been happy?"

Margrit didn't smile as John had hoped she would. "It's been difficult for us. Emil was an inflexible man."

John swallowed hard. "What do you mean?"

Margrit frowned. "His idea of family was like the army. Everything needed to be perfect. Linens pressed, silver shined, son always clean and presentable. There was little joy in our home."

John thought about young Dedrich. "What kind of a father was he?"

Margrit closed her eyes for a moment. "I remember when Dedrich was young, he wanted to be like his father. Even though Emil never showed him affection, he loved his father very much." She wiped away a tear from her cheek. "One day, Emil surprised Dedrich by taking him to the artillery field. He was about five or six at the time. He had a toy gun and kept asking Emil to show him the real guns. When they got back that afternoon, Emil was angry. When the guns started to fire, Dedrich began to cry. Emil made him stay the entire time, even though he was frightened. After that, Emil hardly spoke to him. I never heard Dedrich cry after that."

John could hardly speak. He thought about going camping with his children, taking them fishing and swimming, and even having tea parties with his daughter and her friends. His heart broke that Margrit spent her life with a man like Emil.

"Did he hurt you?" John held his breath.

Margrit shook her head. "No, nothing like that. And I think he loved us, in his own way. But he sort of resented me."

John exhaled. "Why?"

186

Margrit pushed the food around on her plate. "He knew about France. He knew about you and me. He always treated me like damaged merchandise."

33

John held the restaurant door open allowing Margrit to walk past. The familiar scent of her perfume filled his nostrils. Even after all these years, it was the same fragrance.

"Can I walk you home?" he asked.

"I'd like that."

While they walked, John remembered the first time they went for a walk together. He could almost feel her arm around his.

"What have you been doing all these years? Did you keep cooking at a restaurant?"

Margrit shook her head. "Emil wouldn't allow it. He felt my place was at home."

John frowned. "You stopped cooking?"

"I didn't say that." Margrit smiled. "I cooked all the time. Emil liked to have soldiers over for dinner. That was one thing he was proud of. He loved my cooking. I simply didn't get paid for it. Until now."

John's eyebrows rose. "Until now?"

Margrit pointed toward a side street. "I've been working at a little outdoor café most afternoons since I arrived in Nuremburg. It's only a few blocks that way."

John scratched his head. "Why start cooking at a restaurant now?"

"Living in this city isn't cheap."

"Don't you get a widow's pension?" John winced as he heard himself use the word "widow" in reference to Margrit. She was younger than Rose and already a widow.

Margrit took hold of John's arm and stepped over a hole in the street. "Yes, but that barely covers the upkeep on the apartment in

Berlin. I have renters there while I'm away, but when I return home, I'll have to keep working."

Margrit glanced at John and added, "I miss having people to cook for. Why not get paid to do what I love?"

"Well, I'm glad you get to do what you enjoy," John said.

He wanted to say more, but didn't know what to say. For now, he avoided talking about Dedrich. Before he could say anything, Margrit said, "Now, you tell me about your life. Tell me more about your family."

John smiled as he thought about his children and grandchildren. "We have three children. Larry, the oldest is twenty-six. He's a teacher and has two boys. Donald is twenty-four and he also has two children. Twin boys. He's an architect. And my daughter Sandra is twenty-two. She gave birth to her first baby girl a month before I came over here. She's our first granddaughter."

Margit stopped in front of a three-story brick building. "I often wonder how different things would be, if you and I had…"

John stared at the sidewalk. "I've tried not to think about that."

"Why?" Margrit pushed her hair back, much the same way she did when they were younger.

John looked away, trying not to stare at her bare neck that hadn't changed in so many years. "I remember when I first woke up in the hospital, I was devastated. Tom stayed with me the whole time, until Rose arrived. Then they both stayed." He paused and inhaled Margrit's perfume again. "When I recovered enough to get out of the hospital, I still needed a lot of care. I'd lie in bed and imagine I was in France, spending my evenings in front of the fire at Gautier's with you. Even after Rose and I were married, I would daydream about us. It changed when my son was born."

"What do you mean?" Margrit asked.

John's face brightened. "When I first held my son, I knew if things had turned out differently, he would not exist. From that day on, I did not allow myself to imagine how things might be different."

Margrit nodded. "You have much to be happy for."

John wanted to say the same to Margrit, but he knew he couldn't. "After all these years, do *you* still wonder how things might have turned out?" He already knew the answer and didn't know why he had asked.

Margrit's lips turned down at the corners. "It's different for me. When I returned home, I didn't have many options. You were dead and I couldn't tell people I was in love with a man from the country that defeated us."

"I'm so sorry," John put his hand on her arm. "I wish you didn't have to—"

Margrit shook her head. "It's not your fault. I don't blame you. I don't know why things worked out the way they did, but we both made our choices. I married Emil and lived with the consequences." Margrit paused, seemingly lost in thought. "I used to think about killing myself. I thought it would be easier than going on without you."

"Why would you do that? Was it that bad?" John asked.

Margrit spoke in a whisper. "The real question was why didn't I? And the answer was Dedrich. I think if something had happened to him, I would have done it."

John sighed. "I'm so sorry, Margrit. I know there's nothing I can say to change what has happened."

Margrit's shoulders sank. "I guess the answer is I think about how different things might have turned out every day. When I felt the most alone, I imagined you were Dedrich's father. You would come through the door, maybe you had been playing soccer in the yard. I dreamed it more for my boy than for me."

John tried to picture a young Dedrich. He only encountered the man Dedrich had grown to be. The man who was filled with hate and anger. And how was it possible with a mother like Margrit?

"Will you help him?" she asked.

John expected this question but still didn't know how to answer. He hesitated before saying, "I'm not sure what I can do for him, but I'll look into it."

Margrit's eyes glinted in the moonlight. "Will you come for dinner sometime? I'd like to visit some more."

John hesitated again. "Sure. I'll be away for the next day or two, but I can come when I return."

Margrit kissed John on the cheek before walking into her building. "I'll see you in a few days then."

"I hope it's a good idea," he mumbled, as he walked away.

# # #

Knowing he was to leave for Siegen, John interviewed Dedrich again before he left. He hoped to find a redeeming quality that would motivate him to help the young man. He entered the same dark gray room he had interviewed Dedrich the previous day. He found it difficult to feel the disgust he experienced the day before. John tried to remind himself that Dedrich was an ordinary prisoner who deserved the same treatment as the rest. When he looked at the young man, all he could see was Margrit's deep brown eyes staring back at him. He remembered thinking that he looked familiar. Now he knew why.

"Mr. Haussman." John spoke in a quieter tone. "I need to ask you a few more questions for the report."

The young man, who wore the same gray uniform as the other prisoners, looked uninterested. "What else is there to tell you?"

John tapped his pen on his yellow notepad. He swallowed hard and tried to think of Margrit. He had to remain calm. "Mr. Haussman, do you understand what my job is?"

Dedrich's face remained expressionless. "To waste more of my time, it would seem."

John looked Dedrich in the eyes. "Do you really have something better you could be doing? I'm your only chance to get your story into the official record. If you have any chance of not being executed, I'm it."

Dedrich laughed. "I'll take my chances."

"All the same, Mr. Haussman, tell me more about yourself." John picked up his notebook and pencil.

Dedrich stared at John for a moment before sighing. "All right, what else do you want to know?"

John thought for a moment. "Well, you're a young man. It will matter if you were indoctrinated from a young age."

"Indoctrinated?" Dedrich spoke with disdain.

"Yes, Mr. Haussman. Like it or not, that is the word we use in reference to groups like the Hitler Youth. Were you a member of that organization as a child?"

Dedrich's face darkened. "Yes, I was a member of that *organization*. My father enrolled me when I was thirteen. It was a great experience for a young boy to learn how to protect his home and country."

John wrote in his notebook, trying not to stare. "And your father, tell me about him."

"My father was a soldier. He loved his country and died for it in Russia."

John looked up, absentmindedly adjusting the insignia on the front of his uniform. "Yes, but as a child. Tell me about him. What kind of father was he?"

Dedrich's expression hardened. "I said he was a soldier. What more is there to tell?"

"Well, did he take care of you? Was he kind?" John already knew the answer but needed to hear it from Dedrich.

Dedrich rolled his eyes. "I said he was a soldier. He took care of us. What more is there to say?"

John nodded. "Okay, then tell me about your mother."

Dedrich's face contorted into a snarl. "My mother is not someone I will talk about with you."

John rubbed his stubbly cheek. "The guest registry shows she has been to visit you every day for the last three weeks. How does she feel about this?" He gestured to the chains around the young man's wrists.

Dedrich rocked forward in his chair and glowered into John's face. "She is not a part of this. I will not talk about her."

"Why?" John asked. "She has to know what's going on. Maybe I should interview her."

Dedrich slammed both hands on the table. The chains dented the tabletop and dug into his wrist. "She is not a part of this! You will not talk to her!"

John flinched when the young man screamed. Guards rushed into the room and restrained Dedrich, pulling him out of the room.

"She has nothing to do with this." Dedrich's voice echoed through the hall. Trickles of blood from his wrists dotted a path on the floor where the guards dragged him away.

34

The following morning, John boarded a train to Siegen, his parents' birthplace. On this trip, he traveled alone. Tom convinced the General more research was needed on other death marches, but the old man would only allow one person to go. John was secretly relieved. He needed time alone to ponder what to do about Margrit's son.

He found it difficult to relax on the plush brown seats in the well-appointed train car. He once dreamed of the opportunity to enjoy the German countryside. As a young man, he imagined visiting the place of his parents' birth. Now, he could not stop thinking about Dedrich. He felt both revulsion and pity for the young man.

John brought a few files with him and planned to study his cases while he traveled. He made sure the file for Dedrich was included in those he stuffed into his briefcase. He glanced at the picture of the young man for a moment before turning the page. His eyes skimmed over the names and dates. Birthday, April 18, 1919. Height, 6'1. Weight, 190. Hair color, black. Place of birth, Berlin. The file included information about Dedrich's parents. Father's name, Emil Haussman, mother's name, Margrit Haussman. Parents' anniversary, December 12, 1918. None of it really mattered to John. He wasn't sure he should even be involved in the case.

John thought about how Dedrich protected his mother, even in the face of his own execution. Would he really rather be executed than allow his mother to be a part of his defense? The train slowed to a halt near Siegen and John still wasn't sure what he would do. The ethical decision would be to remove himself from the case due to conflict of interest. For now, he would push it aside and concentrate on the search for his family.

John stepped off the train with a small bag in one hand and his briefcase in another. He walked out of the run-down brick depot late in the morning and looked for a taxi to take him to the hotel. Seeing none, he asked an old man working in the ticket booth how to get to the hotel.

The old man smiled through yellow teeth and pointed his crooked finger. "Start walking that way. It's the only building left standing on its block. You won't miss it."

John couldn't believe the city was more damaged than Nuremburg. The old man was right. Most of the city was gone, reduced to either piles of rubble like the ones he saw in Nuremburg, or empty fields with nothing but the foundation of buildings that once stood. Every so often, warped metal beams stuck out of a concrete foundation where a building had collapsed. A twisted reminder of war.

He made his way through the street, studying ruin after ruin. The eerie silence in the city caused John to walk a little faster until he reached the hotel. He couldn't figure out how every other building on the street was gone, but this small three-story hotel remained. After checking into the dark hotel, which he discovered had lost power sometime the night before, John immediately began the search for his family. His train was scheduled to depart early the following morning, so he didn't have much time for his search.

He wasn't sure exactly where to look. All he remembered was that his grandparents owned a small farm at the southern edge of the city. Studying a map, he guessed the farm was about two miles from the hotel. Seeing no sign of a working automobile, much less a taxi service, John ventured out on foot.

He wished he had brought more comfortable attire than his army uniform. The tight collar of his dress shirt pulled at his neck on the damp spring day. Along the way, he asked passersby if they knew of his grandparents or recognized the name "Bayer." No one had heard of his family and they all eyed the American uniform with suspicion.

Approaching the southern edge of town, which was greener and less impacted by war than the rest of the city, John turned toward a small café. Other than the restaurant at the hotel, this appeared to be the only place to eat. Smelling the aroma wafting through the open front door, John's stomach rumbled.

He imagined, on a busy day, bumping elbows with customers in the small diner. On that day, he was the only customer. He stood at the glass counter to the right of the entrance and considered the German pastries in the case. A middle-aged woman with a white and red plaid scarf tied around her hair entered through the back door carrying a tray loaded with bread. She smiled at John before placing the tray on an empty table.

"How may I help you?" She glanced at John's uniform and spoke in broken English.

"I'd like to get a bite to eat." John spoke in German. "I'm also looking for someone, or a few people who used to live around here. Have you ever heard the name Bayer?"

The woman's brown eyes brightened when John spoke German. "Yes, there used to be quite a few Bayers in this area."

"Used to be?" John tried to mask his disappointment. "Where'd they go?"

The woman squeezed her lips together. "Now let me think. We bought produce from them. Before the war."

Well, this is a start, John thought, before he asked, "Do you know where their farm was?"

The woman studied John's army uniform. "Why do you want to know?"

John pointed to the nametape on his chest. "My name is Bayer. My parents grew up in this town. I'm trying to find any family that might still be here."

"Oh, well then." The woman practically screeched, standing on her toes to see over the counter. "That's another story. Let me get you something to eat before we talk."

John settled into a chair at the nearest table while the woman brought him a plate of pot roast and vegetables smothered in sauerkraut and a dark brown sauce. John was famished and ignored that he had not ordered anything.

The woman must have noticed the surprised expression on John's face as she approached. "We only have one item on the menu each day, other than the pastries in the front case."

"It's perfect." John speared a chunk of meat with his fork. "Do you have a few moments to sit and talk?"

195

Even as the words left John's mouth, the woman pulled a chair over. Before she got comfortable, she set another plate on the table with two pieces of apple streusel. "I'm afraid I don't know much that you want to know. My husband knew your family better than I did, but he died in the war."

John stopped eating and considered the woman. She appeared younger than him, maybe in her mid-forties, but she looked tired, with dark bags under her eyes. She had black hair with a few gray strands that escaped her scarf.

"I'm sorry to hear about your husband," John said. In a country where millions perished, everyone had lost at least one family member.

John took another bite. "About my family, are you sure they are gone from this area."

The woman's eyebrows furrowed. Her pursed lips turned into a frown. "Yes, I am pretty sure they left when the…"

"When the what?" John asked, a knot building in his stomach. He already knew the answer.

"I'm sorry, I forgot." She gasped, almost as if she was out of breath. "Those terrible things happened back then and we tried to forget about all of it."

"You mean the Jews?" John spoke gently, trying not to upset the woman any more.

"Yes. I think your family had to leave when the Jews were forced out of our district." The woman's eyes watered. "I'm sorry, I don't know where they were sent."

John's heart sank, although this was the news he expected. "If you could send me in the right direction, I'd like to at least visit the farm if I can find it."

The woman nodded. Her shoulders drooped as she gave John directions to the farm. After that, she didn't seem to want to talk. She stood from her chair and hung her head. "I'm sorry. I forgot what happened to your family. It was such an ugly time I don't like to think about it."

35

While John plodded down the quiet country lane, he dreaded what he would find. He imagined his dad walking the same road as a young boy and was glad he had not lived to see what happened to his family. John wasn't sure he would tell his mother what he discovered, if it really was as bad as he knew it had to be.

With the help of his map, John reached the location of the family farm. He expected the property to be run down from years of sitting vacant. Instead, he spotted a well-maintained farm with cattle in the fenced field and the clucking of chickens from behind the house. The white barn looked like it was recently painted and reminded John of the one in France, although it was smaller in comparison and had a dark gray roof. The two-story brick house had a tidy appearance, with a fresh coat of brown paint on the trim. Seeing the home occupied made his stomach tighten.

John approached the house and almost hoped it was the wrong farm. A young man emerged from the rear corner of the house and froze when he saw John. Wearing blue jeans, a dirty white T-shirt, and work gloves, the man made a hesitant step toward John and stammered in his best attempt at English. "Help you?"

John smiled and looked at his uniform. He was getting used to people looking at him with suspicion.

"Yes." John spoke in German, trying to ease the man's nerves. "I hoped I could look around. Maybe ask you a few questions."

The man ran his gloved fingers through his sweaty brown hair. "Of course. I thought for a minute that you were here for, well, forget it. What can I do for you?"

John reached out his hand and took a step towards the man. "I think my father grew up on this farm. I wanted to see it while I am in Germany."

The man's shoulders tensed. He made no effort to shake John's hand. "Your father?"

John dropped his hand. "Yes, his name was Rudolph Bayer. Is this the right house? My grandfather's name was Alders."

The man removed his gloves and put his hands in his pockets. He didn't look at John. "Yes, this was the Bayer farm."

"Good." John smiled. "I'm John Bayer. My grandparents used to live here. Can you tell me, if you have any idea, when they left?"

The man didn't offer his name in return for John's and stared at the ground. "I don't know for sure. We bought it in 1939."

John leaned in to the young man. He was used to people not looking him in the eye. "Bought it from whom?"

"It was owned by the government when we took possession." The man raked his fingers through his hair again

John took another step toward the man. His heart raced. "They were forced out by the government and you came in and took it? Is that right?"

The farmer stepped back. "We paid for it. We didn't take it. We didn't know how the government got the place before we bought it."

John clenched his jaw. Everyone in Germany knew why houses were empty back then. He knew it wasn't this man's fault that his grandparents were gone, but he had no one else to be angry at. "They didn't have a choice, did they? They were told they have to leave and probably ended up in one of *your* camps. What an opportunity it must have been for you."

"I'm sorry. I don't know what to tell you." The man took another step back. "We were young and borrowed the money from my wife's parents to buy the farm. We didn't ask questions."

"You have no idea what happened to the people who lived here?" John swung his arm, gesturing at the farmhouse.

The young man rubbed the back of his neck. "We learned a little from the neighbors since we got here."

"Tell me what you know about what happened to them?" John's neck was hot, but he knew the man could throw him off the land. Like it or not, the German owned the farm now.

The man nodded. "I talked to the old couple who lived next door when we moved in. That was before I had to go fight in the war. We talked a lot back then." He paused and glanced over his shoulder at the house. A woman and three children stared out the front window. "The neighbor said the old man who lived here wasn't a Jew and could have stayed. But it was against the law for him to be married to a Jew."

"Why did he leave?"

The man shrugged. "According to the old neighbor, he chose to."

"What?" John scowled.

The man swallowed hard. "They came for the woman."

"My grandmother." John hated that he said "the woman."

"Yes, they came for her and the others who were Jewish. They were going to leave the old man here because he wasn't a Jew. But he wouldn't let her go without him." The man took another nervous step back.

"And what else? Where did they go?" John took a step forward and stared hard at the farmer.

The man wagged his head. "That's all I know. I swear. I don't know where they were sent."

John looked around the yard. "What about their possessions? Did you keep it all?"

"No, no. There was nothing." The man shook his head again. "When we got here, everything had been taken away. The front yard had a patch of grass that was scorched. I think they burned a lot of their stuff and took the rest." The man paused for a moment. "We found a picture in the back of a drawer in the kitchen. I'll get it for you."

John followed the man onto the porch of the old brick farmhouse.

"Please wait here." The main raised his hand to John's chest.

John scowled at the man's hand. "I want to see the inside of my grandparents' house. I think I deserve that."

The farmer eyed John from top to bottom before opening the door. The young woman and children who watched through the window were huddled in the corner of the living room.

"Take the children out back for a while." The man pointed towards the back yard.

When the family was outside, John surveyed the living room. The house had been in his family for over a hundred years. He looked at the peeling floral wallpaper going up the stairs to his right and imagined his young father brushing against it as he ran down the stairs. Then he imagined his old grandfather scurrying down those same stairs with a single suitcase. Forced out of the only home he had ever known.

John looked into the kitchen where the young man rummaged through the drawers. He imagined the grandmother he had never met cooking at the old wood-burning stove. He closed his eyes and inhaled the aroma of the old house mixed with the smell of fresh bread wafting from the kitchen. This was his heritage and he once expected to enjoy discovering it. Now, standing in the home that was ripped away from his grandparents, he only felt anger.

The farmer stumbled back into the room clutching the old photograph. John gently took the picture and looked at two young men posing with broad smiles on their faces. John glanced over his shoulder. He realized he stood in almost the same spot, in front of the big window, that the two youths in the picture stood when they posed so long ago.

John blinked at the picture of his father and uncle. His mind was playing tricks on him. He turned away before looking back at the photograph. His legs wobbled and took a step backwards, nearly tripping on a table. The farmer stepped forward and grabbed John's arm.

"Are you okay?"

John ignored the man and stared at the picture taken sixty years ago. A familiar face stared back at him. Margrit's son seemed familiar the first time John met him, and it wasn't because of Margrit. Dedrich looked so much like John's father as a young man, they could have been brothers.

"He's my son."

The outside world faded away. John closed his eyes. He didn't care that the farmer watched him. He had a son who he never knew

200

existed and who was now, more than likely, going to die. John didn't care, in that moment, what Dedrich had done. He cared that Dedrich was his son. He cared that Margrit was forced to marry a man she didn't love. And he cared that she lived an unhappy life because an unmarried pregnant woman didn't have any other options.

"But he sort of resented me," Margrit had said. Now John understood why.

36

John didn't visit any other sights in Siegen. He had found what he was looking for. He returned to Nuremburg the next morning and went straight to work. After interviewing more SS commanders in the afternoon, he and Tom parted ways at the Palace of Justice. Tom found a card game and John went to Margrit's for dinner.

John walked slowly down the dimly lit hallway toward Margrit's apartment. He held a scrap of paper in one hand and a bottle of wine in the other. The old wood floor squeaked with every step. When he reached the apartment door, he checked the numbers on the paper. Raising his hand to knock, he paused.

Should I go to her apartment?

He could send one of the privates with a note to cancel. Margrit would understand, she knew John was busy. He took a step back from the door before it swung open. Margrit smiled from inside. He looked at Margrit, who wore the same black dress she wore at the café. Her hair was tied up in the back with one loose strand dangling to the side. John remembered admiring that strand when he was younger. He shook his head, trying not to linger on the thoughts about how beautiful she still was.

"Come in. Please." Margrit stepped aside, allowing John to enter the small apartment. He held his breath and squeezed by, unable to avoid rubbing against her. He could not avoid the familiar scent of her perfume either. Over the years, when John would smell a similar aroma, he'd have to catch his breath and drive the memories from his mind. Now he was in her apartment, and the scent brought to the surface feelings he had long ago buried.

Standing in a bit of a fog, John studied the small apartment. His dining room at home was larger than Margrit's entire flat. A tiny black table and two chairs were set up in a kitchenette on the far side of the room. On John's left was a closed curtain that did a poor job of hiding the bed behind it. On the right was a narrow door which led to, John assumed, a bathroom or closet. A light smoke from the frying pan filled the room and reminded him of Gautier's.

John stammered. "I brought wine. Mom used to say I should always bring something when invited to dinner." He considered bringing flowers, but thought wine was safer. Now he wasn't sure.

Margrit smiled and accepted the bottle before returning to the kitchen and stirring something on the stovetop. "Thank you. I hope you aren't too uncomfortable in my little place."

John looked at the bed behind the curtain. It wasn't the size of the place that made him uncomfortable. "No, not at all," he lied. "Can I ask why you have such a small place?"

Margrit removed a pan from the tiny oven in the corner of the kitchen. "It's all I need while I'm here. I'll go home to Berlin when this is over."

Ignoring his reservations, John inhaled the aroma of the braised meat steaming in the pan. "This brings back memories of France, doesn't it?"

Margrit set two plates next to the steaming pan. "I think if I closed my eyes, we would be back at my uncle's. I can almost hear him roaring somewhere in the old place."

John's heartbeat pounded in his ears. All he could think about was his son. "I know about Dedrich."

Margrit ignored the sizzling in the pan and stared at John.

"I know he's my son," John added, with more purpose in his voice.

"How did you figure it out?"

John wanted to be angry with Margrit for not telling him. "He looked familiar when I first met him. I thought it was because of you. When I saw a picture of my dad from years ago, I realized Dedrich looks just like him."

Margrit exhaled. "When I got back to Germany, I didn't know what to do. I was unmarried and pregnant. My grandmother almost kicked me out of her house, but my mother stopped her. Emil was a friend of my fathers before the war. He checked in on us after my father's death. When my grandmother told him about the baby, he offered to marry me to protect our family name."

John stood still, holding his hat. "Does Dedrich know anything about me?"

Margrit pleaded with her eyes. "No, and I don't want him to know. When he was a teenager, he figured out I was pregnant before Emil and I were married. We allowed him to believe Emil got me pregnant before we were married. He knows nothing about my time in France."

John nodded. "I won't tell him. But why didn't you tell me?"

Margrit kept her eyes on John as she scooped food onto the plates. "I struggled with this the last few days. I thought it would be easier if you didn't know."

"Easier than finding out on my own?" John's eyes narrowed, although he tried to be gentle.

"No." Margrit shook her head. "Easier than finding out you have a son who's probably going to…"

John understood. "So what do we do now?"

"I don't know." Margrit's hand trembled. She set the plates and two wine glasses at the small table.

After they began to eat, John said. "I know it's not easy, but we need to talk about Dedrich."

Margrit nodded. "I know you're going to tell me I should prepare for the worst. I read the newspapers when Goring and Hess were on trial. I know what could happen."

Not could, will, John thought.

He took a deep breath. "Margrit, I don't know how to tell you this, but I don't see any other outcome for your son. For our son."

John thought about the word "our." Dedrich was his son, and he had been too shocked to fully understand what it meant. His son committed unimaginable acts. John wasn't even sure he believed all of the reports before he arrived at Dachau. Now, he was faced with the real possibility that his son would be executed for crimes against his own race.

Margrit sank in her chair. "Do you think I don't know that? I saw what happened to the others. I know these are probably the last weeks I have with my boy. But I am his mother and I will not stop hoping and praying for him."

John sighed. "I know."

"You don't know," Margrit blurted. "I have one thing left in this world. When I was young, I had the hope of a young woman. When the innocence of youth died, I had Dedrich. Can you imagine having a little boy you love more than anything? Imagine every time you look into his face seeing the man you loved with your whole heart. Being reminded there was a dream that almost was."

John nodded, a lump building in his throat. He remembered holding his son for the first time.

Margrit barely held back her tears. "Now imagine this boy, with the only father he knew, who looked at him with contempt. All he wanted was for his father to love him. But because of what I did as a young woman, he would never have that. A young boy could not understand why his daddy didn't look at him like the other fathers looked at their sons."

John took Margrit's hand. He had never regretted his night with her, until now. He realized the actions of his youth impacted more than just the two people involved. He squeezed his eyes, holding back tears. This was not his moment.

"And now my boy is going to die, and I know that." Margrit burst into tears, her body racked by the sobs. "And there is nothing I can do about it. All I wanted was to protect him. To love him."

John nudged his chair closer and placed his arm around her. Margrit wept, resting her head on his shoulder. His eyes filled with water.

He wouldn't say it out loud, but as Margrit sobbed, he wished he'd never met her. Never fallen in love with her. She would have lived her life and grown old as a happy woman. She was beautiful and could have married any man she wanted. She would not have had to marry Emil. And John would still have returned home to Rose.

He wanted to tell her he was sorry for ruining her life. He knew his words were meaningless. How many times could he say the same thing? Soon, she would lose the only thing, besides him, she had ever been able to call her own.

"If we could," John paused, trying to gather his thoughts. "If we could get it in the testimony, from Dedrich, how he was raised to do the things he did. Maybe he would only go to prison. Other soldiers have been sent to prison for the same crimes Dedrich committed."

Margrit still cried, but her eyes sparkled. "Is that possible?"

John thought for a moment, leaving his arm around Margrit's shoulder. He knew it was unlikely, given that the young man seemed proud of what he had done. He didn't want to give Margrit false hope. "I think you would have to talk him into it. I didn't tell you this, but I interviewed him again after we went to the café the other night. It didn't go well."

Panic flashed across Margrit's face. "You didn't tell him anything about us, did you?"

John shook his head. "No. And I agree it's not a good idea. But when I mentioned that the visitor registry showed you had been to see him, he became angry. He doesn't want you involved at all."

"What do I need to do?" Margrit asked. "I will do anything."

John scratched his head. "All I can think is that you tell him to talk about his father. We need it in the record that his father indoctrinated him. Maybe the court will have mercy on a twenty-nine-year-old kid who grew up in the Hitler Youth."

John struggled with his words even as they left his mouth. After witnessing Nazi brutality, he wasn't sure Dedrich deserved mercy. But Dedrich was his son too.

"I don't think he'll do it." Margrit frowned. "His father taught him to hate many people. Now that Emil is dead, I think Dedrich would consider it an insult to his father's memory."

John reached for his glass of wine, pausing to consider if he should have another drink. "Maybe you should tell him he's Jewish."

Margrit shook her head. "We can't. I don't think I could bear his hatred if he found out."

"But it might keep him alive?" John tried to create a little internal enthusiasm for his plan.

"Let me try talking to him first." Margrit tilted her head, looking into John's face. "I'll tell him I found out about your investigation and I sought you out. That way, he won't be angry with you for speaking to me. I'll go first thing in the morning."

"Okay," John said. "I'll re-interview him in the afternoon and hopefully he'll cooperate." He closed his eyes and inhaled the aroma of Margrit's perfume again. "I'll have to tell Tom the truth, too, and try to get his help."

John knew Tom would help.

Holding Margrit, John closed his eyes and forgot for a moment when and where he was. There was a vague thought in his mind of someone else, but he was exhausted. Was he really in the little apartment, or was he back in another apartment above Gautier's?

Margrit rested her head on John's shoulder. "Thank you for coming tonight."

John opened his eyes. Margrit's lips were close to his. It was a familiar sensation. He looked at the crimson lipstick hypnotically.

"I forgot how much I missed you," she said.

John still watched her lips. He felt Margrit's arms wrap around his waist and squeeze him. He moved his free arm around her and squeezed her tighter, feeling the familiar curves of her body. She had barely changed in twenty-nine years. He looked into her eyes. He wanted to move his lips closer, but he remembered Rose. He remembered his children and grandchildren. Thoughts of his family poured in and his body tensed.

"What's wrong?" Margrit asked.

John forced a smile, letting his arms slip from around Margrit's body. "I have to go. Tom will wonder where I am."

Margrit bit her bottom lip. "Yes. It's getting late."

"Thank you for a lovely dinner." John stood and moved toward the door, leaving the mostly filled glass of wine on the table.

Margrit smiled politely. "It was good to see you."

"We'll talk again." John reached for the door and his hand trembled. He squeezed the handle to steady himself. "You know where to find me."

"I named him after you," Margrit said, before John opened the door. "His middle name is Johann, the German version John."

John swallowed hard and stepped out the door. As he walked down the hall, he heard the sound of crying. He stopped and rested his hand on the wall. Peeling paint crackled and floated to the floor. He took a deep breath before he clinched his jaw and walked down the stairs. The echo of Margrit weeping followed him through the corridor.

37

"You've got to be kidding." Tom looked like he wanted to laugh, but also that he might cry, after John told him about Dedrich. "I guess I shouldn't be surprised considering all that has happened since we arrived here."

John sat in a green chair across from Tom in the sitting room of their hotel suite. "I'm not sure what's funny about it."

Tom swung his feet onto the floor from the little table in front of his chair. "It's not funny at all. I don't know what else to do though. I'm starting to feel sick again."

"You and me both." John's stomach churned. "But I did have a little more to drink tonight than I usually do."

Tom didn't hide his smile when he heard John talk about drinking. "What are you going to do?"

John rubbed his eyes, still lightheaded from the wine. "I guess I have to give him a chance," John paused, before saying what he had been thinking at Margrit's. "Although, I'm not sure he deserves a chance."

"I think I need a drink." Tom rocked out of his chair and shuffled to the white buffet at the side of the room. After consuming the entire contents of his glass in one swallow, he refilled it. "You know what you have to do. Like it or not, he is your son."

John joined Tom at the little bar to pour himself another drink. "I know he's my son. But we saw what the Nazis did. Justice is justice."

Tom swallowed his drink again before considering another refill. "Think about all the Nazis who got off with jail time. I'm not saying he doesn't deserve punishment. But that won't be for you to decide. Your job is to report the facts. It's up to you which ones you want to emphasize in the report."

"I know," John said. "The worst part is the kid doesn't even know he's Jewish. Probably never will." John returned to his seat without a drink, realizing he'd already had too much to drink.

Tom held another full glass of Scotch swishing in his hand when he returned to his chair. "So what do we do next?"

John smiled when he heard his friend ask, "What do *we* do next?" He wasn't alone, even if it felt like he was.

"I think you should join me when I interview him again." John leaned his head on the chair back and yawned. "For now, I'm going to bed."

John pushed himself from his chair and hesitated. He looked at Tom, who was sitting with his eyes closed. "Why are you here?"

Tom didn't open his eyes. "Because I'm too tired to walk to bed."

"No, I meant that you could be home with Fran and the grandkids. You didn't have to come to Europe. Why did you come?"

Tom's eyes remained closed but he smiled, tipping John that a joke was coming. "I guess I needed another adventure. Twenty-nine years is too long between them."

John sat quietly. Part of him wanted to chastise his friend for not giving a serious answer. The other part wanted to laugh. "Well, goodnight then."

Tom opened his eyes. "When I was a kid, my friends and I played at an old flour mill on the river. It had a huge paddle wheel that still turned with the river, even though the machinery was long gone. The mill had been empty since before I was born, so we thought it was a great place to play. We jammed a board into the wheel to keep it from moving and crawled out and dropped a line into the water. We spent entire days at the old mill during the summer."

John settled back into his chair.

"One day, my friend James wanted to go fishing. I didn't feel like going, so I lied. I told him I had chores. All I did was stay home and play with the dog. He went without me, all by himself. That night after dinner, his dad showed up at our place looking for him. He wasn't worried because he thought Jimmy had stayed at our house for dinner."

Tom paused to take a breath. "I remember sitting on the wood floor in my kitchen, already knowing what happened to my friend. There was Jimmy's dad, completely unaware. But I knew he would have been home already if everything was all right." Tom stared into his empty glass. "My dad and Jimmy's dad took a couple lanterns to the mill to look for him. I prayed that my friend wasn't dead. I promised God I would always be the best friend I could be, if only Jimmy was alive."

John leaned in. "And?"

Tom breathed slowly, dramatically, before a smile broke across his face. "He was fine. He'd gone to another friend's house for dinner."

John laughed. "You bum. I thought he was dead."

Tom snickered. "No, but a promise is a promise. God might strike me dead if I don't look after you."

John stood. He wasn't sure if the story was true or fiction. He decided it didn't matter. His friend was here for him, again. "Well, like I said on the train. Thanks for coming."

John stopped at the door when Tom spoke again. "He died though, after that."

"What?" John looked over his shoulder, waiting for the punchline that didn't come.

"When we were in high school, the summer after our junior year, he got his arm caught in a piece of machinery at the farm. Bled to death before his dad could shut it off. He was my best friend."

John was silent. He didn't know what to say. He swallowed and was about to say something like "I'm sorry" when Tom added, "I thought you should know."

John nodded and walked into his bedroom.

It's not that he wasn't tired, but John lay awake most of the night. He couldn't stop thinking about Margrit and Dedrich, and Tom's friend who died. When he finally forced himself out of bed in the morning, it was hours before Tom would be awake. After nursing his headache with aspirin, John slowly put his uniform on and went for a walk.

Exiting the hotel into a misty rain, John pulled his black overcoat tight. The familiar ache below his shoulder returned and he stretched his arm to work out the pain. Not sure where to go, John walked in the general direction of the Palace of Justice. After a few blocks of steadily increasing rain, he scanned the street for a place to get out of the deluge. The doors to the Catholic Church across the street were wide open. John jogged across the street, avoiding the potholes filled with water, and entered one of the few buildings still standing after the war.

Not being Catholic, John bypassed the holy water inside the door and glanced at the statue of the Virgin Mary holding a baby. He slid into the back pew as quietly as he could. The sanctuary of the old church was dark, with the exception of a few dozen candles burning to the right of the altar. John detected the aroma of incense burning near the candles.

He laughed to himself as he remembered the old rift between the Lutherans and Catholics in his hometown. His mother was firmly on the side of the Lutherans. Whenever he was curious about something that wasn't his business, she would say, "We're not Catholic, we don't talk about those things." He smiled when he thought of how irritated she would be to see him in this church.

John hadn't prayed in years. He had mumbled a prayer when he was in a mud filled hole in no man's land many years ago, but that was the last prayer he remembered saying. Rose brought the kids to church. On holidays, John accompanied the family, but he didn't repeat the prayers with the minister. At bedtime, it was Rose who knelt beside the little beds with the children.

John wasn't sure why he stopped praying. He was grateful to have survived the war, but losing Margrit seemed to change something in him. The joy of a beautiful family didn't heal some old wounds. Not that he was ever someone who prayed much before the war.

Sitting in the pew of an unfamiliar church, John thought maybe this was the perfect place to say a short prayer. He didn't know exactly what to pray for, but he also didn't know what led him into the church in the first place. All he knew was he needed strength in the coming days. He would endure two things that were almost unbearable. First, he would try to help a young man who committed crimes John deemed worthy of death. Second, he would likely watch as the son he had never known went to the gallows. Try as he may, John couldn't ignore the fact that his son—his flesh and blood—would die.

His thoughts were distracted by a sound bouncing through the church, as a woman maneuvered a squeaky wheelchair up the aisle. A frail old man with a checkered blanket draped over his lap sat limply in the chair. Something about the man drew John's attention. He watched the two from the shadows of the sanctuary.

The woman pushed the old man to the front of the church near the altar. John watched as she took hold of the man's arm to steady it. He reached out and lit two candles. The pair remained in the front of the church as the man mumbled quietly. John watched the shadow of the old man's head bob up and down.

After a few minutes, the woman turned the old man around and pushed the loud chair back toward John. In the old brick building, the repetitive squeak of the wheels reverberated through the church. Noise that would have been barely noticeable outside echoed against the brick walls. The woman stopped and whispered into the man's ear.

"No, take me home." The old man slurred his words in a raspy German voice.

John tensed at the sound of the man's voice. A cold wave rose up his neck, followed by goose bumps. He squinted at the man who didn't seem to notice him. John remembered the words spoken by the same raspy voice years ago. "I know because we grew up together in Nuremburg. We lived down the street from each other. Raised our families together. Went to Mass together."

With light beginning to peek through the door and windows, John was sure he recognized the man. He jumped to his feet, ignoring the pain as his knee rapped on the pew in front of him.

"Hey, wait a minute," John yelled in German, not caring that his voice echoed in the building.

The woman looked over her shoulder. John darted from the pew and approached them.

"You. What's your..." John realized it wouldn't help to ask for the man's name. All they ever called him in the prison camp was "Die Stimme." The Voice.

The old man strained his eyes at John, pulling his blanket a little higher onto his shivering body. The woman protectively stepped beside the old man and stuck her chin out.

"What do you want?" She studied John's uniform.

John pointed at the old man. "Was he in the first war?" He didn't wait for the woman to answer, instead crouching to eye level with the old man. "Were you in the Great War?"

The old man nodded. Before he could speak, the woman squeezed herself between John and the Voice. "Why do you want to know?"

John's eyes narrowed. "Because I think we've met before." He looked at the man again, craning his neck to see around the woman's legs. "Were you in a prison camp near Verdun? It would have been in 1918."

The old man nodded again.

The woman exhaled. "My father is old and sick. He doesn't need to be bothered, especially in church. Now if you don't mind."

John stood and faced the woman. "As a matter of fact, I do mind. I want to talk to him."

She surveyed John's uniform again before mumbling, "Make it quick."

John crouched in front of the old man again and studied his face. More light crept into the church as the sun rose above the horizon outside. John noted a hint of recognition in the tired eyes.

"You remember me, don't you?" John shifted his weight, his legs aching in the crouch.

The old man's voice cracked. "Yes."

John couldn't believe the old man was still alive, let alone sitting in front of him. After so many years, he still imagined beating the Voice to death with his bare hands. If it weren't for this old man, so many things would be different.

"Everything would be different," John whispered, with a pause. He thought about Rose and the children. He considered his grandchildren, and realized if it wasn't for this demented old man, they would not exist. This man, who John always hated, was responsible for his life.

John looked up at the woman. "You said he's sick. What's wrong with him?"

She crossed her arms. "It's his lungs. We don't know exactly what it is, but the doctor said he only has a few weeks left. The rain doesn't help. It's hard for him to breathe when it's wet."

John returned his gaze to the old man. "Did you ever tell your daughter about your time in the prison camp?"

The old man grabbed John's arm and stared into his face. The strength of his grip surprised John. It reminded him of another instance when the old man took hold of him in a humid train car, nearly choking him to death.

"No," the old man whispered.

John rose to his feet and jerked his head at the old man. "Why are you so protective of him?"

Defiant, the woman replied, "Because he's sick and doesn't need to be bothered."

John shook his head. "I can tell that's not it. I knew your father when I was a younger man." John looked at the old man, whose eyes pleaded with him. "I'm an investigator for the U.S. government. I could cause a lot of trouble for him."

The woman crossed her arms. "If I tell you, will you leave us alone?"

"You have my word."

The woman's voice quivered. "Before the war, when we tried to get certain groups to leave our country—"

"You mean the Jews?" John glowered.

"Yes," she said. "And others. Back then, my father no longer worked, but his health was strong. He was involved in helping organize the groups to get them out. To get them to leave on their own."

"On their own?"

"Yes." The woman gripped the handle of the wheelchair. "Before all that stuff at the camps, all we thought they were doing was forcing people to leave the country." She paused and looked at her father, stroking his smooth, bald head. "He helped with that. He wasn't an important person, just a retired man volunteering his time for his country."

John reached back and massaged his sore shoulder.

"We thought he was doing a good thing. Everyone back then thought so. One day there was a knock at our door." The woman paused again, still caressing her father's head. "We didn't expect the SS to knock on *our* door."

"They came for your father?" John asked.

Tears ran down her cheeks. "No. I had a sister with the palsy. She was in a wheelchair. The disabled disappeared first, but we thought we had hidden her from them. We don't know how they found out about her. One of the neighbors must have reported her."

John looked at the trembling old man, too old for tears. "They took your sister?"

The woman took a deep breath. "When they came, my father wasn't home. He was at one of those foolish meetings. My mother tried to stop them from taking her. One of the soldiers hit her on the head with the butt of his rifle and they loaded my sister in the back of a truck. I still remember the look on her face when they closed the doors. She was terrified.

"By the time we could find my father, my mother was in a coma. She never awoke and we never saw my sister again. My father didn't even say goodbye to my sister when he left that morning because he didn't want to wake her. He knew how tired the seizures made her." The woman crouched and put her arm around her shaking father.

"He loved my sister so much," she whispered. "He would have done anything for her."

John stared at the two, his stomach turning. "What did he do when he got home?"

"What could he do?" she answered. "Those things happened to everyone back then. He's been here to light a candle for my mother and sister every day since."

"That doesn't explain why you don't want to talk to me."

The woman looked at her father. "We know people are being charged with crimes for what happened back then. We have often wondered if there would be another knock at our door because of his role in organizing the deportations."

"There won't be." John reassured. "No one's looking for a sick old man. At least not this one."

"I'd like to talk to him alone for a minute," John added.

The woman looked at him hesitantly before nodding and stepping outside the door. John crouched and stared at the old man. He silently looked into the man's eyes.

215

The old man rasped, barely loud enough for John to hear. "Thank you."

"For what?" John whispered.

The old man turned his head toward his daughter.

John looked at the woman, who waited in the rain with her collar pulled high, before looking back at the Voice. His body was weak and withered, but his eyes were still clear. John thought of all the names he imagined calling him over the years, but couldn't bring himself to say any of them. "Children shouldn't suffer because their parents fail."

As John stood, the old man grabbed his hand and repeated, "Thank you."

John nodded. He thought about Rose and the kids before saying, "No, thank you."

He leaned against the archway and watched the woman push her father out the door. She turned down the sidewalk and the two disappeared around the corner. John lingered a few minutes in the church before stepping into the rain.

38

John and Tom entered the interview room to find Dedrich chained to the table. After his last outburst, the guards were ready at the door to remove him at the first sign of trouble. The two friends sat at the table across from Dedrich with a clear view of the guards through the door's window.

"Mr. Haussman," John said. "I'd like to start by informing you that your mother came to visit us yesterday."

Dedrich's eyes darkened. "My mother?"

John tapped a pencil on his notepad. "The only reason we're here today is that she asked us to meet with you again."

John and Tom decided they would begin by mentioning Dedrich's mother. They knew she had seen Dedrich earlier in the morning, and expected him to respond more favorably during this interview.

"Why would she want you to talk to me?" Dedrich asked.

"Frankly, Mr. Haussman, I don't know and I don't care." Tom veered from their strategy. "I can't see why she cares either. The only reason I'm here is because a mother begged us to help her son."

Dedrich glared at Tom, who had not introduced himself. "Why would you care to help her?"

Tom returned the young man's expression with a sneer. "Like I said, I don't care what—"

"Mr. Haussman," John raised his hand. He knew Tom changed tactics so John could be the good guy. "We're here to get a full history from you. Your mother delivered her testimony, which will be included in our official record. We need you to provide more details."

"What do you hope to gain from another interview?" Dedrich's voice softened.

Tom shook his head. "I don't hope to gain anything. Your mother thinks you didn't have a choice. That you were bred to commit the crimes you're accused of."

"Crimes?" Dedrich's lip curled down.

Tom reached into his leather bag and retrieved a stack of pictures. "These are a few of the bodies found by our soldiers. Can you guess whose troops are accused of killing these people?"

Dedrich glared at Tom.

"Your troops. You and your troops committed these *crimes*," Tom said.

"What about them?" Dedrich looked away.

John rubbed his forehead. "Your mother thinks you were forced by the regime to commit these crimes. What do you say about that?"

"Are you asking me if I had a choice?"

Tom cracked his knuckles. "Tell us about your father. Colonel Bayer reported that, the last time you were interviewed, you were reluctant to talk about him."

"As I said before, my father was a soldier," Dedrich said. "What else is there to tell about him?"

Before Tom could respond, John said, "What kind of father was he? Was he a loving father? Caring? What activities did you do together?"

"This is absurd," Dedrich yelled, causing the guards to peek into the room. "What does it matter?"

Tom exhaled with a level of exasperation John thought might have been over the top. "Do you want to die? Is that what this is about? If it is, then we can pack up and leave."

"Why do you care what happens to me?" Dedrich spoke with a mix of defiance and curiosity.

John pinched the bridge of his nose. "Your mother believes if the whole truth is told, you will only receive a prison sentence. We agreed to write the most thorough report possible."

Dedrich glared at Tom before turning to John. "My father showed us love by providing for us."

"What activities did you do together?" John repeated.

218

Dedrich clinched his jaw. "We didn't do what other kids did. He took me to watch the soldiers practice. He was dedicated to the army. His devotion was to Germany."

John wrote in his notepad. "You never played soccer with your dad? Went to the beach with him? Nothing like that?"

Dedrich's scowl returned. "He provided a warm home, clean clothes, and good food. What else is there?"

John tried to sound nonchalant. "What about your mother? Do you have positive memories with her?"

Dedrich said, "When I was a child, we played games. When I grew older, my father would not allow that sort of thing."

Tom sat back and allowed John to handle this part of the interview. "Tell me, what sort of things did your father want you to do? I mean, rather than play games," John asked.

Dedrich closed his eyes. "I was expected to read a lot. The first book my father gave me was about Bismarck, the great unifier of our country. He also practiced marching with me. By the time I was ten, I could march better than most professional soldiers."

John cringed, not so much for the young man, but for the mother who was forced to watch her child become a soldier. Instead of hide and seek, he marched. Instead of children's books, he read war books. "And remind me when you joined the Hitler Youth?"

"When I was thirteen," Dedrich answered. "On my birthday."

"What a birthday present," Tom said sarcastically.

The scowl returned to Dedrich's face.

Tom put his hands on the table and leaned toward Dedrich. "Can we get to the point? What we need to know is where you got your beliefs."

"About what?" Dedrich's eyes flashed at Tom.

Tom raised his hands. "I give up. About what? About the people you murdered."

"I told you before, I did not commit murder."

Tom stood, allowing his chair to crash to the floor behind him. The guards peeked through the window again. "I've read the report Colonel Bayer prepared after your first interview. That's not going to cut it. I'm done wasting my time with you."

Tom gathered his belongings and slammed his hand against the door. Before the guards opened it, he glared at Dedrich. "You're going to die and leave your mother childless. I hope you can you live with that."

Dedrich raised his chin. "Better to die with honor than live as a coward in his mother's arms."

After Tom left the room, John thought about what to say next. He knew Tom had intentionally planted the seed about Margrit losing her son.

"Your mother believes the reason you obeyed orders is that you were trained from a child to follow orders. What do you think of that?"

Dedrich's jaw twitched. "I followed orders because it was the right thing to do. I, and my men, made our country better for what we did."

"But you lost the war."

Dedrich pressed his hands together. "Winning or losing doesn't matter. Our nation can now rise to greater heights than ever before."

"You don't regret anything you did?" John spoke softly, forcing himself to not show his true feelings.

Dedrich shook his head. "I didn't say that."

"What do you mean?" John asked.

"I don't want to talk about it."

John opened his hands, palms up. "Mr. Haussman, this is your only chance. What don't you want to talk about?"

Dedrich turned toward the window. He took a deep breath before speaking. "There was one day we had a group of prisoners on a march in the countryside. It was toward the end of the war. My men were tired and hungry, so we stopped for a rest near a grove of trees. I remember watching the new spring flowers sway in the breeze."

Dedrich gestured across the table. "Can I have some water?"

John filled a glass and slid it to Dedrich.

"Thank you." Dedrich spoke almost respectfully. "When we stopped, we heard a baby crying. We hadn't noticed him earlier. Maybe he woke up when we stopped or we were too busy to notice him while we marched."

John's forehead creased. "A baby?"

Dedrich grimaced. "I don't know where he came from. They, the children, were usually the first ones to disappear in the camps."

"You mean get killed?" John said.

Dedrich nodded. "He wouldn't stop crying. He screamed and his mother tried to calm him. She kept saying, "Shhh, it's okay. Shhh baby boy.'"

Dedrich wagged his head, his face pale. "She tried to put him on her breast, but she didn't have any milk. How could she? She looked like a skeleton. One of my men screamed at her to shut the baby up."

John swallowed hard. "And?"

"As he screamed at the woman, the baby cried more loudly. I guess he got tired of the noise because the soldier raised his rifle and fired at the baby."

Dedrich stared at his hands.

"And then what?" John didn't really want to hear this.

"He missed, sort of. I don't know how, because he was so close, but he hit the baby in the leg." Dedrich rubbed his temples. "The bullet practically tore his little leg off and continued into his mother's belly. Now she moaned and the baby screamed. It was a sound like I have never heard before."

Dedrich closed his eyes. "The second and third shots didn't miss. The screaming and moaning stopped. All I heard was the sound of the other prisoners whimpering. It sounded like a flock of sheep the way they carried on. And I could hear the soldiers laughing. The one who shot the baby laughed and said 'Did you see his little leg explode.'"

John took a deep breath. "Why do you regret that, of all the things that happened?"

Dedrich looked at John. "I never took any joy in it. I did what needed to be done, but it was an ugly job. I never thought we should eliminate the children."

John raised his eyebrows. "Why not?"

Dedrich clasped his hands together. "I never thought they were born evil. I thought if we could take the young, maybe ten years and younger, away from their parents, we could raise them as good Germans. It was the older ones who needed to be eliminated."

John rubbed his neck. "Hundreds of thousands of babies were killed. Why do you regret this one?"

Dedrich frowned. "I had never had a child on one of my marches. They were the first to go when they were rounded up. I heard stories of trucks loading children and hauling them away. It was only adults on my marches. Until that day."

John leaned forward and studied the young man. This was his opportunity. "I told you we interviewed your mother. We went over your history with her. She didn't seem to think you had a happy childhood."

Dedrich's eyes flashed. "What does that matter?"

John raised his hands. "I'm not trying to upset you. I just thought you should know."

"What are you getting at?"

John ran his fingers through his hair. "I thought it was interesting that you were born so soon after your parents were married."

"So?"

John shrugged. "It seems to me your father was still away at the war when your mother got pregnant."

"And you're wondering if he is my real father?" Dedrich tried to cross his arms with the chains holding them tightly apart.

John shook his head. "Not wondering if he is your father, wondering if you know he may not be?"

Dedrich's mouth curved into a smile. "I figured it out when I was a teenager. My mother thought I believed her story that I was conceived when he was home on leave. But I knew the truth."

"How did you know?"

Dedrich's smile soured. "I could tell by the way he looked at my mother. He hated her. There is only one reason a man could hate someone so beautiful. I could tell by the way he treated me. He didn't exactly hate me like he did her, but he tolerated me. I was more like one of the soldiers under his command than his son."

Dedrich paused before his expression darkened. "And I knew because he told me how she became pregnant."

John's eyes widened, his thoughts scrambling. "In the interview, your mother told me Emil didn't know who your real father was."

Dedrich shook his head. "After they were married, my grandmother told my father the truth."

John held his breath before blurting, "And what is the truth?"

222

A muscle in Dedrich's cheek twitched. "Around the time I wondered if he was my father, he brought me to the artillery field like he did most Saturdays. I still remember the smell of sulfur and dirt in the air from the explosions." Dedrich coughed before taking another drink. "When we got there, he told me about how she lived in France during the Great War. When the war was almost over, a young Jewish soldier in the French army raped her. That's how she became pregnant."

John exhaled, almost too stunned to speak. "And you didn't ask your mother about it?"

Dedrich's expression softened when he spoke of his mother. "My father said it was too painful for her to talk about. He had never hit me, but I knew if I mentioned this to my mother, he would beat me. After that, he started calling me his little Jew when she wasn't around."

"That's why you hate them?"

"Wouldn't you?" Dedrich scowled. "It's proof of what they grow up to become."

John's shoulders sagged. "I might feel that way. But that's not the story your mother told us when we interviewed her."

"What did she tell you?" Dedrich asked.

John was unsure how much he should reveal. "She told us she fell in love with a young man in France, but he died in the war. She told us he was your real father. And she said he was part Jewish."

Dedrich's breath quickened. "No, she just doesn't want to admit what happened. Father was right about how much it hurt her."

"I don't think so." John sighed. "Tell me this. Who was more likely to tell the truth? Your father, or your mother?"

Dedrich pushed his chair back and pulled at the chain around his legs. "It's not true. She only said that to keep me from being executed. She would do anything to save my life."

"The rape story would be more favorable to the court," John said. "I think she was telling the truth."

Dedrich's eyes raged. "No. It's not true. My mother wasn't some run of the mill whore in France that slept with a Jew. This is another game you're playing with me."

John ignored Dedrich's anger. "I'm sorry."

"No, you're a liar." Dedrich lunged at John, jerking back when the chains reached their limit. "I told you to never speak of her."

John flinched backwards, forgetting that Dedrich's chains would prevent him from reaching him. His chair tipped and he fell into the wall. Lying on the floor disoriented, John couldn't stop the guards from wrestling Dedrich out of the room. The last thing he heard before he blacked out was Tom's voice. "You okay, buddy?"

39

"He'll be fine. He has a concussion and will have a headache for a while." A strange voice reached John's ears. "But there's no permanent damage."

"Thanks doc." John recognized Tom's voice.

He fought to open his eyes and found himself lying on the floor of his office. Tom sat next to him.

"You just missed the doctor. He said you'll have brain damage forever." Tom snickered.

"I heard." John pushed himself up and leaned against the wall. His head pounded. "How bad is it, really?"

Tom reached for a file from the desk nearby. "The doc said you have a minor concussion."

"Minor?" John blinked, painfully aware of the light. "Doesn't feel minor."

"Any damage to your head has to be minor." Tom laughed, still looking at a file. "You sure got him worked up. What'd you say to him?"

John fingered the back of his head. A bump was already forming where he hit the wall. "We talked about his father. Actually, about how his father isn't really his father."

Tom set the notepad on the floor and leaned back in a stretch. "Why did he get so angry?"

John rubbed his temples. "I don't think he was actually angry at me. Imagine you had been told you were the result of rape, and the rapist was a Jew. You might feel the same way about them as Dedrich, right?"

"So?"

"Now imagine learning that everything you believed was a lie. The hatred that allowed you to kill thousands of people was based on a fabrication," John said. "I think he is angrier with his father, or himself, than with anyone else right now."

Tom thumbed through John's notes. "What's the deal with the baby story? It seems a little strange."

"Not so strange when you consider the entire picture," John said. "Think about it. He hated adult Jews but felt compassion for the children. He believed Jewish children could be raised as good Germans. Why?"

Tom shook his head. "Because he's nuts?"

John smiled. "Probably. But remember, he was a Jewish baby who grew up, at least in his mind, a good German. If it were natural that all Jews were bad, in spite of upbringing, then he would have to accept that he was inherently bad. But he made an exception for Jewish children like himself."

Tom shrugged. "Okay, you've found a little humanity in him. Now what?"

John scratched his head. "I don't know. None of it changes the fact that he, and the men under his command, committed terrible crimes."

"Again, now what?"

Ignoring the pain in his head, John reached for the file. "We've known that all we'll do is write the report. The verdict isn't up to us, right?"

Tom tilted his head. "Can you live with that?"

John sighed. "No, I don't think I can."

"Then what are you going to do?"

"I think we need to take him into the country, to one of the massacre sites." John said.

"What good will that do?" Tom asked.

John shrugged. "Maybe none. But I need to see how he reacts. Can you get us a car?"

Tom smiled. "You know I can, but it'll take a few weeks."

"Good." John smiled. "Let's start working on it."

40

Tom stood next to a car in front of the Palace of Justice, holding the rear passenger door open. The car, painted the same army green as the one they had borrowed in France, had no stars marking the rank of its user. John and Private Chamberlain exited the main doors of the building, one on each side of a German prisoner shackled at the hands and feet. Dedrich had a blank expression on his face as he walked to the automobile.

John smiled at Tom as Dedrich lowered himself into the back seat of the car. "Couldn't get the general's car this time?"

Tom shrugged. "Cheaper to get one from the motor pool. And less questions."

John sat next to Dedrich in the back seat while Tom hopped in the front passenger seat. Chamberlain got behind the wheel. "Where are we headed?"

Tom pulled a map from his pocket. "About thirty miles west to Ansbach. Then, follow the highway north ten more miles. We'll have to figure out exactly where to stop when we get closer."

Chamberlain shifted the car into gear and drove slowly through the city. Tom looked over his shoulder at John. "How did you manage to get permission to take him on this little expedition?"

John glanced at Dedrich before answering. "I told the truth. Said we needed to do some field research."

"It was that easy?"

John shook his head. "Not really. The prison commander was worried that we, who haven't been combat ready in years, are taking a young, well trained soldier out of the complex without a guard."

"So how'd you get him to agree?"

John smirked at Dedrich. "He kept the keys for the handcuffs and leg irons. Figured if we get overpowered and he escapes, he won't get far in prison clothes with chains on."

Dedrich stared at his hands. "I have no intention of running."

Tom laughed. "That's good. It would be embarrassing for the three of us to get overpowered by a lone, chained prisoner."

Dedrich didn't smile. "Will I be allowed to know where we are going?"

"We're going to a field north of Ansbach." John stared at Dedrich, studying his reaction. "You probably remember which one I'm referring to."

"Why would we go there?" Dedrich's face tensed.

"It was the site of a huge massacre," John said. "We need you to tell us about it."

"I know what happened there. I was the commanding officer." Dedrich said. "And I would rather not go there or talk about it."

Tom looked over his shoulder again and opened his mouth to speak. He paused a moment before looking at John. "Are you sure this is a good idea?"

John half shrugged. "Maybe not, but we're on the way now."

#

After a few wrong turns, the car slowed to a halt on the side of a narrow paved road a little over an hour after they had left. They sat twenty yards from a small, rectangular brick building. The structure had clearly been empty for years, predating the war. All the windows and doors were boarded, and strips of metal flashing pulled away from the roof.

John turned to Dedrich. "Is this the right place?"

Dedrich nodded. "Yes."

John reached for the door handle. "We need you to show us the exact spot. Will you do that?"

Dedrich swallowed hard and nodded again. He crawled out of the car without a word. Tom nudged Chamberlain. "Stay with the car for now, but keep your ears open. If he blows up, we'll need your help."

Chamberlain exited the car and leaned against the fender. He lit a cigarette and watched the three men walk away.

John and Tom followed Dedrich around the side of the building to an open field. About ten yards behind the building, a tall granite gravestone was bordered by a low black fence. The area around the marker was mowed and maintained. The rest of the field was overgrown.

"Is this it?" Tom asked.

Dedrich's face drained of color. "This is the place, but why did you bring me here?"

John surveyed the field. "We just want you to tell us what happened here."

Dedrich shook his head. "You know what happened. You showed me the pictures from your file. What can I tell you that you don't already know?"

"You can tell us the story, from your perspective."

Dedrich shook his head. "Will it make a difference?"

"It might."

"O.K." Dedrich took a deep breath. "It was almost the end of the war. We all knew it would be over in a matter of weeks. As you know, our orders were to march prisoners around the country. Every few days we received a message from command, updating our orders. They were always the same. They told us to keep marching until the prisoners 'had expired'. The day we arrived here, we received a different message from command. It said 'Surrender imminent. Liquidate remaining prisoners.'"

"Which meant to kill them, right?" Tom didn't hide the contempt in his voice.

Dedrich nodded. "Yes."

John thought for a moment before saying, "I know the prisoners were killed, so I don't have to ask if you did it. But were you even a little reluctant to do it?"

Dedrich's shoulders sagged. "There were men under my command who suggested we let the prisoners go. They said there

229

was no reason to kill them. But I ignored them and moved ahead with the liquidation."

Tom wagged his head. "Why? I don't understand why you couldn't let them go when you knew the war would be over soon."

Dedrich stared at Tom, but not in anger. The young man's demeanor had changed in the weeks since their last meeting. "You must understand two things. First, I thought we were doing the right thing. I believed, win or lose, the Reich would be a better nation without them."

"And second?" Tom asked impatiently.

Dedrich shrugged. "I never questioned orders. I always accepted that the leadership knew what was right."

John took a step towards Dedrich. "The first time I interviewed you, you were proud of what you did. Now, you seem to have regret. What's changed?"

Dedrich frowned. "After we last met, I spoke with my mother. She confirmed the story you told me."

John rubbed the still sore bump on his head. "And you accept that she is telling the truth. That she's not making it up to try and save you."

Dedrich slowly nodded. "I am the son of a Jew. It is as you said. My father lied to me all those years ago."

"I'm sorry," John said.

Dedrich shook his head. "I do not ask for your pity. I accept the circumstances of my birth and I make no excuses for my actions."

John took another step toward Dedrich. "Do you see now, what your mother has been saying? You were ordered to commit these crimes and you always followed orders. From a child until the end of the war, it was drilled into you to do what you were told."

Dedrich stepped away from John. "That is true. But I know now that I can't hide from what I have done."

"Even if it means you'll die?" John asked.

"Yes," Dedrich said, before walking towards the car.

John waited a moment before he followed Dedrich. Tom stepped beside him. "What are you going to do now?"

"I wish I knew."

41

John sat in a hard wooden chair, twirling his hat between his knees while he waited for his appointment. He looked at the row of chairs against the gray wall and felt like he was in school waiting to get called into the principal's office. The room was filled with smoke as two clerks puffed on cigarettes while they worked. The shades were closed and the only light emanated from a single bulb dangling in the center of the room.

John couldn't figure out why the General chose this drab area for his office, considering the many well-appointed rooms in the Palace of Justice. Even the General's office in Washington at the Judge Advocate's headquarters had a nice view overlooking the Potomac River. Not this place. It looked more like an old storage room with a few desks moved in to make it functional.

John wished the windows were open. Sweat beaded on his forehead. The stuffy room reminded him of working in the attic at his parents' house on a hot summer day. The two clerks typing in the center of the room had taken off their jackets, but still sweated through their shirts. John was happy he wouldn't be here long.

He heard the voice of the General over the tat a tat of the typewriters. The old man wasn't yelling, not really. The General had the booming voice of a proud Texan. John swatted a fly away from his salty face and thought about the General. *Why are Texans so proud of Texas*? He wondered.

While he pondered his Texan superior, the door to the General's office swung open and slammed into the wall. Two white faced lieutenants scurried out with their arms full of papers. John was surprised to see them, given the only voice he heard through the door was that of the General. He assumed the old man was on the telephone.

"Next," the General yelled, from inside his office.

The inside of the old man's office looked almost the same as the waiting area, although much smaller. Three wooden chairs sat against the wall to the right. John selected the chair in the middle of the row, directly across from the worn out desk. The chairs were so close to the desk, John's knees nearly touched it as he sat.

The window in the General's office were closed and the blinds shut. The single light bulb in the smoky room barely illuminated the area. A small black metal fan at the corner of the desk blew directly at the General. John pulled at his sweaty collar, wishing he could turn the fan in his direction.

The General's chair creaked as he leaned back. The old man's head of white hair made him appear older than he actually was. He didn't look nearly as uncomfortable as he should have in the sweltering office. "I suppose you're wondering why the hell we keep all the windows shut when it's ninety degrees outside?"

John pulled at his collar again. "Yes, Sir. I was wondering about that."

"It's those damn Krauts." The General waved his hands. "During the trials last year, we got all sorts of threats. I don't know about you, but I want to make it home when all this is over. So we keep the blinds closed, just in case."

The General added, "I don't mind the heat anyway. Some days were so hot in Texas, today would have felt like winter." John wasn't sure, but he thought he noticed the old man's chest puff out a little, when he said "Texas."

"Well, Sir, I'll get to the reason I requested this meeting." John handed the General the file he had been clutching. "It's about one of the men whose trial starts soon. His name is Dedrich Haussman."

The General reached into his drawer and pulled out a small white pack of cigarettes. "That's some nasty business, isn't it? Those sons of bitches did some pretty awful things."

"Yes, Sir." John wiped his forehead with the back of his hand. "About Haussman, I feel like he won't have the same chance to defend himself as the other prisoners."

The General thumbed through the file, still holding the pack of smokes. "What do you mean? Is someone out to get him?"

John shook his head. "No, Sir. Nothing like that. I mean he won't defend himself. We've given him every opportunity. He won't take it."

The General snorted. "Why should we care about whether some Kraut won't defend himself?"

"I'm not saying we should care, exactly, but it seems to me the judges should know the whole story." John wiped a bead of sweat off his nose. "They should hear how remorseful he is."

The General placed the file on the desk and pulled a metal lighter out of his shirt pocket. He lit a cigarette and took a long drag. "It's not our job to defend these people. They have their own lawyers for that. We just investigate and report the facts."

John took a deep breath. "Yes, Sir, that's what I mean. The rest of the men on trial will stand, in front of the judges, and wag their heads. They'll say how sorry they are for following orders. It will get a few of them off with, maybe, ten years in prison."

The General's eyes narrowed. "And how is this son of a bitch, what's his name, Haussman, any different?"

John rubbed his forehead. "Well, Sir, he actually admitted to what he did during the war. The rest of the prisoners are lying, of course. This is the only honest one in the bunch."

The old man pushed himself from his leather chair and shoved the file toward John. "It sounds to me like it's a done deal. Guilty. Let the judges sort the rest of it out."

Although the General signaled the meeting was over, John did not take the file. "Sir, are we doing justice if the other men, who committed the same crimes as Haussman, are given prison time and he is executed because he won't play their game?"

The General lowered himself into his seat, still holding the file. "That's not up to us. If he won't play the game, that's his choice." The old man paused and thumbed through the file. "You shouldn't care about that though. Tell me what the hell this is really about."

John tried to swallow some saliva to wet his dry throat. "It's about justice. It's about giving the same—"

"Hogwash!" The General stood again and tossed the file across the desk. This wasn't the first time John had witnessed the old

233

man's legendary temper. "Now if you're not going to give it to me straight, this meeting is over."

"Yes, Sir." John took a slow breath. "It's the young man's mother, Sir. She's here, in Nuremburg. She's asked us to help him."

"And?" The General leaned over his desk, ignoring the cigarette burning perilously close to his thumb. "Don't they all have their mothers or wives here asking for leniency?"

"Sir, the kid is Jewish. Well part Jewish, anyway," John said. "According to his mother, she became pregnant before she met the man Haussman grew up thinking was his father. His adopted father told the kid a Jew raped his mother. That's why he hated them so much."

"And you believe this?" the General asked.

John nodded. "Yes, Sir. Real nice guy, the father was."

The General settled into his chair with a scowl. "Let me get this straight. A woman shows up, claiming she's this Haussman's mother? Not only that, but she has an unbelievable story about how her son is really Jewish, but he hates Jews? Am I right so far?"

"Yes, Sir."

"And now," the General continued. "He feels total remorse but won't admit it to the judges?"

"Yes, Sir, but—"

"But nothing!" The old man's face turned red. "I can tell a ruse when I see one, and you're getting hornswoggled. That damned Kraut and his so-called mother probably planned this all out, hoping to get some soft hearted fool to help him."

John jumped to his feet. "That's not what's going on. We have done our due diligence. We investigated the story. It's true."

"So what?" The General shrugged, instantly calm again. "What if their amazing story is true? Who cares? He led a squad of soldiers throughout most of the war whose only purpose was to kill prisoners or deliver them to a place where they would be killed. Why should we care that his sob story is true?"

John started to sit before he stopped and stood straight up again. He knew the General was right. "It's not about guilt. We know they are *all* guilty. Every one of them. I'm concerned about justice. Maybe I feel bad for the mother. But I can't stand the thought that some of those murderers will walk away with a little prison time, just because they lied about what they knew."

John leaned across and pointed to the file. "At least this guy told the truth. And he is genuinely remorseful about it."

The General sighed. "How do you know he is remorseful? That he's not just playing you?"

"Do you remember, a few weeks ago," John said. "When I got knocked out while interviewing a prisoner?"

The old man nodded.

"Haussman is the prisoner I was interviewing when I fell backwards." John rubbed the now healed wound on his head.

"That's the son of a bitch you are here to help today?" The General's eyes widened.

John nodded. "Yes Sir. The thing is, I have spent a fair amount of time with him over the last few weeks."

"And."

John half shrugged. "It took a while, but with the help of his mother, I was able to get through to him. I believe he is truly remorseful."

The General's eyes narrowed. "Why would you spend so much time with this particular prisoner?"

"I guess he reminds me of someone I knew a long time ago." John swallowed hard, knowing he couldn't tell the old man the whole truth. "And I feel bad for his mother."

The General leaned back, taking a long drag from his cigarette. "Okay John, we've known each other a long time. This isn't like you to get involved in a case. Especially one as clear-cut as this. What, exactly, are you asking me to do?"

"Help me give him a fair chance," John said. "Let his mother testify, even though he doesn't want her to. I think that would help."

The General rubbed his chin. "You know we can't do that. Haussman gets to decide how his defense is handled, with his own people. If he doesn't want to defend himself, we can't stop that. I'm not going to tell the prosecutor to call the mother to the stand to help save him."

The General paused to take another drag of his cigarette. "And frankly, I don't know that I'm inclined to help him, even if he is remorseful. He's guilty, plain and simple. At least one of these murderers will get what's coming to them."

"But, Sir—"

"No buts." The General waved his hand. "Now unless there is anything else, I think that will be all, Colonel."

42

John returned to the hotel room Tom had secured for their three-month stay in Nuremburg. If he was in a better mood, he would have laughed that Tom's bag looked about half the size it did when they left D.C. *How much did it really cost him to stay in this hotel all this time.*

Tom read a newspaper in the green chair that had become *his* chair, in the sitting area of their suite. John mixed a drink at the little mini bar before collapsing in the seat across from his friend.

Tom looked over his German newspaper. "Went that well with the old man, huh?"

"You were right." John kicked his shoes off. "It didn't do any good. All I can do now is cross my fingers and hope for a miracle."

Tom folded the paper and set it on the dark wooden table next to his chair. "At least you tried. I know you would have regretted it if you hadn't."

John shrugged. "I guess."

Tom leaned back and crossed his legs. "Did you tell Margrit?"

John shifted in his seat. "I didn't want to get her hopes up. There's no point in telling her now."

"What's your next step?"

John's face contorted. "What do you mean? There's nothing left to do."

Tom scratched his head. "I know, but what are you going to do anyway?"

"What the hell do you mean?" John immediately regretted snapping at his friend.

Tom ignored John's tone. "Your son is going on trial soon. Maybe you didn't watch him grow up, but he is *your* son. What are you going to do?"

John clenched his jaw. "I still don't know what you mean."

"Yes, you do." Tom was resolute. "Chances are, your son will be hanged for his crimes."

John rested his forehead on his hand. "I can't stay here and watch him die. I can't do it."

"You have to. You know you have to," Tom said.

"How?" John asked. "How do I walk my son to the gallows and pretend to those around that it means nothing?"

Tom shook his head. "I don't know, but I know you will do it. Maybe it doesn't matter if you don't hide your tears."

John took a deep breath. "It matters. Survivors from the camps will witness the execution. There might even be survivors from one of Dedrich's marches. They deserve to watch justice unfold in peace. It's the only satisfaction they will ever receive."

"Then you know what you have to do."

John stood. "I have to talk to him. I have to try once more."

43

When John arrived at Dedrich's cell, he found the young man reading what appeared to be a Bible. Dedrich was in bed, holding the book up to the light shining in from the hallway. The young man didn't move when the guard opened the cell door.

John sat in the metal chair attached to the brick wall. "Good reading?"

Dedrich closed the book and sat up. "Not really. It's all they'll let me have. The priest gave it to me, even though I'm not Catholic." He paused before adding, "What brings you here at almost midnight?"

"You."

Dedrich's forehead creased. "What for?"

John smiled. He had visited Dedrich on a regular basis since their journey to the mass grave site. Being an American officer, he was allowed to visit more than Margrit.

"It's the trial," John said. "If you don't take the stand and express remorse, you have no way of avoiding the gallows."

"We've talked about this, Mr. Bayer. I'm not going to do that," Dedrich said. John didn't know why he called him "Mr. Bayer" instead of "Colonel."

John stood and leaned against the brick wall, looking through the bars out the tiny window. "Then I can guarantee what will happen. When you are found guilty, which you most certainly will, you will be given the death penalty."

Dedrich remained silent, his face unblinking.

"Is that what you want?" John still had mixed feelings about what should happen to Dedrich. When he reviewed documents

239

related to other Nazis who had been tried for similar crimes, he found many who were given relatively short sentences of ten years.

"It doesn't matter what I want." Dedrich shook his head. "What matters is justice."

John sighed. "Then think about your mother."

Dedrich leaned on his elbow. "That would be easy, wouldn't it? I could go on the stand and tell them how sorry I am. I could talk about how I was following orders. But that wouldn't bring justice to the people I..."

As Dedrich trailed off, it occurred to John that the young man often avoided talking about those he was responsible for killing. Other than the story of the baby, Dedrich never shared details of his actions.

Dedrich sat straight up. "No, I will stand like a man and accept what the court decides based on my actions. If everything is in your report, as you say, then justice will be done."

John thought about how different Dedrich was now than when they first met not so long ago. At first, he resisted the truth of his birth. He slowly accepted it and came to realize what it meant. Now, Dedrich was determined to accept responsibility. And he wasn't going to allow his remorse to cloud the verdict. He was guilty and would accept the consequences.

Although he refused to imagine what life with Margrit might have been like, John often imagined how different Dedrich's life could have been. He ached for the son he wasn't able to raise. John knew all the people Dedrich was responsible for killing would likely still be dead, but the blood would be on someone else's hands.

John thought about the crimes Dedrich was going to die for. "How many people do you remember killing?"

"Me, personally?" Dedrich asked. "Or the men under my command."

"Both."

Dedrich avoided eye contact. "Thousands. Tens of thousands probably. I only remember the first one. The rest are all kind of a blur."

"Tell me about that one." John sat on the end of the bed.

Dedrich grimaced. "I wasn't a commander the first time. I was still in Junkerschule, the SS academy near Munich. It was in the spring of 1938. They had us, all the members of my class, on a march. We trudged through the countryside all morning.

"It was almost noon, and we hadn't eaten all day. We came across a farm where prisoners worked. At that time, the camp had been running for a few years and local farmers paid the government for cheap labor. Our commanding officer marched us into the field where the prisoners worked. He looked around, searching for his victim. An elderly man in prison clothes about five sizes too big worked nearby. He struggled to push a handcart through the muddy ground. I remember the collar of his shirt was so big, it kept slipping down his shoulder."

Dedrich sat on the bed and his bare feet touched the floor. He turned away from John and stared at the wall, clutching his book. "Our commander grabbed the old man by the back of the neck and dragged him to the middle of our group. The soldiers in class howled with laughter as he fell into the mud. Our commander looked around and asked for a volunteer for a 'special exercise.' That's what he called it, an 'exercise.'

"No one raised a hand, so the commander selected the soldier closest to him, which was me. It was a lesson, he explained, on how to shoot prisoners without blood and brain splattering on our uniform." Dedrich paused before mumbling, "It was really strange."

"What was strange?"

Dedrich shook his head, as if waking himself up. "There was no question *that* we would kill people. What was important was that we knew *how* to do it correctly. He showed me the angle to use when I aimed the gun and how far back I should stand. Then he cleared the class out of the way and said, 'Go ahead.'"

"What'd you do?" John already knew the answer.

"At first I thought it was a joke. I asked if I would get in trouble. I remember his laughter. He said, 'No one's going to worry about a lazy Jew who can't push a cart through a field.'"

John pictured the scene in his mind. He almost felt sorry for his son.

Dedrich exhaled slowly. "I was nervous. The gun shook in my hand as I pointed it at the back of his bald head. The old man was on his knees, shaking as much as I was."

241

Dedrich paused and closed his eyes. "He actually pissed himself. I was shaking and he was shaking, and the other soldiers were laughing at him. Laughing at a man who was about to die for no other reason than being in a potato field at the wrong time."

John held his breath.

"The commander said we could go back for lunch after I demonstrated the proper way of executing 'criminals.' That's what we called them. My classmates cheered for me to hurry. I closed my eyes and squeezed the trigger. I remember wondering, before I opened my eyes, if the gun had blanks and it was just a test."

John exhaled. "It wasn't a test though, was it?"

"No." Dedrich frowned. "When I opened my eyes, the old man was crumpled on the ground in front of me, pants wet from piss and half his face missing. I remember how dark the blood was as it disappeared into the dirt. The worst thing though, was the sound."

"Of the gunshot?"

"No." Dedrich turned to face John. "There were about thirty of us. At first, they were totally silent and we could hear a gurgling coming from the dead man. When the echo of the shot died away, the sound of their cheering was deafening. Like the howling of a pack of wolves. Before I could really process what I did, the group whisked me away. A hero."

John scratched his head. "It sounds like you didn't want to do it. Couldn't you have refused?"

Dedrich leaned against the brick wall. "I don't know. I was shocked, but the thing is, I kind of liked it."

John's expression hardened. "Liked killing a man?"

"No, not that. I was the first one in my class who killed anyone. I liked the respect the rest of the soldiers gave me. I ignored the feeling I experienced when I pulled the trigger." Dedrich sighed. "They made me into a hero after that. It was the start of my SS career."

John shook his head. "There's one more thing we should discuss before I go. If things don't go your way, there's an appeals process. You will have three days—"

"No." Dedrich snapped.

"Now wait a minute," John said. "Hear me out."

Dedrich shook his head. "There will be no appeal. If I am found guilty, I will accept the consequences."

John said, "You know that means you'll die, right?"
"Then I'll die."

44

Early on the morning of the trial, John walked to the Palace of Justice. He was expected in his office, but first went to the courtroom where the proceedings would be held. He walked through the two huge wooden doors, into an empty courtroom that might belong in any courthouse in America.

To the right were three rows of wooden pews behind a short wood paneled wall separating spectators from the court members. That is where John would observe the proceedings. On the left, against the far wall, was a slightly taller wooden wall with five raised chairs where the judges sit. Between the two walls, an assortment of tables for interpreters and lawyers, and a section with twelve chairs where the accused sat.

John stood in the quiet room. While he was lost in thought, the doors behind him burst open. Two soldiers entered the courtroom, each carrying an overflowing box of papers. They marched to one of the large tables and unpacked their materials. John recognized one of the soldiers as the man who would be prosecuting the case for the government. The other was a lawyer who also worked on the case. John didn't remember either of their names.

"Colonel Bayer, what brings you here so early?" The lead prosecutor looked at John while he unpacked his box.

John shook his head. "Nothing really. Just taking in a few moments of quiet before the circus starts."

The prosecutor stopped unpacking and glanced around the room. "Won't be much of a circus, not like last year. We have all the evidence we need to nail these guys. We expect at least half will get the death penalty. The other half will go to prison for a long time. They're all guilty and it will be easy to prove."

John wondered which group Dedrich would fall into—death penalty or prison? He nodded at the prosecutor and mumbled, "Good luck today," before leaving for his office.

45

"Guilty."

When the judge read the verdict, Dedrich took a deep breath and muttered something John couldn't hear. Margrit gasped, but John dared not look at her, even when he heard her quiet sobs. He hated that she cried alone with no one to comfort her. A few observers in the courtroom clapped. They had every right to be happy with the outcome, John thought. He was not.

In the end, Dedrich refused to testify, or to allow his mother to appear on his behalf. There was no way to force the prosecution to call Margrit as a witness without the support of the General. The report John prepared was the only evidence that had a chance of keeping his son from execution. The rest of the trial consisted of the prosecution reading interviews from witnesses to the crimes and the testimony of the other officers who were on trial.

No witness took the stand. When the prosecution rested and it was time for Dedrich's lawyer to offer a defense, all he said was, "Commander Haussmann does not wish to take the stand. The defense rests." In all, the trial lasted less than four hours and it seemed to John the young man wanted to die. His wish would be granted in four days.

When the courtroom was cleared, John sat alone in the back row, the verdict ringing in his ears. It took three months to gather all the evidence and write the reports, but John was surprised at how quickly the trial was conducted after it began.

Exiting the courtroom, John knew his time in Europe was almost over. After their reports were complete, it took some persuading on Tom's part for the General to allow them to stay until all the trials were over. John knew it wouldn't be long before he would go home. Before he would leave, Dedrich would be hanged.

John made his way through the corridors of the old building to his office. The sound of his footsteps on the marble floor reverberated around him. Entering the office, Margrit sat quietly in a chair against the wall. She clutched a handkerchief in her hands. John looked around the nearly empty room. The two privates and Tom were not around. They had already packed the office, so there wasn't much for them to do anyway.

"They went to lunch," Margrit said. "Tom said I could stay and wait for you."

"I'm glad you came." John lied, not sure what to say. He remembered holding her on the bank of the river almost thirty years ago and in her apartment a few months ago. He knew there would be no easing her pain today.

Margrit's lip quivered. "Is there anything you can do?"

John frowned. "I went to the General yesterday morning to see if we could do something. He denied my request. We're out of options."

Margrit closed her eyes. "I have always felt things happen for a reason. When life was at its worst, I believed there was a reason for everything. Maybe it's childish, but I believe there is a reason that you, of all people, are here. You have to do something."

John slumped in his chair. He was totally helpless. "I wish there was something I could do. But if he won't sign the appeal, his attorney can't submit it."

"We could make a fake one. Appeal without his knowing." Margrit spoke quickly in between crying hiccups. "I could testify on his behalf."

"All appeals are in person. It won't work unless he changes his mind." John reached to take Margrit's hand. "I'm sorry."

Margrit pulled her hand away. "No. There has to be something you can do. He's all I have."

John reached again, forcefully taking Margrit's hand. "I know he is. I tried to convince him but he wouldn't listen."

Margrit tried to pull her hand away. John stretched his arm around her shoulder and pulled her close.

"I'm sorry," he repeated.

Margrit collapsed into his shoulder in uncontrollable tears. She sobbed the mournful tears of a mother who was about to lose her only son.

John reached with his free hand and rested it on Margrit's hands. His throat tightened. It was his child, too, who would die.

Margrit's tears ebbed and she tilted her head to look at John. "What does it all mean? Why does this have to happen?"

John could hardly speak. "I don't know why you have to go through so much." He wiped a tear from his cheek. "You said you thought things happen for a reason. I've never really thought about it, but I think it might be true."

Margrit shook her head. "If you're not here to save him, how can it matter that you're here? You get to go home to your life while I stay here."

John lowered his head. She was right. He would go home to his family and she would have nothing. He tried to console her. "I can only think about what happens after we're gone. I believe there is life after death and I know there is no way we can stop what is going to happen to our son." John winced when he said "our son." He recomposed himself. "I believe in eternal grace and eternal judgment. Maybe my being here was the only way Dedrich could find forgiveness."

Margrit still shook with tears, allowing John's arm to rest on her shoulder. "That doesn't give me any relief."

"No." John shook his head. "It doesn't give me much either. But at least I know the mistakes made in this life can be forgiven in the next."

Margrit leaned back, looking closer into John's face. "What will you do when it's over?"

John rubbed his eyes. "I'll be sent home."

"And what will you tell your family," Margrit asked.

"Everything," John said. "What will you do when it's over?"

Margrit's lip quivered. "I'll take him home to be buried next to his father."

John blinked, trying to purge the image of a lonely Margrit dressed in black, standing beside the grave of her dead son and husband. "Then what?"

Margrit gently pushed John's arm off her shoulder and stood up. "I guess I'll go home and try to live my life. What else is there?"

46

The morning of the execution, John lay awake in bed. He hadn't slept the entire night, or much the last three nights for that matter. Dedrich would be hanged in an enclosed courtyard of the Palace of Justice at eight in the morning. Military personnel and death march survivors would be in attendance as witnesses. There would be no appeal. No pardon was possible. John quietly dressed and walked to the prison section of the palace, not bothering to stop by his empty office.

"I'm sorry, Sir." The corporal guarding the cell stepped in front of John. "No one's allowed inside the cell the day of the execution. They get a little edgy on these days."

John sat in a chair next to the cell door. Dedrich reclined on his bed and read the Bible John had seen him with the night before the trial. John said nothing, already feeling the weight of what was to come. He surveyed the dingy cell and thought it was an ugly place for anyone to spend their final hours. The room consisted of unpainted brick and metal furniture attached to the walls.

Dedrich glanced at John before returning his gaze to the book. "I've been reading this since the priest gave it to me. Do you believe what it says in here?"

"Says about what?" John asked.

Dedrich shrugged. "The stuff about forgiveness."

John's throat tightened. "I guess so. What do you think?"

Dedrich leaned forward, still holding the book. "I'm going to die today and I know I deserve it."

John clenched his jaw. "You might deserve it. It's not up to me to decide."

Dedrich shook his head. "I know I deserve it, but I wonder if there is any hope for me after I'm dead."

John tried to smile, wanting to ease his son's mind. "I've never been a religious person. My folks made me go to church, but I haven't thought about it much. Until now."

"And what have you decided?" Dedrich looked at John the way a child would when he hoped for a specific answer.

"I remember the story of the Apostle Paul." John raked his fingers through his hair. "He used to help kill people, and he ended up writing most of the New Testament. I guess there is hope, if you believe in all that."

Dedrich exhaled slowly. "I hope you're right. I know I deserve this, but I'm scared."

John squinted away the tears. He needed to be strong as long as he could. "I know. I wish I knew what to tell you."

"You don't have to say anything," Dedrich said. "I know I have to face this."

The door opened down the hall and John glanced over his shoulder. Another soldier entered the cell block. "I thought that would be your mother."

Dedrich closed his eyes. Tears streamed down his face. "Last night she said goodbye. She told me she couldn't come and watch me..."

John's heart sank. He remembered Margrit telling him, when she was younger, if it wasn't for Dedrich, she would have killed herself. He was concerned she was not at the jail for Dedrich's last hours. He would worry about it later. For now, he needed to be with his son. "Is there anything I can do for you?"

Dedrich nodded, tears still falling from his unshaven cheeks. "Stand in front. When it's time, I mean. I want to see a kind face before they put the cloth over my head."

John couldn't speak. He pictured the moment a thousand times over the past few days, but didn't want to experience it.

"Thank you for being so kind to me." Dedrich struggled with the words. "I know I don't deserve it."

John nodded, then glanced at his watch. "It's almost time. Before they come for you, may I ask you a question?"

Dedrich looked up.

"Why haven't you asked why I've spent so much time with you? I'm sure you wondered."

He was surprised when a smile appeared on the young man's face. "I'm not a father, but I imagine one would want to spend time with his son. A real father would anyway."

John's eyes widened. "How long have you known?"

The door opened again. Three soldiers and a priest entered the corridor. "It's time," one of the officers announced.

Dedrich ignored the officer and kept his eyes on John. "Mother told me a few weeks ago. She said I should keep it quiet. That it might get you into trouble. But she wanted me to know the truth."

John exhaled. An officer behind him tapped him on the shoulder. "I'm sorry, Colonel, it's time."

John stood and moved out of the way. Dedrich gazed at John while his hands and feet were bound with metal chains. One of the guards nudged John's elbow. "You need to go out the visitor entrance and make your way to the courtyard."

"Can't I walk with him?" John pleaded.

The soldier looked at the other two and shrugged. "I guess so. You seem to be his only friend."

John stood tall as he walked through the corridor next to his son. He took hold of Dedrich's arm, pretending to help guide him through the maze of hallways that led to the courtyard. John tightened his grip as Dedrich stumbled. The young man's legs started to give out when he approached the exterior door.

Stepping into the courtyard, John walked Dedrich to the wooden stairs of the gallows. Before ascending, Dedrich silently looked into John's face and smiled. John ignored the spectators and reached his arms around to give his son a hug. It was the only time he would ever hug him, and because of the chains, Dedrich could not hug back.

After John let go, Dedrich took a deep breath. He turned and lifted his right leg as high as the chains would allow. Dedrich climbed the seven stairs to the hanging platform and shuffled to the center of the wooden stage. The sound of dragging chains jingled in the courtyard.

John looked around the courtyard for a moment, noticing fewer witnesses than he expected. The General stood near two officers whom John did not recognize. Two rows of wooden chairs were set up, but no one used them. A group of journalists, in wrinkly suits, stood a few feet from the General. One witness wore a yarmulke. A survivor of one of the marches. Margrit was not in the courtyard.

An American army officer walked to the front of the platform and jolted John back to reality with his booming voice. He held a piece of paper to eye level. "Dedrich Johann Haussman. You have been charged with war crimes and crimes against humanity. You have been found guilty on all charges and have declined to appeal the ruling. Per international law governing war crimes and U.S. army regulations, you have been ordered to be hanged by the neck until dead. Your sentence will be carried out immediately. Do you have any last words?"

Dedrich's voice was barely audible. "I'm so sorry."

The soldier squinted. "Anything else?"

Dedrich shook his head.

"Then your sentence will be carried out."

Two soldiers guided Dedrich beneath a noose that hung on a wooden beam, supported on both sides by two larger beams. Before the black cloth bag was placed over his head, Dedrich gazed at John. John gritted his teeth and looked Dedrich in the eyes, willing himself not to cry. He was determined tears would not cloud this last image of his son.

The cloth bag was placed over Dedrich's head and the noose tightened around his neck. When John was sure Dedrich could not see him, he turned and tiptoed through the small crowd. The priest stood in front of Dedrich and read from a Latin prayer book. As John reached for the door handle, the release of the wooden trap door echoed through the courtyard. John leaned against the door. Hot tears streaked his face.

John waited, leaning against the door, until the creaking wood of the scaffold became silent. Dedrich's lifeless body had stopped moving. John opened the door and walked out of the courtyard, refusing to look back.

Epilogue

The old man smiled as he stood in the shade of an oak tree, reading a letter that arrived in his mailbox that afternoon. He re-read the letter to make sure he soaked in every word. Looking up, he smiled and watched his wife walk toward him from the old yellow farmhouse. Stuffing the letter into the back pocket of his dirty blue jeans, he reached out and took the hand of the woman he had been married to for more than two thirds of his life.

John and Rose strolled down the dusty road as the sun lowered over the horizon. They had been married fifty-one years, and for the last twenty-two, they walked together down this same road every evening. Today, children chased each other in the grassy front yard, and the sounds of laughter reached their ears. Everyone knew grandma and grandpa liked to walk alone.

John pondered the contents of the letter and remembered another walk, a frantic walk that turned into a run. Twenty-three years ago, John sprinted from the Palace of Justice to the little apartment where Margrit had been living. Running up the stairs, he was out of breath when he reached her apartment. He pounded on the door, but got no response. He pounded again, still no response. He grabbed the door handle, furiously turning it. His sweaty hands found it difficult to grip the handle that would not turn. It was locked.

John backed away from the door and prepared to slam his body into it.

"She left this morning."

John jumped at the sound of the voice, spoken in broken English. He turned. An old woman peeked through her barely open

254

door. The chain was still latched on the door and the woman peered at him with a wary expression.

"Do you know when she'll be back?" John spoke in German, leaning against the wall trying to catch his breath.

The old woman shook her head. "She won't be back. She left."

"For good?" John wiped the sweat from his brow.

The old woman nodded before closing the door as quietly as she had opened it.

John didn't know where to look nor did he have time. His flight was scheduled to leave early the following morning. He wasn't even able to stay in Germany long enough to go to Berlin to bury his son. The Soviet Union limited access to the city by rail and automobile, and the few seats on the airplanes allowed into the western part of the city were difficult to acquire. As a resident, Margrit would have no trouble traveling to Berlin. John could only return home.

He limped to the hotel, his feet aching from running in his dress shoes. Tom and the two privates waited for him on the curb with his suitcase. Tom had offered to accompany him to the hanging, but John said he needed to go alone.

Returning home after a long flight, John told Rose the entire story. He informed her that when his enlistment was complete, he would retire from the army. He had served his country long enough. The following year, he retired. He and Rose sold the Washington, D.C. home in which they had raised their children and moved into a small place in rural Virginia, not far from the city.

John suggested they could move back to Nebraska, but Rose was unwilling to move away from the children and grandchildren who all lived near the nation's capital. This was their home now. And, she joked, Tom and Fran would probably have to follow them all the way to Nebraska if they moved back home. John considered opening a small law firm in their new town, but with an army pension, he had the freedom to do whatever he wanted. He bought a small farm instead, and the only time he practiced law again was to get Tom out of trouble in traffic court.

John always wondered what happened to Margrit, until the day the letter arrived in his mailbox. As he strolled with Rose, he reached his free hand back to feel the paper in his pocket.

Dear Mr. Bayer,

My name is Frederic Beaulieu. My wife and I have owned a small café in Paris for nearly twenty years. It's a little place that serves German and French cuisine in the heart of the city. The restaurant is named after my wife, Margrit. Perhaps you remember her? She speaks fondly of her time with you and her uncle in Verdun.

I hope this finds you well, as the American army was reluctant to provide your contact information. I was fortunate enough to persuade a clerk to help me. He guided me in the right direction and provided me with your mailing address after I explained why I needed it.

I am writing to invite you to a celebration we have organized. It is nearing twenty years since Margrit moved to Paris and we opened the restaurant. The staff would like to surprise her with an anniversary party. Our restaurant is small and most have been with her since the beginning, so there are few people outside the café we know to invite. Margrit speaks often of you and has expressed a wish to meet your wife. I believe it would be a wonderful surprise if you could attend.

We have scheduled the celebration for the weekend of July 18th of this year, and would be delighted if you could make it. I know it is a great distance for you to travel. If you are unable to join us, I understand. If you are able to attend, please respond to the address below.

Sincerely,
Frederic Beaulieu

P.S. I know you and Margrit have not been in contact over these many years, but please know she is still the wonderful woman you met so long ago.

John smiled as he imagined Margrit cooking in her own restaurant. He often felt sad when he imagined her a lonely widow in an empty Berlin apartment. He was pleased to think about her, at her own restaurant, with employees that had become family.

Rose glanced at John and squeezed his hand. "What are you smiling about?"

John put his arm around his wife and pulled her close. "I was just wondering how you would feel about a trip to France?"

Acknowledgements

As a college student nearly twenty years ago, I had the idea for this book. I sat down at least a dozen times and tried to peck out the story, only to quit after a few pages. It took the encouragement of two friends who wrote their own novel to motivate me to see the project to completion. Without the support of so many people, I would not have accomplished this goal.

To Aaron and Allan Reini, thank you for showing me that a normal guy can write a book. Your amazing novel Flight of the Angels is an inspiration, and I look forward to reading your next work.

To my sister Sandy, who dreamed with me over the years about this project and offered timely and poignant advice. Your honesty was sometimes hard to hear but certainly needed.

To my beta readers: Marie Westlund, Cindy McIntyre, Barb Kruger, DeeAnn Lindholm, Paul Jacobson, Tony Harkonen, Donnie Farnsworth, Franz Tezel, Becca White, Becky Reini, Craig Hattam, and Steve Potts, thank you for the honor of reading a rough draft that still needed work. I have not taken the sacrifice of your time lightly.

To my dad, for always teaching me that hard work pays off. Without that work ethic, I would never have finished this book.

To my writing coach, Larry Leech, thank you for helping me turn a bloated novel into a book worth reading. Sometimes our work was tough, but well worth it.

To my beloved wife Jamie, for putting up with my writing and for reading and rereading and rereading my work, even though you had a million other things to do. You are my love, my inspiration, and my joy.

About the Author

Robert Farnsworth received his bachelor of arts degree from the University of Saint Thomas in St. Paul in 2000. He has been a teacher for nearly twenty years, starting out teaching history but most recently teaching students with special needs. He earned his Master of Science degree in Emotional Behavior Disorders from Minnesota State Mankato in 2009. Robert, his wife Jamie, and their four children live in Hibbing, Minnesota.

Made in the USA
Middletown, DE
27 June 2018